NOT MY MOTHER

THEO BAXTER

INKUBATOR
BOOKS

Published by Inkubator Books
www.inkubatorbooks.com

ISBN (eBook): 978-1-83756-365-4
ISBN (Paperback): 978-1-83756-366-1
ISBN (Hardback): 978-1-83756-367-8

NOT MY MOTHER is a work of fiction. People, places, events, and situations are the product of the author's imagination. Any resemblance to actual persons, living or dead is entirely coincidental.

PROLOGUE

I jerked the car into the left lane, my gaze sliding to Jake, the ten-year-old in the back seat. He had a death grip on the armrest and the door, a look of terror on his face. I had to get away from the brown sedan. My heart was racing in my chest, beating a million miles a minute. I tightened my grip on the wheel as I pressed the gas, making the car jump forward.

I knew Jake was scared. I could see it on his face in that millisecond of a glance. I was beyond scared too. What if this was it? What if I couldn't get away? The brown sedan just kept coming, racing after us, and nobody was stopping them. Why was this happening? How did we get to this point? Why wasn't anyone doing anything to help us? Everything was all a blur in my head.

"Carly!" Jake shouted, his body going rigid in the seat. "Look out!"

I had taken my eyes off the sedan for less than a moment. It was a blink, a mere fraction of a second, but it was enough time for that sedan to get in front of us and slam on their brakes. I yanked the steering wheel to the right, praying I wasn't about to hit anyone or anything. If I did, I knew we wouldn't survive. The person in the sedan would make sure of it. I swerved, narrowly missing the back bumper of the sedan.

I pressed hard on the accelerator and glanced at the driver as I careened by the sedan that had come to a stop. In that moment when my gaze connected with theirs, I could see that they weren't pleased. But I was. I'd managed to avoid another car that had moved into the right-hand lane in front of the sedan, and several pedestrians on the sidewalk who scattered when they saw me coming before I got the car straightened back in the right-hand lane. All those years playing Mario Cart were paying off, I thought with a smirk.

Now I just had to find a way to lose this sedan for good and keep Jake safe. That wasn't such a big ask, was it?

I glanced in the rearview mirror. The sedan was once more riding my bumper.

"Hang on, Jake. We're going to find a way out of this, I swear!"

1

The clock chimed four thirty and I set my paintbrush down on my palette. I'd been at it since just after breakfast, which was more than seven hours ago. I was working on a landscape; the sky was my favorite muse. I took a step back to look at my work and decided it was coming along nicely.

Raising my arms above my head, I stretched, feeling my back crackle as I unkinked it. Right now, this painting and many of my others were just for me, but one day I hoped to be able to show them off in a gallery. That was my dream. My day job consisted of painting as well, but only for children's books. The pay was nice, but it wasn't what I wanted to do forever.

I stretched a little more and then began cleaning up. Once everything was wiped down and back in their proper places, I turned out the light in my tiny studio and headed to the kitchen. I'd yet to decide what to make for dinner and I wondered if Nelson would be showing up. Maybe I'd order take-out. It wasn't like he expected me to cook. I wasn't his wife, only his mistress.

I snorted at that. Once upon a time, I'd thought Nelson was the love of my life and I was the love of his, despite the fact that he didn't tell me he was already married. Oh sure, he'd promised for years that he was going to leave his wife, Amanda, but he never did. I needed to end things with him, but every time I tried, he somehow managed to talk me round in circles and we'd wind up in bed. It wasn't a healthy relationship by any means.

Picking up my phone from the kitchen counter, I scrolled through my take-out options and landed on Scheswans. I sent him a text.

> Hey, are you coming by? I'm ordering Chinese.

Within thirty seconds, Nelson texted back.

> Order me my usual. Be there in thirty. Oh, and Jake's with me.

> Great. I'll order enough for him too.

Sighing, I called Scheswans and placed our order, then I headed to my bedroom to shower and change clothes. My hair was short, cut pixie style, so it didn't take long for me to wash it, or the rest of me. I pulled on a pair of shorts and a t-shirt, then ran a comb through my raven hair.

Buzz.

I set the comb down and hurried to the intercom by the front door. "Yes?"

"Delivery from Scheswans."

"Come on up." I pressed the button to unlock the outer

door. I grabbed my purse and pulled out enough cash to cover the meal and a tip, then headed back to the door and set it on the side table. I lived on the eighth floor, so it would be a minute before they arrived. While I waited, I returned to the kitchen and pulled down plates and cups.

Knock, knock.

"Coming," I called out as I moved toward the door and pulled it open. "Here you go. Keep the change." I handed him fifty-five dollars, and then took the bags from him. "Thanks."

"My pleasure." The deliveryman headed down the hall just as Nelson and Jake exited the elevator.

"Carly!" Jake called and raced down the hallway toward me. He slammed into me and wrapped his slender arms around my waist, his backpack sliding down off his shoulder to hit my hip.

"Hey, Jake. Come on in. I got your favorite."

"Sweet and sour chicken?"

"You bet."

"Yes!"

Nelson strolled in a moment later and kissed my cheek. "Hey, babe."

"Hey." I sighed as I closed the door behind him. As much as I loved Jake, I really wished Nelson had left him with Amanda, because we needed to talk. Jake already knew too much about my relationship with his father. I carried the bags to the kitchen and began unloading them.

"Did you get anything done today?" Nelson asked as he bit into an eggroll.

"I'm about halfway done on the landscape I'm working on. Why?"

"I was thinking of reaching out to a gallery for you."

I arched a brow at him. Nelson was always offering to reach out to someone on my behalf. Of course, it never came to anything, despite the fact that he was a very lucrative and sought-after artist himself. "Oh?"

"Can I eat in the living room? I wanna watch TV." Jake held his plate in both hands and looked like he was about to race off to the other room.

"Sure," I agreed.

Jake scurried from the kitchen, leaving me and Nelson alone.

"You were saying?" I glanced at Nelson then back to the take-out.

He bit into another eggroll. "Yeah, so, it's a new place, small, just getting started. Probably won't get much traffic... maybe it's not a good idea. Forget I said anything. It'd probably just hurt your career to have your work shown there."

My jaw ticked. It was just like Nelson to throw out an offer and then pull it back, though this time was faster than normal. Usually, it took him more than an hour. He was overachieving today.

"Right." I turned and scooped lo mein noodles onto my plate, then added some chicken.

"You're mad."

"No, I'm frustrated." I turned back toward the table with my plate in hand.

"Babe, you know I just want the best for you, right?"

"You say that, but you never actually do anything to help me." I set my plate down hard, half afraid that I cracked it with the force, but it seemed okay when I looked at it. I pulled out a chair and sank into it.

"What are you talking about? I help you all the time. Didn't I introduce you to my manager?"

"Who apparently has no interest in managing my work, since he's not once called me."

"Well, your style isn't really his cup of tea, you know?"

"Right." I picked up my chopsticks and began to eat. "So why do you have Jake tonight? I thought he had soccer and Amanda was picking him up."

"He did, but Amanda called and said she was having dinner with a friend and asked me to do it."

"Of course she did. I was just hoping we could talk, and it's not the kind of conversation I want to have with Jake here."

Nelson chuckled and gave me what he thought of as his sexy smirk. "Is that what we're calling sex? It can still happen after Jake goes to bed—"

I glared at him. "No. That wasn't a euphemism for sex. I mean it. Nelson, I'm tired of this. I'm tired of being fourth in your life. You come and see me as the whim takes you, half the time you use me as a babysitter—"

"But you love watching Jake."

"I do, of course I do! That's not the point though. You put everyone and everything else above me. You've been promising me that you'll leave Amanda and here we are, five, nearly six years later and you're still married to her. Nothing's changed."

"This is about the gallery, isn't it? Look, I'll call them, but I can't promise they'll even look at your—"

"This isn't about the gallery. Or my career. Sure, that's a part of it, but mostly this is about us. You and me. You don't value me. You treat me as an afterthought. I think... I want my key back."

"Don't be like this," he whined. "I swear, things are going to get better soon. I just have to go gently with Amanda. I can't leave her right now. She's too fragile. I am working on it, for you. By this time next year, we'll be married. Jake loves you. I love you. We'll be a proper little family, okay?" He gave me sad puppy-dog eyes.

"I don't want to wait that long anymore," I murmured, turning my gaze from him, because if I looked at him a moment longer, I'd cave. "I'm not getting any younger and I want to live a normal life. I want to have a family. I want to be important to the man I'm with."

"Babe, you are." Nelson reached toward me and put a finger under my chin, turning my face to his. "It's going to be perfect. Just give me a little more time."

I raised my eyes to his and I would swear the man could hypnotize me with just a look. The look that was in his eyes at the moment, which was filled with love, and affection, and desire. It was a look that said, *trust me, I've got you, I'll never let you down,* and damn me if I didn't fall for it again.

"Okay," I whispered, knowing that I shouldn't give in, that he was only going to take advantage of me. He always did.

Nelson leaned forward and pressed his lips to mine. "I love you."

"Me too," I answered back but it nearly stuck in my throat.

He shifted in his chair and scooped the last of his food into his mouth. "Could you watch Jake tonight?"

My chopsticks clattered to my plate, and I stared at him. "What?"

"I've got a meeting with Glenn in about an hour. You don't mind, do you?"

I was reeling. Hadn't he just said that we could have sex after Jake went to bed? Not that I was actually wanting to have sex, but his words implied that he was going to be here for that to occur. I clenched my fingers into a fist beneath the table. "Are you coming back here after?"

"Maybe. Depends on how late the meeting runs. If it's late, you can keep him overnight and take him to school in the morning."

It wasn't a question. He wasn't asking me; he was telling me what I would do. There was no use arguing with him about it. "Sure."

I knew I only had myself to blame. I'd walked right into that. He'd talked me around and now he was pawning Jake off on me for the night. It wasn't Jake's fault that his parents were completely irresponsible. I'd never blame him or take my frustration out on him.

"Thanks, babe." Nelson stood up, then bent over and kissed my cheek. "I'd better go, or I'll be late." He headed for the door, leaving his plate for me to clean up. "Jake, buddy, I've gotta go. Come give your old man a hug."

I remained in my chair, still stupefied at what had occurred. I'd set out to break up with him and here I was, not only still involved with him, but now I was babysitting for him. Again.

"Bye, Dad. See you tomorrow," Jake's voice carried from the front door.

I heard the door close and a moment later Jake appeared in the kitchen doorway. "So, kiddo, ready for seconds or do you want dessert?"

Jake's face lit up with a lopsided grin. "Dessert."

"Okay. Help me clean up and we'll make some ice cream sundaes; how does that sound?"

"Perfect." Jake turned and sped off to the living room, only to return a few seconds later with his plate.

"I'll wash, you load. Deal?"

"Deal." He began grabbing things from the table and bringing them to the counter for me to wash and then he loaded each dish, utensil, and cup into the washer.

Once it was cleaned up, I pulled down bowls and got the makings for the sundaes. "You have homework?"

Jake nodded as he took a bite of his sundae. "Just some math, and spelling."

"Then after you finish that sundae, sit down at the table and get it done. I'll let you watch another show once you're finished."

Jake sighed melodramatically. "Fine." He drew out the word so that it had about ten syllables.

I shook my head at him and smiled. "Did you bring clothes?"

"In my backpack. This morning Dad said I was staying with you and that you'd take me to school in the morning so I should pack extras."

"Smart thinking," I replied, but inside I was seething. The asshole had known this morning that he'd be leaving Jake with me and that he wouldn't be here.

As much as I loved Jake, I really needed to get out of this relationship and move on. How I was going to do that was a question I'd probably ponder all night.

2

I woke up to find Nelson already gone, if he'd even come back last night. I wasn't sure, considering he wasn't here when I'd fallen asleep around ten. I grabbed my phone from the nightstand to see if he'd messaged, but there was nothing. It figured.

I climbed out of bed and straightened it, then got ready.

Once I was dressed in a red blouse, a black knee-length skirt, and a pair of low black heels, I knocked on Jake's door. "Hey, kiddo, time to get up."

"'Kay," he called back. "Carly?"

I opened the door and poked my head into the room. "Yeah?"

"Can I have scrambled eggs?"

"Sure. I'll have it ready in a few minutes. Get your backpack ready and get dressed." I closed the door, then headed for the kitchen. I started the coffee maker and then began his breakfast. Glancing at the clock, I saw we had a little under forty minutes before we needed to leave.

"Jake, it's ready," I called.

A minute later, Jake slammed himself into a kitchen chair and dropped his backpack on the floor next to him with a thud.

I poured him some orange juice and set it on the table next to his plate.

He grabbed the glass and took a gulp, then sighed.

I turned to look at him. "What's wrong?"

Jake shrugged.

I sank down into the chair next to him. "Okay, spill the tea. What's going on?"

"It's them."

"Who, your parents?"

Jake nodded. "They fight all the time."

"Oh?" I said, trying to keep the curiosity out of my voice. I wanted to ask what they were fighting about, but pumping him for information would be wrong.

"Dad got drunk the other night and yelled at Mom. Mom threw a vase at him. Yesterday she moved to the penthouse."

I wasn't too concerned that Amanda had moved out. She frequently left Nelson and went to the penthouse, but she always returned to their townhouse within a week.

"Mom doesn't want me there. That's why I'm with you."

I frowned. "What do you mean?"

He shrugged again and scooped a spoonful of eggs into his mouth.

"Jake, has your dad been drinking a lot?"

I knew Nelson liked to drink, but when he did it to excess, he got mean. I always cut him off before that happened. Amanda apparently didn't. Or he'd done his drinking elsewhere and then gone home to fight with her.

"Almost every night." His voice was barely above a whisper. "They've been arguing about me."

I blinked in surprise. "You? Why?"

"Mom wants to send me away to school. Dad said no. They fight about taking me to school, picking me up, and other stuff." Tears filled his eyes and started to spill down his cheeks. "Carly? Why does my mom hate me?"

I opened my arms, and he got up from his chair and threw himself into me. I hugged him tightly. He cried softly into my shoulder while I rubbed his back.

I wiped his cheeks with the palms of my hands and looked into his watery eyes. "Jake, your mom doesn't hate you. She just doesn't know how to be a mom. It has nothing to do with you. You're a great kid."

Jake sniffled. "But she never wants to be with me. And Dad barely tolerates me. He pushes me off on you every chance he gets." His eyes suddenly widened, and he added, "I'm not complaining. I love you and I love coming here. I didn't mean—"

I smiled. "I know, kiddo. I love you too and you know you're welcome here anytime, right?"

He nodded and hugged me again, his slender arms tightened for a moment, as though he was afraid that I would disappear, and then he let me go and returned to his seat. "Thanks, Carly."

"No problem." I stood. "Come on, finish up and go brush your teeth, then we've got to go."

He scooped up more eggs and was finished before I could drink my first cup of coffee. He jumped up and started out of the room.

"Hold up there. Where do your plate and cup belong?" I asked, not raising my voice at all.

Jake paused and then turned back. "Sorry." He grinned, grabbed the plate and glass, rinsed them off in the sink and stuck them in the dishwasher, then charged off toward his room.

After rinsing my cup, I brushed my teeth and then we headed off to the parking garage for my car. Forty minutes later we pulled up in front of his school and he waved goodbye to me.

My phone rang as I crossed FDR Drive to get on the Brooklyn Bridge. I hit the answer button and since my phone was connected to Bluetooth, it went through my car speakers. "Hello?"

"Carly? Why do you sound so far away?" the cultured voice of my agent, Vivienne, came through in a crackly blast.

"I'm driving. You're on speaker."

"I thought you were working today. Don't you have the cover for Marjorie Timmons due this afternoon?"

"It's already finished, Viv, and I've couriered it over to her office."

"That's wonderful news, dear. I have another possible booking for you. Jasmine Fortune is looking for an illustrator for her new young-reader series, and I think you'll be perfect for it. She's asking a few artists to submit a zoo scene to her by the end of the month."

"What kind of zoo scene? Did she have a style or a medium in mind?"

"That is the only direction she gave. I'm sure whatever you submit will be fine. Now, I've got to run—"

"Wait! I wanted to ask you about finding a gallery—"

"Carly, darling, we've spoken about that. It really isn't your forte, now, is it? You are exactly where you need to be in your career. I really must dash. Bye, now."

Silence crackled over the airwaves. Vivienne had ended the call.

I sighed.

Vivienne had a particular vision for my career, and it didn't include my work being shown in galleries. She was absolutely certain that going that route was the wrong career move for me. But it didn't take away my desire to have my art hanging in galleries.

It wasn't that I was unhappy. I loved doing illustrations for various books and working with a variety of authors, and I had a modicum of success. I was easily able to afford my three-bedroom apartment in Brooklyn. Granted, the rooms were small and cozy, but it allowed me a room for work plus a guest room for when Jake stayed overnight. And I could afford a few luxuries. Still, I wanted more success. Heck, I wanted to be as famous as Van Gogh and Monet and I didn't want to wait until I was dead to reach that goal. Was that too much to ask?

I pulled my car into the garage and parked in my assigned space as my stomach growled. This morning I'd made Jake scrambled eggs, but I'd only had coffee. Now I was starving. I rode the elevator up to my floor and let myself into my apartment, dropping my keys in the bowl on the table by the door. I pulled the leftovers from last night's dinner out of the fridge and fixed myself a plate. Cold Chinese wasn't my favorite, but it would do, especially since I didn't want to cook.

As I sat down at the table with my food, I thought about Nelson and shook my head in frustration. I should have stuck to my guns and broken up with him. I needed to break up with him. I had to for my own peace of mind.

Really, my only concern was Jake. But I supposed he

would be okay. Nelson and Amanda had more than enough money, and they'd make sure Jake was taken care of. Even if he did end up going away to a boarding school. Maybe that would be the best thing for him. He'd be away from his parents' fighting at the very least, and maybe he'd grow up to be more responsible and stable than either one of them.

My phone sprang to life with *We Are Family* by Sister Sledge, and I knew it was my brother Blaine calling. "Hey."

"So? Did you drop the asshole?"

I sighed. Blaine didn't like Nelson, but mostly he didn't like the fact that Nelson was married and I was his mistress. We'd had a falling out over it when I'd first gotten with Nelson, but after Mom died, we'd grown closer again. That didn't stop Blaine from constantly harassing me to break up with him.

"Carly, you said you were going to break up with him last night. Did you?"

"I tried, but he had Jake with him—"

"Let me guess, he left Jake with you so he could run off and do whatever the hell he wanted." Blaine slammed something down and I had to pull the phone from my ear. "If Dave pulled this shit, I would be filing for divorce. I can't believe you won't stand up for yourself. This guy is nothing but a user."

"I had every intention of breaking up with him. But then I look at him and he pulls on my heart strings and brings up Jake and talks about us being a family. I'm the only stable adult in that kid's life."

Blaine sighed. "I know, but he's not your responsibility. Seriously, this isn't good for you. The asshole does nothing but make you promises he doesn't keep. He's never going to leave his wife. He's never going to make a real family with you and Jake. He's just going to keep stringing you along. You aren't important to him. I hate sounding so harsh, but you never listen."

"I do listen. I hear everything you're saying, and I know you're right. My biggest concern is Jake."

"And the asshole knows it. He uses your affection for him to manipulate you. I know you don't want to hurt the kid, but this relationship is toxic, and you need to end it."

"I know," I replied, putting my chin in my hand. "It's just really hard."

"Welcome to being a grown-up. It's full of making difficult decisions, sis. Figuring out what to do about Jake should help. Maybe you can work something out with Nelson about still being able to see the kid, but a clean break would probably be best."

I was shocked that he'd used Nelson's name, but he was trying to appeal to my good sense. "Maybe."

"After all, you're his free babysitting service. He wouldn't want to lose that." Blaine was back to his snarky self.

I groaned. "Why can't I just tell him I'm done? Why do I let him talk me around every time?"

"Because you're too soft-hearted," he replied. "Next time you see him, tell him you're done and get it over with. Like a Band-Aid, just rip it off quickly and then the sting will go away faster. And come for dinner this week. Dave misses you, though I don't know why."

I snorted. "Because I'm nice to him and not a snarky ass like you."

"Hey, I'm nice to him." Blaine laughed. "Just last night I was *very* nice to him—"

"I do *not* want to hear about your love life." I giggled. "I'll see what my schedule looks like and let you know."

"Bye, sis."

"Bye." I hung up, but continued to sit at the table for a few minutes thinking over the conversation. He was right. I needed to end things with Nelson. And soon.

3

———

I picked Jake up after school and we headed to his mom's penthouse because she couldn't be bothered to get him. I felt like a glorified babysitter, and I resented it. Not Jake. Never Jake. But Nelson and Amanda, oh hell yeah. Most definitely.

"I wish I didn't have to go to Mom's." Jake flopped back against the back seat.

I glanced at him in the rearview mirror. "She's your mom, Jake. She wants to see you."

He frowned. "No, she doesn't. She just wants to say she's doing equal to what Dad does, but it's not even Dad taking care of me, is it? It's you."

"Your mom loves you, in her own way. She's just..." I had no idea how to finish that sentence.

"I wish you were my mom," he said softly. "You're the only adult I trust."

His words filled my heart with sadness. No kid should feel like his parents were untrustworthy. "I couldn't ask for a better kid—if I were your mom." I smiled over my shoulder at him.

We pulled up to his mom's apartment building. I found a fifteen-minute space and parked the car. "Come on, I'll walk you in."

I unbuckled and got out, then went around the car to open his door on the sidewalk side. I took his bag from him and walked with him to the building doors, which were opened by a doorman.

"Visiting?" the doorman asked.

"I'm coming to stay with my mom. Amanda Carter. I'm Jake Carter."

"Ah yes, I was told to expect you, Jake. I'm Davidson." The doorman looked at me. "And you are?"

"Carly Michaelson. Friend of the family."

"I see. Jake, if you go into the lobby, and up to the reception counter, someone will take you up to your mother's penthouse."

"Thanks," I murmured as he let us in. Once we reached the lobby, I gave Jake a hug. "You've got my number. If you need anything, call me."

Jake nodded. "Bye, Carly."

"Bye, kiddo. Be good for your mom, okay?"

"Yeah," he muttered and headed for the reception counter.

I waited until the lady at the desk guided him to the elevator and then I hurried outside to my car. I hated this. I hated that I was the one bringing him here. It should have been Nelson. It wasn't that I didn't want to take care of Jake, but Nelson dumped all his parental responsibilities on me, and it wasn't fair. But then, if I weren't still with him, I'd never see Jake. I felt stuck between a massive boulder and a mountain and surrounded by a pride of hungry mountain lions. In other words, not a good place to be.

When I got home, I sank down on my couch and pulled up Nelson's number. I hesitated for a moment, and then hit dial. The phone rang with no answer. Frustrated, I left him a message to call me back.

I had no idea where he was or what he was up to. He never told me anything. It was always vague. Maybe I was overreacting and he really was busy with gallery showings, or creating something new, or just meeting with his manager.

I decided to do a little digging. Maybe he had something listed on his website that said what he'd been doing this week. I went to his website and took a few minutes to admire some of his work. He was a gifted artist; it was one of the things that drew me to him in the first place.

As I scrolled, I noticed he'd added social media links. Under Instagram, it said:

Click here for all my latest news.

I clicked it and the first thing that popped up was an image of him and some woman I'd never seen looking cozy in a posh restaurant in Manhattan.

My stomach sank. I started scrolling, looking at images and dates, and the more I scrolled the sicker I felt. While I was here taking care of his son, he was out hooking up with all these other women. It was beyond humiliating. And I was done.

I closed the app and went into the bedroom. I pulled his suitcase from the closet and then crammed all his clothes and crap into it. Then I dragged it to the little area by the door and left it there.

Returning to the sofa, I sat down and tried calling him again without any luck. Finally, I resorted to sending him a text message.

> I'm done. You can come and pick up your shit and then stay away from me.

I hesitated before hitting send, not because I wasn't done and didn't mean it. I totally did. However, sending it would mean not seeing Jake. As much as I loved that kid, I had to end this. With tears sliding down my cheeks, I pressed the button to send the message.

Sniffling, I then sent Jake a message too. I didn't want him to feel like this was because of him. I didn't want him to hate me for breaking up with his dad.

> Hey, kiddo. I hope you're doing okay. I wanted to let you know that I've broken up with your dad. I love you so much, and I hope you will forgive me. You can call or text me anytime and I will be there for you as much as I can.

Funnily enough, it was Jake who texted me back first.

> This sucks. I already miss you! I'm not mad at you. I love you. I still wish you were my mom. Mine's mean. Dad did this. I hate him.

> It does suck, you're right. Why is your mom mean?

I hoped he was okay. I had a sudden urge to go get him, but I didn't have the right to do that.

She keeps yelling at me. Saying I'm being too loud, but I swear I'm not. I've got the TV on low. She's just being mean because she doesn't want me here.

Maybe she just doesn't feel good? Also, don't hate your dad. He's the only one you've got

.

Until Mom decides to remarry some lame guy. Then I'll have another person who hates me being around.

I snorted and shook my head. This kid.

Nobody could hate you. You're amazing. I better go. Text me if you need me. And be good for him and your mom, okay?

Yeah. Okay. Bye.

Bye, kiddo.

My heart shattered and I curled up on my sofa and cried.

4

"Carly! Open the door!"

I sat up on the couch and rubbed my eyes.

"Carly!"

I turned toward the door and sighed. It was finally time to stand my ground. I pushed myself up and walked to the door, but I didn't unchain it. Instead, I pushed Nelson's suitcase into the opening, squishing it through the door. "Take it and go."

"Why are you doing this?" Nelson pushed his face into the crack between the frame and the door. His expression was full of hurt, his eyes sad and watery.

I knew it was all an act to get me to cave. He'd done it to me before. I had to be strong. I couldn't let him get to me.

I crossed my arms over my chest. "You know exactly why. This isn't working. You need to take your stuff and go home. I'm done. For good this time."

"Please, can't we talk about this? I love you. I thought we were going to be a family. You, me, and Jake. The three of us, making the perfect life together." He stuck his hand through the crack and tried to reach for me.

I took a step back. "Go home. I can't do this anymore. And I want my key back."

He drew his hand back and stuck his face in as far through as he could. "No. I'm not giving it to you. We can work this out. You mean too much to me."

"I don't mean anything to you. You've spent the last couple of days with other women, and you've barely even said hello to me. You've left your son with me to take care of without any help. I love Jake, but I'm not his parent. I'm just the adult he gets stuck with. I'm tired of being your babysitting service."

"Babe, please, open the door. Let's talk about this."

"There's nothing more to talk about. I'm tired and I'm going to bed. Don't bother about the key. I'll just get the Super to change the locks tomorrow. Goodbye, Nelson." I closed the door.

"I'll give you time to cool down," he called, "but I'm not giving up on us." His voice carried loudly, and I was afraid the neighbors would start complaining.

I pressed my forehead into the back of the door. "Just go," I whispered, but I doubted he heard me.

"I mean it, Carly. I'm not giving up. We belong together." He sounded further away now, as though he was walking down the hallway.

I pressed my ear to the door, trying to hear what he was doing. After a few minutes, the hallway was silent and then I heard the faint ding of the elevator and I prayed that meant he'd left. I didn't check though. I wasn't about to open the door and give him a chance to come in. Instead, I went to the bathroom and turned the shower on as hot as I could make it. I stripped and got beneath the spray. The water felt good sluicing over me.

I don't know how long I was in there, but the water was chilly by the time I got out. Drying off, I pulled on a sleep shirt and then climbed into bed. I planned on sleeping in. I didn't have too many chores to do, and the grocery shopping and work could wait.

I woke to my phone ringing. I groaned as I saw who it was. Nelson. I knew I should have turned the ringer off. I grabbed it and swiped to answer. "What do you want?"

"You can't leave me," he slurred. He sounded as though he'd drank an entire bar full of alcohol. "I won't let you."

I sat up in bed and looked at the clock. "What the hell, Nelson, it's four in the morning!"

"I won't let you leave me. I'll have you black-balled in every gallery across the US. I'll make sure you never work in the industry again. Not even for book covers. Nobody will touch your work ever—"

"Why are you doing this? You don't even want to be with me. You don't love me," I muttered into the phone as I wiped a hand down my face. I tilted my head to stretch my neck. I was tense and had a banging headache. You would have thought I'd been the one to drink an entire bar full of liquor with the way my head hurt, but I hadn't touched a drop.

"I love you so fucking much. I can't stand it, Carly. I can't stand it that you want to leave me. I won't stand for it. You have to stay." His tone was whiny, and half his words slurred together.

"You don't love me if you're blackmailing me into staying, Nel. You're an absolute fucking asshole. Right now, I think I might actually hate you." At this point I really did think that.

If I never saw him again it would be too soon. If he were here, I might even punch him in the face.

"Don't say that. You love me. I know you do. You have to stay. Jake—"

"Don't you *dare* bring Jake into this."

"I won't let you see Jake ever again if you don't stay with me."

He'd apparently figured out that Jake was the leverage that would keep me around. I hated that he was using his kid that way. It was emotional blackmail. I sat there fuming, breathing hard as tears of frustration slid down my face. I was seething. "Stop threatening me. I'm hanging up."

"No! You can't leave me. I need you. I can't survive without you."

"You mean you've got no one to take care of Jake. That's all I am to you. A babysitter."

"That's not true. I love you, damn it!" He slammed something down hard and I heard things breaking and tumbling to the floor in the background. "You stay and things will get better. I swear."

I didn't know how I'd put up with Nelson and his lies for so long. I'd allowed him to manipulate me for years. Anytime he wanted something, I gave in. I changed my life to suit his. I had done everything he asked of me because I wanted him to love me, and now I didn't think he ever did. All he'd done was use me. I gave him everything and got nothing in return. Well, nothing except for getting to know Jake. He made it worth it.

"Go to bed, Nelson. It's over." With that I hung up and turned my ringer off.

As I set my phone down, I felt a weight lift from my

shoulders. I was free. Free of Nelson's manipulations, free of his whining. Free of his wheedling.

It felt really good.

5

The next morning, after talking to the Super about changing the locks, I called Blaine to tell him the good news. But first I decided to mess with him a bit. "I saw Nelson last night," I began.

"So did you do it?" he asked hesitantly.

"Do what?" I replied.

He sighed. "You know what. Did you break it off with him?"

"I did. He threatened to ruin my career and never let me see Jake anymore, but I stood my ground."

Blaine blew out a breath. "Wow, I guess I owe Dave fifty bucks. I didn't think you'd ever drop Nelson."

I chatted with Blaine for a few minutes and then my phone beeped. "Hey, I have another call, can we talk later?"

"Sure thing. Bye, sis."

He hung up and I switched to the other line. "Hello?"

"Carly?"

"Jake, what's the matter?" I was immediately on alert. Something in Jake's tone told me he was really upset.

"It's my mom—she's gone," he mumbled over the phone, his voice catching on a hiccupping cry.

"What do you mean? Where did she go?" I glanced at the clock; it was ten in the morning. "Why aren't you in school?"

"She didn't come home. She said she was going to a reunion, and I had to stay here. She went out and left me alone."

Of all the irresponsible, stupid things the woman did, this one took the cake. Leaving her son alone to worry about her all night. I could throttle her. "Did you call your dad?"

"He's not answering his phone." He sniffled and I could tell he was trying hard not to break down into full-out sobs.

"It'll be okay, kiddo. Let me grab my stuff and I'll come get you." I rushed to my bedroom to change clothes. I'd put on junk clothes this morning because I was painting. They weren't fit to wear outside of my studio.

"What about Mom? Where is she?"

"I don't know, but we'll find out." To get his mind off the topic of his missing mother, I asked, "Did you eat breakfast?"

"No. Mom doesn't have any cereal here."

"I'll grab you something on my way there. Anything particular you want?"

"Can I have a donut?"

I laughed. "Sure, but how about a sandwich too? It'll be nearly lunchtime by the time I reach you."

"Yeah, okay."

"Do you want me to stay on the phone with you, or are you going to be okay until I get there?"

"I'll be all right. I'll go play my Switch."

"Good man. I'll text you when I get there."

After we hung up, I climbed into my car. I was fuming as I made the forty-minute drive into Manhattan. I made two stops along the way, one for the donut at a convenience store and another at a fast food joint for burgers and fries and iced tea. I'd tried calling Nelson, but it kept going to voicemail. I left a terse message, demanding that he call me as soon as possible.

Just as I pulled up to Amanda's building, my phone rang. I parked and grabbed the phone.

"It's about damn time. Where the hell have you—"

"Amanda's in the hospital," Nelson interrupted me.

"What?" I sat in my driver's seat in shock.

"I got a call from them, but they didn't tell me anything. I'm headed there now. Can you bring Jake?"

"Yeah, of course. I'm already here. Jake called me when he couldn't reach you. Go find out what's happened, and we'll be there soon."

"Thanks," he gave me the address and then hung up.

I grabbed my purse, got out and locked the car. I texted Jake as I walked toward the building. I didn't have to wait long for Jake to come hurdling out of the elevator and into my arms. "Hey, kiddo. Come on, your dad called."

"He did?" Jake looked at me wide-eyed.

"Yeah. He's headed to the hospital. We're meeting him there."

"Why? What's wrong with him?"

I could hear the fear in his voice as we practically ran back to my car. "Nothing. He got a call saying they had your mom. Something must have happened to her and that's why she didn't come home."

Jake burst into tears on the sidewalk next to my car. "Is she okay?"

I bent down and gathered him in my arms. "Oh, Jake, I'm sorry. I shouldn't have told you like that. I'm sure she's being well taken care of. I don't know what happened, but we'll find out, okay?"

He hugged me tight and wiped his face on my shoulder. "Okay," he said into my shirt and then let me go.

I unlocked the car and opened the passenger door for him. Once he was in and buckled, I hurried around to the driver's side and got in. I handed him the bag of food. "Go ahead and eat. You can have the donut after you finish your burger and fries."

Jake dug into the bag and pulled out a burger. "Are they the same?" he asked, looking into the bag.

"Yep. Hand me one, would you?"

I ate as I drove to the hospital and finished my fries as we pulled into the parking lot. I'd parked near the emergency room entrance, thinking that would be where I'd find Nelson. Jake and I rushed in, and not seeing anyone, we headed for the reception desk.

"Hi. We're here for Amanda Carter. This is her son, Jake. I was told she had been admitted?"

"And you are?" the woman asked, staring up at me.

"Carly Michaelson." I handed her my ID.

She nodded as she took it. After scanning my ID and handing it back, she typed into her computer. "She's in room three-oh-four on the third floor."

"Thank you." I guided Jake to the elevator, and we rode up to his mom's floor. Our shoes squeaked on the tile as we headed down the sterile hallway toward her room.

When we reached Amanda's room, I knocked gently on the open door. Nelson was seated next to her bed, his head in his hands. He looked up at me with bleary, watery eyes, as though he'd been crying hard. My eyes strayed to the woman in the bed. Her head was bandaged, and her face showed signs of bruising. Her eyes were closed, and I wondered if she was sleeping or if she was unconscious.

"Dad," Jake whispered and hurried to him.

"What happened?" I asked as I came further into the room.

"The doctor said she was attacked." Nelson's voice was full of emotion and cracked as he spoke.

"Attacked by who?" I asked.

Amanda groaned and moved around, her eyes blinked open, and she turned to stare at the three of us. Her expression turned hateful. "Who the fuck are you people? What are you doing here?"

6

Nelson jumped up. "Baby, it's me, Nelson... Are you okay? What happened?"

Amanda's expression turned troubled. "What? I... I don't know... I don't remember."

"You don't remember what happened?" Nelson asked.

Amanda shook her head. "I don't remember you. Any of you. Do I know you?" She stared right at me.

"I'm Carly. I'm a friend of Nelson's. I take care of Jake occasionally."

She stared at me blankly.

"Your son?" I indicated Jake, who was standing next to me.

"Can you leave? I need to rest," Amanda said dismissively as she turned her head away from us and toward the window.

A knock sounded on the door and a doctor stepped in. "Mrs. Carter, I'm glad to see you're awake."

"Jake and I will wait in the hallway," I murmured, my

hands on Jake's shoulders as we turned for the door to exit the room.

Nelson barely acknowledged us.

"Why doesn't Mom remember us?" Jake asked, looking up at me.

"Sometimes with head injuries there can be temporary amnesia. Maybe that's what's happened to your mom." I really hoped it was temporary. I couldn't imagine forgetting my own kid. Hell, I couldn't imagine forgetting Jake at all. It hurt my heart to even contemplate it.

"What's that?" He looked confused.

"It's a kind of memory loss. It happens quite often with head injuries. Don't worry, Jake, I'm sure she'll remember everything soon." God, I really hoped she would for Jake's sake.

"I don't know what happened." Amanda's voice carried through the half-open doorway. "I don't know why I was attacked."

"I'm sure... your family... being here..." the doctor's murmur barely reached me as we stood in the hallway.

"Do you want Jake to stay?" Nelson asked. "He's—"

Amanda cut him off. "I don't fucking know who that kid is," her voice shrilled from the room. "I barely even know who you are."

Jake was standing frozen, tears streaking down his cheeks.

I was livid that they were being so loud and hurting this sweet little boy. Jake had enough to deal with on a daily basis with these two as parents. He didn't need one of them now denying he was even theirs. It didn't matter that she was injured and couldn't remember him, the very least she could do was keep her voice down.

I poked my head in the room and glared at Nelson as though it was his fault Amanda was acting like a brat. "I'm taking Jake to my place. Text me later." I didn't give anyone even a second to oppose my decision. I reached for Jake's hand and squeezed it. "Come on, let's go do something fun."

Jake dragged his feet for a moment and wiped his forearm across his face, smearing his tears on his shirt sleeve. His sniffles were subsiding by the time the elevator doors opened on the lower floor. "Are we going to your apartment?"

"We don't have to go right away if there's something else that you'd like to do."

He shrugged. "I left my stuff at Mom's." His words were quiet.

"We should probably go get that, huh? You'll need your school work for tomorrow, and you probably want your Switch."

Nodding, he sniffled. "Can we?"

"Of course. You have a key to get back in, right?"

"Yeah."

"Crap, I bet nobody called the school either," I muttered. When we reached the car, I made the call and explained the situation. I told them that Jake would be out for the rest of the week, and he looked at me with wide eyes.

"Really?" he mouthed.

It was just one extra day. I didn't think it was going to make much of a difference. "After the day you've had, you deserve an extra-long weekend." I winked.

After stopping by Amanda's penthouse to get Jake's things, we headed to my place, only stopping to grab a pizza on the way. We spent the rest of the late afternoon and early evening watching movies and playing board games. Jake beat me three times at Clue. I let him win to make him feel better. Okay, that's not true. I was too distracted to keep good track of what clues he gave me. Still, he was in a better mood by the time I sent him to wash up for bed.

Nelson didn't text at all, not even to answer the numerous messages I sent to him over the course of the evening. I had no idea what the plan was, and I needed some clarification, but I figured he was probably busy at the hospital with Amanda. That was until I looked at his Instagram and noticed he had posted a round of pictures of himself out to dinner with his manager and a few women I didn't recognize.

"Are you fucking kidding me?" I muttered and turned my phone off.

"Night, Carly," Jake said as he moved to the guest room.

"Night, kiddo." I headed to my room and got ready for bed, but it was a long time before I fell asleep.

The next morning, I got up early, turned on the coffee maker, and fixed us breakfast. I flipped the french toast and pulled out the syrup, butter, and powdered sugar. Once it was done, I fixed two plates, adding pads of butter and powdered sugar to each stack. I'd let Jake add his own syrup.

"Jake, breakfast," I called.

The door to the guest room opened and Jake walked sleepily down the hall, rubbing his eyes. "Smells good," he replied as he sat down, still in his pjs.

"Milk or juice?" I asked as I opened the fridge.

"Milk, please." He poured syrup on his stack of toast.

I fixed his glass and then returned the pint of milk to the fridge. "Here." I set it down next to his plate and turned to pour myself a cup of coffee.

We ate together in pretty much silence. All that could be

heard was the clinking of silverware against our plates and the gulping of Jake drinking his milk, and then, out of the blue, he asked me to take him to the hospital to see his mom. I could see that he was really worried about her, and I couldn't blame him. I was worried about her too, and I didn't even like her.

I set my coffee mug down. I was afraid Amanda might still be disoriented, but I couldn't say no. "We'll go after breakfast."

Jake nodded. Then his eyes watered and his lip trembled as he stood up from the table. "What if she never remembers me?"

I pulled him into my arms and hugged him tight. "That's not going to happen. She will remember you, buddy. She's your mom. Moms don't forget their kids. At least not for long." It was a bullshit answer. I knew there were terrible parents out there who forgot their kids all the time, but I was trying to comfort him, and it was all I had.

"That's not true. Some moms do." His voice was barely a whisper.

"Only the really bad ones." I sighed. "I'm sorry, Jake. I'm not very good at this, am I?" I frowned, wishing I could be what he needed, say what he needed to hear.

"You're better than Mom or Dad," he replied with a wry smile. "At least you actually try. Dad shoves me off on you when things get hard. Mom just ignores me." He sniffled and looked away.

"Ah, kid. It's not because they don't love you. They're just bad at showing it. You know that, right?"

"I guess." His lip trembled.

Jake was the best kid on the planet and they both treated

him like an afterthought, if they thought of him at all. It wasn't fair.

If Nelson were here right now, I'd have throttled him.

7

"How is she?" I asked.

The nurse frowned, her hands on her hips as she looked at Amanda asleep in the hospital bed. "When she woke earlier, she was near hysterics. We had to sedate her. The doctor thinks she might have a little swelling on her brain. They took her for a CT scan, but it was inconclusive. He's hoping she'll get better soon."

"So she hasn't recovered her memory yet?" I murmured, keeping my voice low as Jake sat in the chair by Amanda's bed.

"I don't think so. She knows who she is and what day it is, but she doesn't remember other things." The nurse's eyes strayed to Jake. "We try not to force patients to recall things, believing they'll recover the information on their own. Usually seeing family helps."

I nodded. "I hope it does. He's already crushed, with her being injured."

"If you need anything, I'll be out at the desk." She tilted her head toward the door.

"Oh, before you go, has Mr. Carter been here today?"

"No, I don't think so. I've been on shift since seven and I haven't seen him."

"Okay, thanks." I gave her a tight smile as she left the room. I moved over next to Jake and sat down in the second chair. "You okay, kiddo?"

Jake nodded, not taking his eyes off his mom. "Why isn't she awake?"

"The doctors gave her something to help her sleep. It's what's best for her. Do you want to play your Switch while you wait for her to wake up?"

"You don't think she'll be mad?"

"Why would she be mad?"

He shrugged. "Because of the noise."

"I don't think so, but you could turn the volume down some if you're worried about disturbing her."

Jake agreed and I handed him the Switch. I'd stuck it in my purse before we left, just in case he needed something to distract him while we were here. Hospitals could be boring, especially for a kid.

We'd been there for about an hour when Amanda started screaming, "Leave me alone! Stop it! Stop!"

Jake jumped from his seat. "Mom?"

I put a hand on his shoulder and drew him back. Amanda was fighting some invisible foe, and I didn't want her to accidentally hit Jake.

"Where the fuck are you, you asshole?" Amanda sat up and swung a fist at her imaginary opponent.

I slid my hand down Jake's arm to his hand and tugged him toward the door, then popped my head out to look for the nurse. My eyes landed on the nurse from earlier. "She's awake, but she's acting like she's under attack—"

The nurse rushed toward me and then pushed past us into the room. She caught Amanda's arm as she threw another punch. "Mrs. Carter?"

"Let me go!" Amanda screamed. "Where are they? I'll kill them! I'll fuck them the fuck up!"

The nurse was doing her best to contain Amanda as a doctor and another nurse rushed into the room.

I pulled Jake in front of me and held him against me as I plastered myself to the wall so we were out of the way.

"Mrs. Carter, you're fine... Your attacker is gone..." the nurse murmured.

Amanda blinked her eyes open, but she seemed out of it. "Stop it... Let me go," she demanded.

"Do you want to sedate her again?" the second nurse asked the doctor.

"Not if we don't have to," he answered. "She seems to be calming a little bit. Mrs. Carter, I'm Doctor Norton. Can you hear me?"

Amanda struggled for a moment more and then nodded. "What happened?"

"You're safe now, Mrs. Carter. You're at the hospital. Do you remember?"

Amanda stared at him. "The hospital?"

"Yes. You've been here for two days. How are you feeling?"

"I don't understand," she muttered. "Why am I here?"

The nurses let her go as she seemed to calm more.

"Mom?" Jake said, but Amanda either didn't hear him or was ignoring him. "Mom?" He pushed away from me and rushed toward the bed.

"Jake, wait..." I reached for him, but I wasn't fast enough.

"Who the fuck are you?" Amanda said, staring at Jake with disgust.

Jake burst into tears and turned and slammed into me.

I rubbed his back and bit back the cuss words I wanted to shout at her.

Amanda turned to me. "Who are you people? What are you doing here?"

Dr. Norton drew her attention again. "Mrs. Carter, I understand your confusion. You have a head injury, and it seems to have caused some brain swelling which has led to what we hope is temporary amnesia."

Amanda shook her head and then groaned, her hand going to the bandage wrapped around her head. "What? That's not right. I know who I am. What I don't know is who they are." She tossed a glare toward me and Jake.

"Yes, sometimes it's only partial amnesia. Meaning you can remember some things and other things can slip away. It will all come back to you with time and patience. Can you tell me what you do remember?"

Amanda pursed her lips and her brow furrowed as she ignored me and Jake, which was a little hard with him sobbing loudly against my stomach. "Can you shut that brat up? I can't think," she muttered.

Jake cried harder.

If I could have, I'd have punched her in the face, but I needed to cut her some slack. She was dealing with a brain injury and wasn't herself. I rubbed Jake's back and drew him toward the door, but we didn't leave.

"Mrs. Carter?"

"Yes... sorry... it's just my head is banging."

"We'll get you something for the pain in a moment," the doctor said. "Can you tell me what you recall?"

She nodded slowly. "I was attacked."

"Do you know who attacked you?"

She paused and a play of emotions crossed her face. "No. I don't remember."

"Do you remember where you were?"

Again, she paused. "I went out. I had dinner with someone... I was attacked from behind..."

"You're doing very well... Now, can you tell me who you are? What's your name?"

"Amanda Carter."

"Excellent. Anything else about your life?"

"I have a penthouse apartment."

Funny, that was what she remembered but she couldn't remember her own son. I was back to wanting to clock her.

"Do you know where?" the doctor asked.

Amanda gave him the correct address.

"That's good. Now, do you remember your husband? Or your son?" The doctor indicated Jake, who was clinging to me.

"That's my kid?" She seemed overly shocked considering Jake had called her 'mom' just a few minutes earlier. Did she think he was lying?

I glared at her.

"If he's mine, who are you?" she asked me with suspicion.

"I'm Carly. I take care of Jake occasionally for you and your husband." I didn't give any further details. It was none of the hospital staff's business that I used to be Nelson's mistress.

She shook her head slowly. "So, you're his nanny?"

I snorted. "No. Just a friend."

"We're friends?" She sounded skeptical as she looked me up and down.

"Not exactly. I'm more a friend of your husband's."

"Where is my husband?"

That was a great question. I would have loved to know the answer to that myself. "I don't know," I answered honestly. "I haven't seen Nelson since you were brought in."

"Nelson... that sounds familiar."

"It should; it's your husband's name," I replied sardonically. I couldn't help it. If I didn't know better, I'd think she was playing this up for some melodramatic reason.

Amanda narrowed her eyes at me. "Why are you here?"

"Jake was worried about you so I brought him to see you." I patted his shoulder.

His sobs had subsided, and he'd somewhat dried his eyes. He looked at Amanda leerily, waiting to see what she'd say.

Amanda studied him. "I'm sorry I don't remember you," she said softly, almost gently, which was very much out of character. "I'm sorry about getting freaked out earlier and shouting at you."

Jake nodded.

"I'm sure you're a good kid and all... I just... I don't... I didn't know who you were."

Sniffling, Jake wiped his nose as his eyes teared up again. "It's okay, Mom. Carly told me you've got temporary amnesia."

Amanda nodded slowly.

"We do hope it's temporary," the doctor added. "As the swelling on the brain goes down, your memory should return to normal, Mrs. Carter."

"How long will that be?"

"We want to keep you here for a few more days. It may

not be safe for you to leave until we can be sure that you don't have a brain bleed or any other complications."

"Hey, you're awake," Nelson said as he entered the already crowded room with a bouquet of flowers.

I stared at them. Red roses. He'd brought her red roses. My eye twitched.

Doesn't matter. You broke up with him, remember? I told myself.

Nelson moved toward the bed and kissed Amanda on the cheek, then handed her the flowers. "How are you feeling? Better?"

"Are these for me?" she gasped and smiled up at him. "You're so sweet."

Nelson turned and caught sight of me and Jake. "Hey, buddy, you doing okay? What's wrong with your face, why's it all red and puffy?"

"My fault, I'm afraid," Amanda admitted. "I don't remember him."

"Huh. That's weird, baby."

"Hopefully it's just temporary, as the doctor said," I nearly growled.

"Well, Mrs. Carter, I'll leave you in the hands of your nurses and guests for now, and I will come back this evening. Nurse Parish, I've noted what to give her for her pain management in her file. I'll leave you all to it." With that, Dr. Norton left the room, followed by the other nurse whose name I never learned.

"Do you want to visit some more before I give this to you?" the nurse asked. "It will make you sleepy if I do."

"My head really hurts. I think I want the medication."

"That's fine, I can come back later, baby. I'm just glad to

see you awake and recognizing me." Nelson grinned at her. "You do, right?"

Amanda nodded. "You do seem familiar. I know you're my husband... that's what they've told me."

"Good. I'm glad you're remembering." Nelson bent down and kissed her again, this time on the lips. "I'll see you later, yeah?"

Amanda smiled as she took the offered cup of pills from the nurse. "Okay."

"Bye, Mom," Jake murmured, staring at the two of them.

"Uh... bye," Amanda replied, looking uncomfortable.

I gave her a tight smile and walked Jake out of the room. I shouldn't have brought him. All of this had to be traumatizing to him. When we got further into the hallway, I stopped, drawing Jake to a halt as well. I squatted down and looked him in the eye. "I'm sorry, Jake. I'm sorry you're having to deal with all of this."

He sniffled but didn't look away. "It's not your fault. You didn't do this to her."

"No, but I brought you to see her knowing she might not have her memory back yet. I should have waited."

"I asked you to bring me. It's not your fault. I'm okay."

I hugged him and stood up as Nelson joined us. He tried to put his arm around me, but I shifted out of the way and glared at him. "No." I held Jake's hand and strode for the elevator.

"Babe," he muttered, jogging to catch up.

I stabbed the button to call the elevator car to us. "Don't." I flashed my eyes at him, letting him know I was beyond pissed off.

"Don't be like that," he pouted, his lower lip jutting out as he turned his sad puppy eyes on me.

I wasn't moved this time. "Do you want Jake to come home with you?"

"I want you both to come home with me."

I stared at him for a few moments, not saying anything.

"Please?"

I pulled Nelson down the hall so Jake couldn't overhear. "We're done. Get it through your thick skull that I'm here for Jake. That's it."

"I thought we were going to make a go of it. You, me, and Jake."

"Tell that to someone who will actually believe you." I folded my arms across my chest. "I can't do this. I'm going home."

"No, Carly, you can't leave," Jake cried out. He raced down the hall and slammed into me.

I rubbed his back and sent Nelson a glare. "Hey, kiddo, I'm sorry but I need to go. Remember that talk we had before? You can call me anytime, okay?"

Tears raced down his cheeks. "Promise?"

"I promise." I hugged him, then kissed the top of his head. Without another word, I strode over to the elevator.

"I hate you," Jake said to his dad.

I glanced back at Nelson and sighed. "With me gone, how exactly are you going to care for him?"

Nelson's eyes darkened. "Plenty of babysitters on Tinder."

8

"Tinder. Seriously? Asshole," I muttered as I headed back to Brooklyn. I knew what Nelson was doing. He was trying to make me angry and manipulate me into begging him not to do that. Well, he was in for a surprise. I wasn't begging him for shit. Yeah, I was worried about Jake, but the kid was resilient. He'd be okay. He had my number, so he could text or call me when he needed to vent about his asshole parents.

I gripped the steering wheel tighter. My knuckles were turning white, I was holding on so tightly. I made it across the bridge and soon I was home in my apartment. My happy place.

It was after six, but I didn't want to cook. I sat down on my sofa and wondered what I should do. I didn't feel like watching TV or a movie. What I really wanted was to be around people. I wanted to be inspired.

I decided to go out and have a good time. I wasn't going to think about the Carter family at all. This was the first step in me moving on and living without Nelson in my life.

I went to my room, pulled open my closet door and flipped through my clothes, looking for something to wear for a night out. I grabbed my little black dress. It reached mid-thigh, had spaghetti straps, and accentuated all my curves. I added a pair of black strappy heels, then went to the vanity in my bathroom to do my makeup. I gave myself smokey eyes outlined in kohl that made my pale green eyes pop. I added red lipstick to my cupid bow lips, then ran a brush through my short raven hair. Finally, I put on a pair of gold hoop earrings and a thin gold necklace with a faux emerald pendant.

After one more look in the mirror, I declared myself ready to hit the town. The only things I needed were a wrap and an appropriate purse, so I switched all my essentials to a black clutch, grabbed a black pashmina, and headed out.

There was a popular bar just a few blocks from my place, so I decided to walk. I wrapped the pashmina tighter around my shoulders and enjoyed the fall evening air.

I found the bar and went in. It wasn't too crowded, which was nice. People were clustered in groups at little round tables with half-moon chairs. Off to the side was a grand piano where someone was playing exquisitely. I was intrigued to see who sat behind the gloss black finish of the large instrument, but first I needed a drink, so I walked over to the bar.

The bartender slowly made his way over to me. "Welcome to Melodies. What can I get for you?"

"Something strong." I had no idea what to order. I wasn't much of a drinker, and I usually stuck to wine, but tonight I wanted to get drunk and forget about Nelson.

"Do you like apple butter?" He arched a brow.

"I don't know, but I'll give it a try." I smiled.

"Then one apple butter old-fashioned coming up." He grinned and began gathering ingredients—bourbon, apple cider, orange bitters, apple butter and a few other things. He mixed it all together and then set the glass before me. "See what you think."

I lifted the crystal glass and took a sip. The bourbon in it burned but the flavor was fantastic. "It's good, thanks. What do I owe you?" I asked as I set the glass down and opened my purse.

"First one's on me," he said with wink.

I blushed and closed my purse. "Thanks." I lifted the glass and took another sip.

"Anytime." He sauntered down the bar to another customer.

I grabbed my drink and sat down at a table with a good view of the attractive man behind the piano. His shoulders were broad, his arms muscular, and his thick black hair hung to his shoulders. His long, elegant fingers stroked the keyboard like a lover stroking his paramour. His voice had a gravelly but rich tone. It was making my insides flutter, or maybe it was the bourbon. Whatever it was, I liked it.

His pale gray eyes caught mine in a heated gaze. It was intense and sexy and made me catch my breath. The honeyed baritone of his voice grew stronger as he continued to sing, and it felt as though he was singing just for me.

My heart began to race in my chest and without realizing it my hand flew up to cover it, trying to calm it. I had no idea what was going on. I'd never had anyone make me feel this way before. Not with just a look and the sound of their voice. And he wasn't even singing to me. It was for everyone. But the way he was looking at me made me feel like the sexiest woman on the planet and that he had eyes only for me.

All thoughts of Nelson and Amanda slipped from my mind. I could do nothing but focus on the man with the sensual tone as his fingers glided over the keys.

The song ended and he began playing "Dancing with Your Ghost". His voice became haunting as he sang the words right into my heart. "...*How do I love, how do I love again? How do I trust, how do I trust again...*"

His eyes were locked on me, and I couldn't look away. My breath caught in my throat as the song came to an end.

The room was silent, like everyone in the entire bar understood the poignant moment and needed time to process the emotions the melody and words evoked. And then a round of thunderous applause filled the room along with whistles and bravos. Still, the magnetic man behind the piano didn't take his eyes from me.

"Thank you," he murmured into the mike. "I'll be back in thirty minutes to play for you some more. In the meantime, enjoy your time here at Melodies." He rose from the piano bench, his lithe and slender body moving with the grace and elegance of an aristocrat. He stood at my table a second later, his lips curved in a small smile, his intense gaze locked on me. "May I join you?"

I couldn't make words come out of my mouth; I was so captivated by him. I gestured to the seat and gave him a nod. Finally, I squeaked out, "Please."

His lips quirked up more, showing off a dimple in his cheek. "I'm Hans Wohlers. And you are..." His last name sounded as though he said Wallers, and his dimple deepened as he shook my hand.

"Carly Michaelson," I replied, feeling a tingle race up my arm at his touch.

"You have the most beautiful eyes. I don't think I've ever seen such a color before."

I blushed. "Thank you." I nodded toward the piano. "You play beautifully. Do you play here often?"

"A few times a week, and every other weekend when I'm not giving a concert. I enjoy being around people."

A waitress approached the table and handed Hans a highball glass of whiskey. "Devon sent this over."

"Give him my thanks," Hans replied.

"Devon?" I asked once the waitress was gone. I wondered if I had somehow misread his signals and he was actually gay.

"The man behind the bar." He tilted his head toward the bar, raised his glass and took a sip. "Tell me about you, Carly Michaelson. You have me intrigued."

I bit my lip and felt my cheeks heat at his gaze. Definitely *not* gay then. Not with the way he was looking at me, like I was the most decadent dessert on the buffet, and he was starving. "I'm an artist." My shoulders lifted in a shrug, and I reached for my half-empty cocktail and finished it.

"Would you like another?" he questioned, his eyes on my lips.

"Sure."

Hans raised his hand and got the bartender's attention then pointed to my drink.

The man behind the bar, who I now knew was Devon, nodded.

Hans smiled at me. "What kind of artist?"

"I work with most mediums. I draw and paint. Right now, I'm mostly working with authors, designing and painting or drawing book covers for them. I really want to be a serious artist. I want my work hanging in galleries."

"And why don't you?"

I sighed. "That, my friend, is a long story."

"And now I am even more intrigued. I'd love to see your work sometime." He reached over and put his elegant hand on my cheek and stroked my cheekbone with his thumb. "You are a very beautiful and fascinating woman."

The waitress arrived with my drink.

Hans let me go, leaning back in his chair. "Put it on my tab, Kathleen."

"Oh, no... I didn't mean for you to buy—" I started, feeling flustered.

Hans grinned. "It's my pleasure."

"Thank you," I murmured as the waitress moved on.

"So, what brought you into Melodies this evening? I don't think I've ever seen you here before."

I pursed my lips, thinking about my answer. I went with honesty. "I didn't want to be alone. It's been a hellacious week."

"Oh? Would you like to talk about it, or just forget about it for a while?" he asked, his intense gaze on my face.

My breath caught in my throat. "I'd like to forget about it for a while, if you don't mind."

"Of course," he answered. "However, should you need someone to talk to, I'm a good listener."

I smiled. "I appreciate that."

He took another drink of his whiskey, finishing it. "Are you going to be here for a while?"

"I suppose that depends." I couldn't take my eyes from him he was so damn sexy.

"On?" He arched a brow.

"Why you're asking," I said with a grin.

His smile widened. "I have another set to play, and then I

thought maybe we could get to know each other some more."

"I'd like that," I replied.

"Me too. I'll tell Devon to put whatever you're drinking on my tab, then I have to get back to the piano for a little bit."

"Okay, I'll be here."

I spent the rest of the evening listening to Hans playing and singing while he eye-fucked me and I did the same to him... well, not the playing and singing part, but yeah.

Once he was done, we talked some more about everything and nothing and then we exchanged numbers. He called me an Uber and walked me out to it, paying for it before helping me in.

All in all, it was one of the best evenings I'd had in a very long time.

9

I woke up with less of a hangover than I thought I would. My head didn't hurt at all, but my mouth was dry and felt like cotton. I stretched and sat up in bed thinking about the night before. It hadn't gone as I'd expected. I wasn't even sure what I expected when I walked into that bar—probably something along the lines of drowning my sorrows in lots of liquor. However, after meeting Hans my night had drastically improved. He was like no other man I'd ever met before and so incredibly talented it was unreal. Just the thought of him made me smile.

I got up and prepared for my day, dressing and making the bed, then headed to the kitchen for coffee. While the coffee maker worked, I pulled out my phone and debated texting him. I wasn't usually the first to make contact, but he had told me to get in touch whenever. I could do that, right?

Geez, it had been so long since I'd done this kind of thing. I was so out of practice. I decided I had nothing to lose, so I pulled up his number.

> Hey, it's Carly. I just wanted to say I had a really great time last night and to thank you for the Uber home. Hope you have a great day.

I read it over about twenty times before I finally hit send. I set the phone down and grabbed my full mug of coffee. I drank it in just a few gulps. I poured a second cup and drank it too, then rinsed my mug and cleaned the coffee pot.

Picking up my phone, I headed for my studio. It buzzed in my hand, causing me to stutter in my steps.

I glanced at it and smiled. It was from Hans.

> I'm so glad you texted, sexy lady. I had a great time too. I wondered if you'd like to go out with me Friday.

My breathing picked up. He was asking me out. I immediately texted back.

> Absolutely. I would love to.

I strolled into my studio feeling lighter on my feet, my mood very much improved. My phone buzzed again, and I looked at it.

> Great. I will pick you up at seven, if that works for you.

> It does. Any hint of where we're going so I know what to wear?

> Thought we might have dinner and check out a club. Do you like to dance?

> That sounds nice, and yes, I do.

> I thought maybe you might. See you Friday night.

> See you then.

I set my phone down and moved to a blank canvas. I had all these energized feelings charging through me and I felt like if I didn't start painting something new, I was going to burst.

I filled my palette with bright colors and grabbed my brush. I had no idea what I was going to paint. Something abstract? Something unique? I didn't know until I started putting paint on the canvas. I added some black and gray to my palette, then some ivory... Soon I had a background of faint colors that looked vaguely like people seated in a joyous place. In the forefront was a grand piano and an elegant man seated with his side profile as the main focus.

I had painted Hans.

He was poised over the keys, his expression one of intense heat as he seemed to connect with the viewer. It was one of many looks he'd given me last night that had sent a singular thrill through me. It was easy to call up the memory and hold it there as I painted. Everything else was slightly out of focus, but he and that piano drew me in. I hoped it would do the same for anyone who got the chance to see it. Normally my paintings took days to complete, but this one... it was like I was possessed.

When I came up for air, it was well after nine p.m. I'd been painting for almost twelve hours straight. My shoulders ached, and so did my lower back, but my heart was full.

Studying the painting, I thought it was one of the best

things I'd ever created.

10

By Friday I'd heard from Jake a few times, but despite my worry, he was doing okay. I was relieved, since it meant I didn't have to see or be around Nelson. I was still angry at him for trying to manipulate me. I was angry at myself for allowing him to do so for so long. I was working on letting that anger go, but it was still sharp and pointy, stabbing me every chance a thought of him passed through my mind.

I was working on a new illustration today, for a new author. I had also sent off one of my watercolor zoo images to Jasmine Fortune. Today's illustration was in watercolor pencils. It was a children's story about aliens, so it was a fun little project.

At five I cleaned up my studio, then headed to my room to get ready for my date with Hans. I searched for something dressy to wear. I chose a pair of high-waisted, flowy black pants and a tight white top. I paired that with black heels, some chunky multi-colored earrings and matching necklace and bracelets. It was a little bohemian looking, but it would do. I grabbed a black jacket and reused my black clutch from the night we'd met.

At two minutes to seven, the downstairs buzzer rang, and I hurried to the intercom. "Hello?"

"Carly? It's Hans."

I pushed the button to let him in. "Come on up. You know the number?"

"I do. I'll be right there."

I nervously waited, fidgeting with my hair in the mirror by the front door.

Two minutes later there was a knock.

I looked through the peephole and then opened the door with a big smile. Hans had a bouquet of colorful daisies in his hand.

"Hi. Come on in." I opened the door wider. "Are those for me?"

Hans held them out to me, and I took them and brought them to my nose. "They are. You look fantastic."

"Thank you, and thank you for these. They're beautiful. Let me get a vase."

He followed me into the kitchen, looking my place over. "This is nice. Larger than I expected."

"It's a three-bedroom. Granted, the rooms aren't very big, but they get the job done. Gives me a studio, and a guest room."

"You paint here?"

I nodded as I filled the vase with water and arranged the daisies in it. I set it on the center of the kitchen table. "Would you like to see some of my work?" I asked, feeling anxious.

"I'd love to."

With trepidation, I moved past him and down the short hall to the room I used for my studio. I opened the door and switched on the light. Front and center was the pencil drawing of aliens I'd been working on earlier.

"That's cute. For a book?" he asked as he moved toward it.

"Yes. It's going to be adorable. I'm having fun depicting these alien creatures in various disastrous activities."

His eyes moved around the room, catching sight of some of my landscapes. "Wow, those are gorgeous."

I felt heat rise to my cheeks. "Thanks."

"What's that?" Hans began walking toward something behind me. "Is that... me?"

I spun around and now my face was flaming. "Uh... yes?"

He looked at me over his shoulder and then back at the painting. He stood there quietly, staring at it for so long I was ready to panic and jump out the window. "How did you capture me so well?" His voice was barely a whisper.

"Well, you're very memorable. I just... I had that image of you in my head and I had to get it on canvas. If you don't like it, I can paint over it—"

"Absolutely not! This is beyond amazing. You are incredibly talented." He pulled his phone out and snapped a picture. "You don't mind, do you?"

Warmth filled me at his high praise. "Thank you. And no, I don't mind."

"How much do you want for it?"

I stepped back and blinked at him. "What?"

"I want to buy it."

"You don't have to buy it. I'll give it to you as a gift when it's finished." I grinned at him. "Just so you know, I may end up painting you again. You've become a muse of sorts."

He chuckled. "I'm all right with that. Shall we go? We have reservations."

"Oh, yes, of course."

He put his hand on the small of my back and led me out of the studio, then toward the door. I grabbed my clutch and locked the door, then we went out to his car. We drove into Manhattan, chatting the whole way. The conversation never lagged. When he pulled up to the Japanese restaurant, I was very relaxed. The meal was delicious, and from there we went to an upscale club that had a line around the corner.

Hans took my hand and drew me with him to the front of the line.

"Don't we have to get in line?" I asked, looking at all the people waiting to get in.

"I'm friends with the club owner, so we get VIP treatment."

Well, color me impressed. I didn't say that, of course, but it was true.

The bouncer on the door recognized Hans and immediately let us beyond the velvet rope.

Hans ushered me through the throng of people, up a roped-off set of floating stairs to a section that overlooked the dance floor. There were leather sofas and chairs, with coffee tables scattered around. Several were occupied by celebrities and athletes.

Hans led me to a love seat that was unoccupied. "Comfortable?"

"Yes. I'm blown away." I grinned at him. "For a first date, I don't think this can be topped." I laughed.

He chuckled as he raised a hand to the waitress.

"Welcome to The Zone," she said. "What can I get for you?"

Hans went with a soda since he was driving, and I ordered a daiquiri.

After our drinks were delivered, and we'd chatted some more and enjoyed them, we headed down to the dance floor, where they were playing music from the eighties and nineties.

I was sweating by the time we returned to the VIP section. I sank down on the sofa, fanning my face. "I haven't danced like that in ages," I said with a laugh. "I'm going to be sore tomorrow."

Hans laughed too. "You should dance more; you're good at it. Is there anything you aren't good at?"

"I'm terrible at sports." I grinned. "Doesn't stop me from playing though."

"Good to know. I'll have to play tennis with you." Hans grinned.

"Did you not hear me say I'm terrible?" I laughed.

His eyes sparkled as his grin widened. "Exactly. So am I," he replied, joining my laughter.

"Bet you're better at basketball with your height." I leaned into him and smiled.

"I'm all right." He drew me closer, his lips a hair's breadth from mine. "You're sexy, you know that?"

"Am I?"

"You are. Can I kiss you?"

My breath caught in my throat at the look in his eyes. "Absolutely."

Hans pressed his lips to mine, and I could taste the sweetness of the soda he'd been drinking. Then his tongue swept against mine and every thought in my head disappeared. My toes curled and my fingers dove into his thick raven hair, as I hung on for dear life. When we came up for air, I knew I was falling for him.

Shortly after that world-stopping kiss, Hans drove me

home. The car ride was just as full of conversation as our ride there had been. He asked about past relationships, and I told him about Nelson. He didn't judge me for it, which was nice, and he understood my connection to Jake, which was even nicer. He told me about his past relationships as well.

Once we reached my apartment building, Hans walked me to my door, and then kissed me again, before wishing me pleasant dreams. I asked him to come in, but he declined, saying he had an early morning, but we made plans to meet up before his trip to Boston.

The next morning, after numerous dreams about Hans and his kisses, I was cleaning my apartment when my phone rang.

"Jake? Everything okay?" I switched off the vacuum cleaner.

Jake sighed. "I guess."

"What's going on?" I sank down on the sofa, filled with concern.

"Dad and Mom are fighting over the tutor and nanny again. I liked them, but Mom keeps firing them or Dad will say something to them he shouldn't, and they'll quit."

I wasn't surprised. Nelson would hit on anything in a skirt and if they were all women, then yeah, he'd consider them fair game. "I'm sorry, kiddo. Maybe see if they'll hire a guy?"

"They aren't asking my opinion. I wish things could go back to the way they were before, and you could watch me. I miss you. I miss my friends at school. I don't want a private teacher."

"I do too. Well, the watching you part, at least. I miss you too. Call me anytime. I'm always here to listen, even if I can't see you."

"I have to go," he grumbled. "Mom's calling me to meet the new nanny."

"Bye, Jake." I hung up with an overwhelming feeling of despair. There was nothing I could do to help him. It was very depressing, and I just wanted to cry and cuss out his parents and make them treat him better. I wished for the millionth time that I was Jake's mom.

Of course, it was a useless wish. That was never going to happen.

11

W eeks passed and I was falling into a relatively good routine. I saw Hans whenever we were both free, and we were growing closer. We weren't intimate yet. I was a little gun-shy about jumping into bed with someone new after Nelson, but I was enjoying the slow build of my relationship with Hans, and he was good with the pace as well. He didn't push for more and often said that when we were both ready for that step it would happen naturally.

Being with him wasn't a chore, or a headache. It was almost freeing, and I often wished I'd met him sooner, but if I had, I might not have been in a place to be as open to a new relationship, so maybe it was serendipity that we met in the exact moment when we needed to. Just thinking about him made me smile.

I'd painted three more images of him, but I'd not allowed him to see them. Not yet. I was thinking about getting a new agent and having them look at these as well as a few others that I was working on, in hopes of finally making my gallery show dream come true. Hans thought it was a good idea, but I was still leery of dropping Vivienne. I'd been with her for so long and she had a good heart.

I set my brush down and glanced at the clock. It was nearly midnight. I had been at it since early this morning. It seemed now that I wasn't with Nelson, I had more time to paint and draw. Probably because I wasn't watching Jake, or driving him back and forth to Manhattan.

I shook my head to push those thoughts away. I had never really minded caring for Jake; I'd enjoyed it, and I missed him.

I decided it was time to clean up and go to bed, so I washed out my brushes and rinsed off my palette, then straightened the studio and flipped off the light.

I had just climbed into bed when my phone rang. I glanced at it with surprise and saw Jake's name.

"Jake, are you okay?" It had to be something dire to have him calling me this late.

"Carly," he hissed over the line in barely a whisper.

"What's wrong?" I asked.

"I don't want Mom to hear me on the phone. She'd be mad. I'm in my closet."

"Jake, what's going on?" I was really worried. Why would Amanda care if he called me? She knew that I took care of Jake and that we kept in touch.

"I can't explain right now, but can you meet me tomorrow? After school?"

"I thought you were being tutored."

Jake huffed. "They couldn't find a new tutor after the last one, so they sent me back to school. So can you meet me? Please, Carly. It's important."

"Sure, but how? Who's picking you up?"

"Mom will send the nanny, but I'll just go with the walkers, and she won't know the difference."

"Okay, I'll meet you at the coffee shop two blocks from the school. You know the one?"

"Yes."

"Be careful walking, and get some sleep. You shouldn't even be awake right now."

"Okay. Night, Carly."

"Night."

I set my phone down and turned off the light, but it was another hour before I finally fell asleep. I was worried about Jake. My dreams were filled with all kinds of horrors involving him, and by the time I woke up, I felt as if I hadn't slept at all.

I didn't have anything urgent to work on today, so I decided to take the day off and relax as much as I could until I had to leave. It might have been better if I'd actually worked, though, because I couldn't keep my mind from creating all these terrible things that were going on with Jake.

By two I was a nervous wreck, so I grabbed my stuff and headed out the door. I made the drive into Manhattan, found the coffee shop, and went in. I ordered a coffee, and got a table. I'd had two full cups by the time Jake arrived. I stood up as he entered. He ran to me, wrapped his arms around my waist and hugged me tight. I hugged him back and just held him.

"Carly." He sighed.

"Hey, kid. What do you want to drink?"

"Hot chocolate."

"Okay. Sit down and I'll get it."

Jake did as I asked, and I went to place his order. I added

a piece of sponge cake as well. Sliding the plate and mug onto the table in front of him, I sat down in the opposite chair. "Now, what's going on?"

Jake looked around. In fact, his head had been on a swivel since he'd sat down, like he expected someone to be following him. "It's my mom. Only, I don't think she's my mom."

I frowned. "Jake, come on. Don't be silly. I saw her. Of course she's your mom."

"No, you don't understand. She looks like my mom, but she's not her."

I folded my arms over my chest and studied him. "Is this about the nannies and tutors?"

Jake swallowed the piece of cake he was eating. "No. This woman isn't my mom. She can't be." He gave me a frustrated look, his brow furrowed.

I relaxed my arms and leaned forward. "Tell me why you think she's not your mom."

He took a sip of his cocoa. "She talks a lot; I mean, she doesn't shut up. Mom never did that. Mom has always been too into herself to talk to me or Dad. And it's not just that she's talking a lot, she's swearing. Mom never swore and would get mad when Dad swore in front of me. Nearly every word out of her mouth now is a swear word."

"Okay, that is odd, but brain injuries can cause changes in behavior. Something could have triggered in her brain and made that part of her inhibitions loosen up."

"It's not just that. She smokes. Mom never smoked before, and she hated the smell of cigarettes. And she doesn't like any of the foods that were her favorites before. Now she thinks cheese puffs are the fucking bomb."

"Jake, language." I frowned at him.

"I'm just telling you what she said. Mom never ate junk like that. If she wanted a snack, it was always fruit. Or a smoothie. Something healthy. She loved avocado toast for breakfast. Now she says it looks and tastes like baby shi— um... poop."

"Okay, that is weird." I couldn't imagine the Amanda I knew eating cheese puffs or smoking. And the swearing was off too. Maybe Jake was on to something? But how was that possible? It's not like she could have been cloned. As far as I was aware that kind of tech was still in progress and the best they'd been able to do was on animals. I hadn't heard of them cloning people yet. Well, not unless you listened to conspiracy theories. Were they right? Had cloning become a thing? But if it had, what happened to the real Amanda? Where was she?

"That's what I'm trying to tell you," Jake said in exasperation. "And she's constantly watching me, looking at me. She still says she doesn't remember me, but she's making me feel weird, Carly. Like creepy-weird."

"Okay. Keep track of all the different things you notice and email them to me. We'll figure this out, I promise." I smiled at him. "Finish that up. I need to get you home before your nanny loses her mind."

Jake rolled his eyes. "She's pretty but not very smart. Dad hired her. She won't last long. That woman who's not mom fires them as quick as Dad hires them."

"Still, we shouldn't take advantage."

"I wish I could come stay with you," he said quietly as he played with his fork and last piece of cake, twisting it about on the plate.

"Me too. I've missed you," I answered honestly.

Jake ate his last bite and swallowed the rest of his hot chocolate. "Okay, I'm ready."

I gathered up our garbage and tossed it in the trash, then ushered him out the door to my car. Once he was buckled in, I headed for his townhouse.

"How's your dad?"

Jake shrugged. "I don't see him much. He doesn't like to come home."

"I'm sorry, Jake." I knew it wasn't my fault, but I empathized with him. He deserved a dad who protected and cared for him. Who wanted to spend time with him. Nelson was none of those things.

"It's okay. I have you," he said softly.

"Always, kiddo. Keep me posted, okay?" I pulled up in front of his house.

"I will." He undid his buckle then turned to me.

I hugged him and kissed the top of his head. "Be good, okay? Get your homework done before you jump on your video games."

He smiled. "Okay. Bye, Carly."

"Bye." I watched him climb the steps with anguish in my heart. I hated that he had to go through this. Go through thinking his mom wasn't his mom. Go through putting up with a father who couldn't be bothered. It wasn't fair.

He turned back and waved before he entered the house and then he was gone. Hidden behind the door where I worried that he was going to be mistreated by the woman he thought wasn't his real mother. The idea that she wasn't the real Amanda sent a chill down my spine. What if I'd just left him with an imposter?

12

J ake had emailed me every night for the last two weeks and the things he'd been observing were more and more disturbing. I couldn't get a handle on it. It was all just so bizarre.

Before the attack, Amanda had been very into body fitness and her health and beauty regime. She had a personal fitness trainer, she did Pilates, and yoga. She ate fruits and vegetables. She drank protein drinks and worried about her skin care. And above all, she rarely drank, and never hard liquor.

From Jake's emails, that had all changed. Now she was drinking tequila shots, and gin and bourbon. She brought home beer and drank a six-pack herself. Jake said she didn't get drunk like his dad did, which for a lightweight drinker was surprising. I wondered if her being drunk was just different than Nelson's, and I'd said as much to Jake, but he'd replied that she swore more, and laughed loudly, but she sounded the same drunk and not drunk.

He had also mentioned that she never put up with his

dad's attitude. She yelled at him no matter who was around. Before the attack, Amanda did her best to keep their fights between them and out of the public eye.

And then there was the fact that she refused to return to the doctor for follow-up visits, even though she had a massive scar on her forehead. Amanda had always cared greatly about her appearance and a scar wouldn't have been acceptable before. It blew my mind that she hadn't already made an appointment with a plastic surgeon to fix it.

His latest email said he'd seen her sneaking out of the house late at night, leaving him alone because his dad wasn't there. And then he'd caught her whispering on the phone a few times. She would immediately hang up if she noticed him nearby, and once she'd whisper-yelled at someone on the phone and when he'd asked who it was, she'd said it was a wrong number. Jake had thought it was all suspicious.

Everything Jake reported had my worry growing exponentially. I was starting to agree with him that the 'Amanda' who had come home to them wasn't his actual mother. I didn't know what had happened to the real Amanda, but I wanted to find out. I just didn't know how I was going to achieve that.

Not until Nelson started calling again.

I ignored him at first. I didn't want to talk to Nelson. I didn't want to hear him whine at me to come back to him. That was never going to happen. I was enjoying being away from him. More than that, I was enjoying being with Hans.

The only reason I called him back was because he'd left a voicemail about Jake.

"What's wrong with Jake?" I asked, out of breath and full of worry.

"Nothing. He's okay."

I let out a breath of relief.

"I need you, Carly. I miss you. Don't you miss me?"

"No. I don't miss you at all. I'm much happier without you," I replied. "If it weren't for Jake, I wouldn't be on the phone with you now, and you know it."

He sighed. "I know. I just don't know what to do. That's why I called you."

"What do you want from me?"

"I can't get a nanny to stay, and I'm struggling to find a replacement. Amanda is being difficult, and I think you might be the only one who can watch Jake without her getting her nose out of joint."

"Is that because you keep sleeping with the nannies? Because if that's the case, I'm on her side."

"I didn't sleep with them all. She's just a jealous bitch. She left me before the attack, but she doesn't even remember that and insists that we play happy family all the time. It's like she forgot everything."

I snorted, but his words intrigued me. Even Nelson was noticing differences in Amanda. "Have you brought up the fact she moved out prior to the attack?"

"Of course I did, but she won't hear any talk of that kind. She said we made vows and we are sticking to them till death do us part. I swear she's just doing this to get back at me."

I so didn't need to hear any of this. I didn't really care if he stayed married to Amanda or not. My concern was Jake. "Good for her."

"I don't know why you're taking her side," he complained. "You're supposed to be on my side."

"I'm on Jake's side."

"Fine, be on his side by watching him for us."

"Why does he need a nanny anyway? Can't Amanda watch him? She works from home."

"She says she's still recovering and that she doesn't understand his homework or how to handle him."

I rolled my eyes. "I'll watch Jake, but there will be rules. First, you will pay me the going rate for nannies these days."

"I can do that," he agreed easily.

"Second, you don't come near me. I don't want to see you, unless I absolutely have to."

"But—"

"No buts. Third, I'm watching him at your place and I'm off duty by six every night, unless I'm keeping Jake at my place over the weekend or if you and Amanda give me notice beforehand—and if I do, then you are compensating me for that time."

Nelson sighed. "Okay. We'll do it your way."

"Good." I was proud of myself for setting boundaries and having a plan of action. "I'll start tomorrow."

"Can't you get him after school today? I promised Amanda I'd make sure he was taken care of today."

My eye twitched. "Fine, I will pick him up from school. I'll have to leave now to be there in time."

I hung up, grabbed what I'd need to spend the afternoon with Jake. The one good thing about all this was that I was going to be able to keep an eye on Amanda and see her in action. Part of me hoped that Jake had exaggerated things the way kids often did, but I had a feeling that wouldn't be the case.

I pulled into the car pick-up line and sent Jake a text.

Hey, kiddo, guess who is your new 'nanny'.

No way! Really?

> I'm in the pick-up line. Want to grab a
> snack?

Yes!

A few minutes later, Jake got in the car and hugged me. I smiled and pulled away from the school once he was buckled. I headed for a hot pretzel shop.

"How was school?" I asked.

"Eh, it was okay. How did Dad talk you into being my nanny?"

"He was desperate, and I missed you." I gave him a grin.

"Does Mom know?"

"She should by now. I guess we'll find out when I get you home. I did tell your dad that I wasn't staying after six."

"How come?"

"Because I've met someone." I smiled at him.

Jake's eyes narrowed. "Who?"

"His name is Hans. He is a pianist and is very talented."

"So you really aren't going to get back together with Dad?" His tone told me he was feeling disappointed.

"I'm sorry, kiddo. I won't be getting back together with your dad. But that doesn't mean I don't care about you and love you. You know that, right?" I parked the car in an open space on the side of the street.

"Yeah. It just sucks."

I reached over and scruffed his hair. "Come on, let's get some cinnamon pretzels, then we'll get you home and tackle your homework."

Jake was quick to unbuckle and jump out of the car.

I hurried around the car, locking it as I went. I dropped

my arm around his shoulders, and we went into the shop, placed our order, and found a seat by the window.

As we ate our pretzels, we chatted about some more of the things he'd observed. I promised him we'd figure it out and I'd keep him safe.

"Thanks, Carly." He smiled up at me.

After we finished, I took him home and stayed to help him with his homework. I also fixed him dinner since that seemed to be something Amanda required from the 'hired help'. She didn't want to worry about feeding the kid.

I stayed until seven that night, only because I ended up listening to Amanda describe what she needed from me while I was there. Jake was right, she really had become a talker, and nearly every other word was an expletive. It amazed me that she could fit so many into one sentence.

By the time I got home it was nearly eight. Hans was playing at the bar tonight and I was supposed to meet him for a drink between sets. I hurried to get ready and then went to Melodies. I got a little thrill to see my painting of him hanging on the wall near the bar.

"Hey, Carly," Devon called with a wave as I came in. "I'll send a waitress over with your usual."

I smiled. "Thanks."

I headed for my usual table, which sported a reserved sign. So much had changed since that first night I'd been in. Well, not that much, but for me it had. I now had a 'usual' drink and a 'usual' table that was reserved for me. It had the perfect view of Hans as he played.

His smile grew brighter as he noticed me sitting down a few feet from him. The song he was playing ended, and he began to play the opening chords to an old Air Supply song.

His rich baritone lifted as he sang, his eyes on me. *"I, I was the lonely one, wondering what went wrong—"*

His eyes sparkled as he came to the chorus, and it felt as if he were singing right into my heart. I was so distracted by him that I didn't even realize that the waitress was standing next to me.

"Ever since you started coming in, his playing has become so much more... I don't know... electric maybe? It's like you can feel his emotions pouring out of him."

I glanced up as Megan set my drink down. "It's different when I'm not here?"

"It's not the same. He's crazy good all the time, but the atmosphere changes when you're here. It's like sex for my ears when he plays for you." She held the tray next to her hip, her eyes on Hans.

I felt my cheeks flush and I lifted my drink, gulping a swallow. I had no idea what to say to that. "I'm sorry?"

She laughed. "Don't apologize. My tips go up dramatically when he plays like this. I mean, just look around... everyone is entranced."

My eyes glided over the other patrons, and she was right. Everyone's eyes were riveted on Hans. It made me smile.

"I'll let you get back to ogling your man," Megan said with a wink before sauntering away.

Hans played several more songs. Our eyes met every few seconds and I felt heat all over my body at his looks.

When he finished his set, he joined me, bending to give me a quick kiss before sitting down. "How was your day?"

I told him about Nelson's call and my decision to help out by watching Jake. He already knew about Jake's worry that Amanda wasn't the real Amanda, and he understood my reasoning for wanting to help keep him safe. It was nice that he wasn't jealous or demanding that I not have anything to do with them.

He reached for my hand and held it. "If this will give you peace of mind, then I'm glad. I just worry you'll be stretching yourself thin with being his nanny and trying to get your paintings done."

I sighed. He wasn't wrong. It was going to take some creative time management for me to accomplish everything, but I wasn't going to let Jake down. "I know. It's not the ideal solution and it's not going to work long term. I don't want to do it long term either, as much as I love Jake."

He smiled. "So, what's your schedule looking like for the rest of the week? Am I going to be able to see you?"

We discussed both of our schedules and made tentative plans for later in the week.

"So I guess we'll have to get in as much kissing as possible tonight," he said, his eyes on my lips for a moment before rising to gaze into mine with an intense heat. He reached for my face, his thumb tracing over my cheek in a gentle caress. "I'm going to miss seeing you as often as I have been."

My heart fluttered. This man. I didn't know how I got so lucky, but I was grateful to fate for bringing me into Melodies that night and into Hans' life.

I had no idea what the future would bring, especially now that I was going to be doing this nanny job for Jake, but I was damn certain I was going to make sure I kept Hans in it.

13

It had been a week of waking up at six in the morning and driving into Manhattan to pick Jake up for school and drop him off, then going back to Brooklyn to get work done for my clients. I did that until two, then made the trip back to pick him back up, take him home and work on homework, make him dinner and get him settled. Most nights I was out of there by six or six thirty.

I had yet to see anything unusual in Amanda's behavior. It was like she was trying to impress me, or maybe more like she was on her best behavior. She wasn't swearing as much, which I took as a good sign that maybe she was returning to normal. She was smoking, and I did see her eating more junk food than she used to, but all those things could be explained away by the head injury.

It was Friday and I had just picked Jake up from school. He got in with a smile on his face.

"Hey, kiddo. Good day?"

"Yeah, pretty good. I'm glad it's the weekend. Can I stay at your place?"

I had plans with Hans for Saturday night, so I wasn't sure that was a good idea. "I don't know. I didn't discuss that with your parents."

"They won't care. They'd rather be rid of me." He stared out of the window.

"Why do you want to come to my place?"

"Because I don't want to hear them arguing all weekend."

"I haven't heard them arguing at all since I've been around. In fact, I haven't seen your mom doing anything really unusual, not anything that couldn't be explained by the head injury. Maybe she's returning to her normal self?"

Jake's brow furrowed. "She's been hiding it. She doesn't know what to make of you."

"What do you mean?"

"She's asked me questions about you, but Dad told me not to tell her anything about you and him. Just that you were friends."

I sighed. "Great. So, he's basically lied to her. She doesn't remember who I am, does she?"

"Nope. She remembers you from the hospital, but that's it."

When we reached the townhouse, I said, "I'll go see what's available to make for dinner. Go put your stuff away."

"Yes, ma'am." He grinned as he ran up to his room to put his bookbag away and change out of his school clothes.

I headed for the kitchen, pulled open the fridge and began to look for ingredients.

"Babe, glad you're here." Nelson walked up behind me and wrapped his arms around me.

I pushed on his arms and moved away from him. "I'm not your 'babe' anymore, and I told you to leave me alone. I don't want you near me." I shut the fridge and turned around to stare at him.

"Babe, don't be like that." He tried to reach for me again, but I pushed him back.

"I'm not doing this. I will walk out that door in a heartbeat if you keep it up."

"What's going on?" Amanda interrupted, watching from the doorway. "Are you hitting on her?"

"What?" Nelson looked startled. "No, of course not."

I folded my arms and glared at him. "Yes, you were, and I told you to knock it off."

Amanda gave me a curious look. "Who are you to him again?"

"Nelson's ex."

Her eyes brightened as she stared at me. "His ex and he is so pathetic he keeps trying to hit on you?"

"Hey," Nelson whined. He looked hurt.

Honestly, I didn't care. "That about sums it up."

"I have no idea why I put up with his shit for so long." Amanda stared daggers at him. "You will leave her alone from now on, do you hear me? I will not have you disrespecting me in the fucking house. Why don't you just go?"

"But—"

"Get out of my house," Amanda demanded. "I will not have you trying your shit with Carly anymore. She isn't interested. Are you, Carly?" She arched a brow at me, a slow smile curving her lips.

"Absolutely not. As I've told you before, I'm seeing someone."

"Who is it?" Nelson asked, jealousy leaking into his voice.

"No one you know, nor anyone who wishes to know you," I replied.

Amanda laughed. "That's my girl."

Nelson sulked for a few minutes and then turned to leave. "It's my fucking house," he muttered as he stomped out of the room. The front door slammed a moment later.

"Ugh, that man. When will he learn?" Amanda stared at the empty doorway.

"When pigs learn to fly?" I tossed over my shoulder with a grin.

"You're probably right." Amanda threaded her arm through mine, and practically dragged me into the living room to sit down. "Tell me more about yourself."

"Um, okay. I'm an artist. That's how I met Nelson, almost six years ago."

"So, he cheated on me with you," she said matter-of-factly.

"Yeah. I didn't know that he was married when we met. He told me he was divorced. Afterward, when I found out, he claimed you were separated... but—" I sighed and looked away. "I knew. I'm sorry. I tried to stop seeing him, but he'd bring Jake around, and I adore him, so I would cave, and it just became this cycle. I know it's not an excuse. There isn't any excuse that would make what I did okay—" I fumbled.

"You're right, there is no excuse for you to sleep with someone's husband, let alone mine." She smiled, but it was creepy, like the smile a predator gave its prey right before it devoured it.

I shivered in response.

"However, I have a feeling I didn't much care what Nelson did—prior to the attack, I mean. I don't exactly care now, except that I don't want to give all of this up." She leveled her stare at me, her eyes boring into mine as she waved her hand about the room.

"Well, the only reason I'm around anymore is to help you with Jake. I wouldn't be here otherwise."

She tilted her head and studied me for a few moments. "I believe you. Nelson has lost his power over you, which is good. As for Jake, I do appreciate your help. I have been having a hard time trying to find someone to fucking take care of him. I just won't be disrespected in my own home by Nelson sleeping with the help."

"I can promise he won't be talking me into sleeping with him again."

"See that you keep it that way," Amanda replied with a sly smile.

I nodded. "I will, of course. Um... can I ask you something?"

She gave me a considering look. "What is it?"

"How did you get Nelson to listen to you? How did you get him to back down and stop whining?"

She shrugged. "He's a manipulative man, but I know how to handle him."

"Did the head injury change you so much?"

"What do you mean? I've not changed. Not really." She stared at me as if to dare me to contradict her.

"Before, you were indifferent, I suppose. You just ignored him and Jake. Now you seem more... involved. More harsh. Not with Jake, exactly, but with Nelson, and don't get me wrong, I am glad to see it; he needs that, and I wish I could do it—"

Her predator grin was back. "Jake is a child. He needs guidance. A firm hand; I hope you'll help with that. As for Nelson..." She shrugged. "Call it a trauma response."

A trauma response? Was she implying it was from the trauma of the attack or something else? After looking at her for a moment, I didn't think it was from the attack. She was talking about something else, but I had no idea what. Amanda was a spoilt, pampered wife. At least she had been prior to the attack. Now she was something different, but I didn't know what. I didn't even think it was my place to figure it out, except that Jake had asked me to.

He was my worry. I knew he was concerned that this Amanda wasn't his mom, but if she wasn't, I had no idea who she really was. Maybe this had always been the real Amanda beneath the veneer she lacquered on to hide her true personality. I couldn't be sure.

I'd need to watch her more intently and see if she slipped up, because there was no way I was going to let her hurt Jake. Ever.

14

Over the following month I had several more dates with Hans, who was very understanding about me helping out Nelson and Amanda with Jake. He didn't like that Nelson was around so much, but he didn't have anything to worry about. Amanda stayed on top of Nelson and his inability to keep his hands to himself.

One day I was chopping vegetables for the meal I was making for Jake, and Amanda sat on the breakfast stool by the counter.

"So, we were never friends before?" she asked, sounding curious.

"No." I set the knife down and looked at her. We'd gotten to know one another better over the last month of me being here every day. "I don't think you'd have wanted to be friends with me before."

"Hmm, probably not." She laughed and picked up a piece of red pepper. "Though we probably had more in common than I knew. Both of us putting up with Nelson's shit."

"True."

"Still, we're friends now, aren't we?" she asked, taking a bite of the pepper, then making a face as if disgusted by the taste.

"Yes," I agreed. I couldn't say that I exactly liked her, but I didn't dislike her either. I still thought there was something very strange about her, but I hadn't discovered proof that she wasn't the same Amanda from before. It was pretty hard to disprove she was that Amanda. She had her face, for heaven's sake.

"I'm so glad." She smiled, but once again it was that predatory smile.

It made me nervous when she turned that particular smile on me. Like I was about to be swallowed whole by an anaconda and there was no escape.

"So... have you remembered anything about the attack yet?" I asked.

Her expression turned sour, and she pursed her lips. "No, I haven't fucking remembered anything."

"Nothing? Not even about who you were supposed to be having a reunion with?" I set the knife in the sink, away from her, then turned to pick up the chopped veggies and put them in the skillet.

"No." She rubbed her forehead. "I don't know what kind of reunion it was. I don't remember shit, okay?" She slammed her hand down on the counter. "Stop pestering me about it."

I cringed, but nodded. I hadn't meant to upset her. I just wanted to know if she'd had any memories come back. It was odd that she hadn't. Well, perhaps it wasn't strange that she hadn't remembered the attack or the events leading up to it, but she should have remembered everything else by now.

She remembered selective things about her life. Like she knew she was married to Nelson. She remembered how she spent her days prior to the attack, not that she seemed interested in going back to living her life as a pampered princess who worked when she wanted to. It wasn't exactly work—more like she'd sat on committees for charities and helped arrange fundraisers.

Then there was Jake. Amanda couldn't remember anything about him. Not his birthday, his middle name, what school he went to. It was very weird. I didn't know what to make of it. It wasn't that she was mean to Jake. She was actually very cordial. But who wanted a parent who was merely nice to you? Who treated you as though you were just some stranger visiting their home. That was pretty much how Amanda treated Jake.

"So, have you decided what you're going to do for Jake's birthday?" I asked, hoping I wasn't going to piss her off.

"When is it?"

I heard a loud pop and turned to see that she'd opened a bottle of wine. I watched as she poured herself a glass. "Next week."

"What is?" She sipped her wine.

I blinked, and then frowned at her. "Jake's birthday? It's next week."

"Oh."

"So, are you planning anything special?" I stirred the veggies and then pulled the oven open to check the chicken.

"Why would I? Isn't that your job? I mean, you're the one we pay to watch him and keep him happy." Amanda shrugged, then gulped her glass of wine and poured another.

I gritted my teeth. I wanted to scream at her. I wanted her to actually care about Jake. To love him. To want to build a relationship with him, even if she couldn't remember giving birth to him. I wanted to shake her and yell at her, but I knew that I couldn't. It wasn't fair to her. She'd been injured. She had amnesia. It was just frustrating.

I could imagine it was even more frustrating for Jake, seeing as he was the one dealing with the mom he loved not remembering him. It didn't seem fair for either of them. Still, it was Jake I felt bad for. I knew I needed to do something to help. Something to make it seem like she actually cared.

"I'd be happy to come up with a party for him, if you want."

"Sure. Just take care of it. Nothing too expensive though. I don't want to spoil him."

"Right." I nodded. "Perhaps a sleepover? He could invite some school friends?"

"What? Here?" Amanda scoffed. "No, I think not. I don't want a bunch of pre-pubescent boys running all over my house."

"Do you want a family party?" I asked.

"No. Can't you just take him somewhere?"

I pulled the pan of chicken from the oven and set it on the stove. "You don't want to celebrate with him?"

"Not particularly, no. I don't have anything in common with an eight-year-old boy."

"He's going to be ten."

"I don't have anything in common with a ten-year-old either."

"He's your son, Amanda."

She sighed. "I know that, but I don't remember him. I don't even know what to do with him."

I frowned and turned off the burner with the veggies. "But he's your son. Even if you don't remember him, you should feel some kind of connection to him."

Amanda shrugged. "Yeah, well, I don't."

I felt sad for Amanda, but my heart broke for Jake. He deserved to be loved. He deserved to have two parents who loved him.

I couldn't say anything. I couldn't even look at her because I knew she'd see the horror on my face. Instead, I busied myself fixing plates for me, Jake, and Amanda. After I got them made, when I felt I could speak without sounding accusatory, I said, "I'll figure something out that he'll enjoy."

"Great. He's a good kid. I want him to be happy."

I supposed that was the best I could hope for at this point. It didn't seem like she was going to make an effort to get to know him or try to be a mother to him, but at least she wanted him to be happy. Or as happy as he could be with a mother who couldn't remember him.

I handed her a plate and then called, "Jake, dinner," before carrying his plate and mine to the table.

"Coming!" he shouted as he ran down the stairs. He skidded to a stop in the kitchen and looked at his mom. "You're eating with us?"

Amanda shrugged. "I've got nothing better to do."

Jake's eyes slid to mine for a moment, then he gave her a slight nod before taking his seat. He looked so depressed as he stared at his plate that I couldn't help myself.

"Hey, kiddo. I was thinking, if you don't already have plans for your birthday, how about we visit Bryant Park and do some ice skating, then maybe check out the New Victory

Theatre? I think they have a new show going on. You could bring a friend."

Jake picked up his fork and looked at me across the table. I could tell by his expression that he knew what I was trying to do. His gaze slid to his mom for a moment, but she seemed more interested in her wine and the food on her plate than him. "Sure, but can it just be you and me? Maybe Hans?"

I nodded. Jake had met Hans once, and he seemed to like him, which I was glad of. "Sure."

"And can I stay at your place for the weekend?"

I looked at Amanda. "Would that be all right with you?" I asked, tapping her wrist.

"What? Sure. I don't care. Whatever you want."

I hesitated for a moment, then smiled at Jake. "So, what do you think, you good with that?"

"Sure." He nodded.

We continued to eat, but I made a mental note to make sure Amanda and Nelson got him a good bunch of gifts for him to open.

I just wished the gift he could really get was his mother's memory back.

15

After an afternoon of ice skating and seeing the show at the New Victory Theatre, we headed back to my place. I had called Nelson earlier that morning to remind him to get Jake some good birthday gifts. I really hoped he would, but I couldn't be sure, so I wanted to do everything I could to make sure he had a fantastic day. Hans had joined us for part of the day, but then had to head over to Melodies to play the piano. Jake asked him to come over for breakfast, which he agreed to do.

"So, what do you want to do now?" I asked as we entered my apartment.

"Can we get pizza and watch a movie?" Jake suggested.

I smiled. "Sure, kiddo. Did you like the new Switch game?"

"Yeah. I've been wanting to play it, but it can wait. I'd rather do something with you."

"I'm honored you'd rather hang with me than play video games." I laughed. "Go get your pjs on and I'll order the pizza."

"Yes, ma'am." Jake took off for the guest room at the rapid speed only a child could achieve.

I called in the order, then headed to my room and changed into leggings and a sweatshirt. Once I was comfortable, I returned to the living room to find Jake wrapped in a fuzzy blanket, remote in hand as he scrolled through the streaming movies. "Did you find anything good?"

"Don't know," he mumbled as he moved the cursor so fast that I could barely take in what was on the screen. He'd pause for half a second then move on.

"You're making me seasick," I said with a laugh as I looked away from the screen.

"How about this one?" Jake paused on a Christmas movie.

"That Santa doesn't look very jolly, and it's titled *Violent Night*... I'm not sure that's a good idea. Let's go for something not rated for adults, okay?"

Jake sighed dramatically. "Fine... how about *Nightmare Before Christmas*?"

"You've seen that one before."

"I like it."

"Okay, I'm up for it." I ruffled his hair, which he quickly straightened back into place.

Before he could hit play, there was a buzz to the outside intercom.

"That's probably the pizza. Just a sec." I went to check and let them in. When they reached the door, I handed over the money and brought our pizza into the living room, setting it on the coffee table. "Let me grab some plates, then we can eat and watch the show."

Two minutes later, we were snuggled on the couch chowing down on pepperoni pizza and watching Jack and

Sally. I'd seen the movie many times before, so I practically knew it by heart, but it was still good.

Jake fell asleep about three-fourths of the way in, but I let it continue to play to the end, then I carried him to the guest room and put him to bed. I cleaned up the living room, then headed to my room for the night, but I couldn't sleep. I was still thinking about all the weird stuff going on with Amanda.

I decided to pose a question to a neurologist on Reddit and see if I could get some answers about temporary amnesia. I didn't want to use names. That stuff was permanent, and I didn't want to be outed or have Amanda or Nelson find out about it. So, I created a new account with a generic email address and random name.

Dear Dr. Adams,

I'm writing because a friend of mine was recently hit on the head and has been experiencing temporary amnesia. I am curious, though, because it seems so strange that she can remember some things but not others. She can remember her life, the fact that she was married, and that she had a particular job, but she's forgotten her child, doesn't recognize them at all, and even knowing the child now, has no real interest in recalling them. She has also had numerous behavioral changes, such as going from an extremely healthy lifestyle to an unhealthy one. On top of that, she often cusses now, where before she abhorred that kind of language.

Is this normal? Will she ever remember or revert back to how she was before? I feel bad for her kid. They believe

she isn't really their mother, but an imposter, and I'm
starting to agree. Is that possible? If it is, what do we do?
Do we go to the police?

Any help or guidance you can give me would be greatly
appreciated.

Feeling bad for the kid,

Ashlee Simon

Since it was late, I doubted I'd hear back from the
neurologist right away. Instead of sitting there anxiously
awaiting an answer, I set my phone aside, turned off the light
and went to sleep.

My dreams were troubled; I kept chasing something that
I could never quite catch, and I woke up feeling exhausted. I
reached for my phone and looked to see if I'd received a
reply. I was excited to see that I had, and I pulled up the
thread.

Dear Ashlee,

I can see your dilemma and I want to assure you that
traumatic brain injuries can indeed cause changes in
behavior such as you've described. It is unfortunate that
your friend no longer recognizes her child, and that the
child fears their mother has been, for lack of a better word,
body-swapped. Amnesia is a tricky disease. It can and
often does go away on its own, allowing the patient to
regain their memories over time, but there is a small

percentage of cases where the mind never makes that
recovery. The memories are lost.

Do not try to force memories onto your friend or demand
anything from her as it will merely frustrate you all and
can sometimes cause more damage than good. I would
recommend giving her time along with as much care and
understanding as you can.

Of course, I suppose it might be possible that your friend
isn't your friend but an imposter. However, that scenario
is very unlikely unless you're living in a fictional story-
book, so I would not suggest going to the police with your
theories. That is, unless you gather more evidence to
corroborate such a theory. In that case, I would be inter-
ested to have you write again because it would be fasci-
nating to see how it was accomplished.

My heart goes out to you, your friend, and her child. I
hope her memory does return soon.

Best of luck,

Dr. Adams

I sighed. That was not a lot of help. He did confirm that it
was possible for her behavior to change, but it all just
seemed too strange to me—the way she remembered some
generic things, but nothing real. Part of me wanted to write
again and give more details but I feared someone who knew
Amanda or me or Nelson would read it and recognize them.

I didn't want to draw more attention to them than necessary. It wasn't fair to Jake.

I set my phone aside and got up. After taking a quick shower and making the bed, I grabbed my phone and headed for the kitchen. As I pulled out ingredients to make pancakes, my phone buzzed.

It was Hans.

> What kind of donuts does Jake like?

I smiled as I replied.

> Anything chocolate and he'll be your best friend forever.

> Got it. Be there in ten minutes, sweetheart.

I replied with a kiss emoji and then started mixing the batter. I turned on some music while I prepped the food. By the time Hans arrived, I had a stack of pancakes made. "Jake? Hans is here," I called down the hall as I headed for the door to let him in.

Jake zoomed past me and reached the door before me, yanking it open. "Hi, Hans," he said, his eyes going to the box in his hand. "What's that?"

Hans chuckled and handed it over. "Exactly what you think." He leaned in and kissed my cheek. "Good morning. Did you sleep well?" he murmured.

"Good morning." I smiled. "I slept okay. You?"

Hans shrugged. "I didn't get much sleep. I was at the bar late. I missed seeing you there in your usual spot." He smiled, his eyes sparkling as he stared at me.

"I missed being there," I replied as Jake headed for the kitchen with us following behind.

"Carly, can I have a donut?" Jake asked as we entered the kitchen.

"You want it before your pancakes? They're ready."

Jake eyed the donut box, then the stack of pancakes on the counter. "Can I have them at the same time?"

I laughed. "Sure, kiddo. Let me get you a plate."

The three of us sat and ate a leisurely breakfast, then I sent Jake to pack up his stuff. Hans and I were driving him home so we could spend the afternoon together, just the two of us.

"I wish I didn't have to go." Jake sulked in the backseat.

I glanced at him in the rearview mirror. "You'll see me tomorrow morning to take you to school."

After dropping Jake off, I reached across the console and took Hans' hand. "So, what are we doing today?" I asked.

"Lunch here in the city?" he asked.

"That sounds nice."

He directed me to an intimate bistro, and we soon found ourselves ensconced in a corner booth with dim lighting and a candle on the table.

Hans draped an arm around my shoulders and pulled me closer to him. "I really did miss you last night."

I smiled and kissed his lush lips. "I know. I would have been there if it weren't for my having Jake. You like him, don't you?"

"He's a good kid. Hard not to like him." Hans smiled. "He adores you. Probably as much as I do." His smile widened to a grin.

I laughed. "Do you?"

"Do I what?" he teased, his pale gray eyes twinkling in the candle glow.

"Adore me," I teased back.

"Utterly. I'm crazy about you," Hans murmured, nibbling on my neck.

I sighed at the pleasure of it, but then the waitress showed up with our food and we had to stop. "I wrote to a neurologist about Amanda's memory lapse," I murmured as we dug into our food.

"Oh? Did they answer back?"

I nodded. "Pretty much what you'd expect. It's just... I don't know, it seems like it's more than just memory loss. It's like those memories were never there. I don't know how to explain it." I shook my head as I tried to wrap my mind around it all.

Hans seemed thoughtful as he thought about it. "Well, to me it sounds as though there are three possibilities."

I gave him a wry smile. "Only three?"

He chuckled. "Well, aside from actual temporary amnesia."

"Okay, what possibilities are you thinking?"

He set his fork down and picked up his water glass, taking a sip. "One, it could be an actual serious mental illness, manifesting as amnesia. Something like schizophrenia or maybe something similar."

"I hadn't considered that, but it doesn't feel right. There's no family history that I know of, and doesn't it run in families?" I frowned as I tried to recall information I'd heard about the topic.

"Honestly, I don't know enough about it to be sure one way or the other." Hans shrugged.

"Okay, let's set that idea aside. What are your other thoughts?"

"Two, it could be she is being influenced by an outside source. Maybe being blackmailed?"

My brow furrowed as I thought about that idea.

Hans reached over and smoothed the crease in my forehead with his finger, then leaned in and kissed me. "You look so pensive."

"I'm just trying to decide if that's a viable theory. It's possible, but I can't imagine who would want to blackmail her into pretending to not know her kid. I mean, what would be the gain other than to hurt Jake?"

"I didn't say it was a good theory." He chuckled.

I laughed and took another bite of my food. "Okay, what's the third idea?"

"The third is that Jake is right and the woman claiming to be his mom is an imposter. A very convincing imposter."

"I don't know about convincing. If she wanted to be convincing, wouldn't she at least pretend to know Jake? Act like his mom? Amanda barely remembers he's around most of the time."

"I don't think so. If you wanted people to believe that you were someone else, it would be easiest to do that if you then claimed to have a form of amnesia that would explain away any mistakes you made about people, places, and things you are supposed to know about, wouldn't it?"

I bit my lip as I realized he was right. That would make it incredibly easy to fool people. You gained sympathy from all the friends and family of the person whose life you were taking over and be excused from any errors you made.

"But wouldn't that mean they'd have to look exactly like that person?" I asked.

"They do say we all have a doppelganger out there some-where. Maybe this person is Amanda's," Hans suggested.

I thought about it for a few minutes while we finished eating. "I suppose all your suggestions are in the realm of possibilities. I just need to figure out which one is true now."

"Are you leaning toward any one in particular?" Hans asked.

I glanced at him and nodded slowly. "I think so. I'm wondering how I can find out more about this doppelganger theory of yours. It has me intrigued. But if that's the case, what happened to the real Amanda?"

16

The following Friday, when I stopped at the townhouse to make Jake breakfast and get him off to school, Amanda pulled me aside. She gripped my arm and drew me into the living room and away from Nelson, who was in the kitchen.

"What's up?" I asked, looking from her to the kitchen door.

"Jake's staying at a friend's house tonight, so you don't have to pick him up."

I stared at her, wondering why that was a secret. "Okay." I turned to head back to the kitchen to get started on breakfast.

Amanda captured my arm again, not letting me get far. "I thought maybe we could go out tonight."

I stopped short and blinked at her. We'd never been friends. Even now, with us acting so cordial, I didn't think we'd ever get to the point where we'd hang out together. "Um..."

"We could go for drinks, have grown-up conversations." Amanda looked so hopeful that I felt bad saying no.

"Well, I was going to listen to Hans play tonight at the bar," I started.

"That's perfect. What bar?"

"Melodies. It's in Brooklyn."

Her lips pursed in distaste, but she quickly nodded and said, "Seven o'clock?"

"Sure." I didn't know what else to do but agree.

"I'm looking forward to it." She gave me that predatory grin again and a shiver slid down my back.

"I should go get Jake's breakfast ready," I murmured and headed for the kitchen again.

After dropping Jake at school, I went home. I had plenty of work to do for my clients, but I also wanted to get some painting time in for the series I was doing for what I hoped would get me into a gallery. As I pulled into the parking garage, my phone rang.

"Blaine? Everything okay?" I asked as I climbed from my car.

"Can't a brother call his sister just to check in and say hello?" he questioned.

I smiled, not that he could see me. "Sure, but is that really why you called?"

"No." He laughed. "Dave wants to invite you to lunch tomorrow. I said I'd call and ask."

"Oh." I considered my schedule. "I've got some work to do in the morning, but I'd love to come."

"Great. So how are things?"

"Good." My thoughts turned to Hans, and I smiled. "Really good."

"Oh yeah?"

I opened my apartment door. "I've met someone."

Gasping, Blaine said, "He's not married, is he?"

"Of course not. I learned my lesson, okay?"

"Sorry. It was a low blow. So, who is this guy?"

"Hans Wohlers. He's a musician."

"You're not involved with one of those buskers on the street, are you?"

I rolled my eyes and practically growled, "He's an extremely talented pianist and gives concerts all over the country, and when he's not away doing that, he's playing at Melodies. He's amazing." I set my purse down on the kitchen table and fumed.

"Sorry, I just get concerned. You're my little sister. I'm trying to look out for you," he added quietly.

"I'm a grown woman, Blaine. Even if he did busk on a street corner for a living, I would still go out with him because he's genuine. He treats me well and I love his company."

"Okay, so long as you're happy. And I'm glad you didn't get back together with Nelson."

"I am helping him and Amanda with Jake, but they're paying me. Amanda was attacked and lost parts of her memory."

"Probably not the best idea for you to still be in their lives. It's gotta be awkward, right?"

"It's fine. In fact, I'm meeting Amanda for drinks tonight."

"Really? Isn't that weird?"

"Oh, it's totally weird. She knows I was with Nelson for a while, but she also knows that I have no interest in being with him anymore." I checked the clock. It was almost ten. "So tomorrow, lunch. I'll see you then."

"See you tomorrow."

I hung up and set my phone down on the counter, then went into my studio and got busy.

At five thirty, I cleaned everything up and headed to my room to get ready for the evening out. I chose an emerald-green sleeveless silk top, a swishy black mini skirt, and low black heels. I added simple, faux emerald drop earrings, and a gold necklace. I put on a knee-length black coat and a long black scarf, picked up my clutch that I'd switched my stuff to, then headed out.

I walked into Melodies at six forty-five. Devon waved to me as I made my way to my usual table, which once again had a reserved card on it. I smiled as I sat down and took off my coat. Hans wasn't at the piano, and I wondered where he was.

I rarely had to order anymore, unless I wanted something different, but usually I went with the same thing I'd ordered that first night. It had become my signature drink. Megan set it on the table in front of me. "Hey, where's Hans?" I asked, stopping her.

Megan smiled. "He headed for the bathroom right before you walked in. Did you need anything else?"

"Not right now. I'm meeting a... friend. She should be here any time."

"You don't seem very confident that she's your friend." Megan gave me a curious look.

"Yeah, it's weird," I answered without going into detail.

Megan continued to give me an assessing look, but then nodded. "Well, if you need anything, let me know."

"I will."

My eyes drifted past her as Hans made his way toward the piano. He hadn't noticed me yet, but when he did, his face lit up with a huge smile. I grinned and waved to him. He gave me a wink as he took his place on the piano bench. He'd played through two songs before Amanda showed up.

She blew into the bar, demanding attention from everyone. Of course, she didn't get it, and huffed as she sank down into the chair opposite me. "This is quaint," she said, but I could tell she didn't mean it as a compliment. Her eyes drifted over the bar, then to Hans, where her gaze lingered longer than I liked. Finally, she turned to me. "What are you drinking?"

"An apple butter old-fashioned."

She made a sound of distaste, raised her hand for Megan, then said, "I'll have sex on the beach."

"Yes, ma'am." Megan turned and headed for the bar.

Amanda unwrapped her coat and revealed a tight white dress with the middle and sides cut out. I assumed the back was just as free of fabric. Her gaze went back to Hans, who was singing an old Frank Sinatra number. His baritone melted into me and warmed places inside me that a year ago I would have told you no longer felt things.

Megan returned with Amanda's fruity drink, as well as a fresh beverage for me. "Can I get either of you anything else?"

"The man on the piano's number?" Amanda's lips curved up in a grin.

Megan's eyes went right to me, and she seemed to panic for a moment. "Um... I don't—"

"It's okay, Megan. Amanda is just messing around. She knows that I'm seeing Hans."

Megan scurried away before she could be asked any other questions. I didn't blame her.

Amanda gave me an innocent look. "Oh, is that Hans?"

"You know it is."

Amanda laughed. "Seeing as you slept with Nelson knowing he is married to me, I thought I should be able to do the same."

My fingers in my lap curled into a fist, biting into the flesh of my palm. "That ended a long time ago, Amanda, as you are well aware."

She picked up her drink and took a sip. "I know. I'm just fucking with you. Hans is not my type." She smiled. "So, what was it? What made you kick Nelson to the curb? Why'd you finally break it off with him?"

I shrugged. "I realized I didn't love him. I hadn't loved him in a long time, if I ever really did. He made all kinds of promises when we first met. He said he was going to help me with my career. He promised me I would be a star in the art world; it was what I had always wanted. I was young and starry-eyed. I thought that meant he loved me. It was just an excuse to get in my pants. Later, when he started bringing Jake around, it was an excuse to get me to take care of Jake. Not that he needed it. Jake's a great kid and I love him."

"I have to admit, you're good with him." She sat for a moment, sipping her drink. "What did Nelson do when you broke it off?"

I picked up my own drink, taking a gulp. "He used Jake to try to get me to keep seeing him. He said he'd never let me see him again."

"That's awful," Amanda gasped.

"He also said he'd get me black-balled in the art community and that no one would ever touch my work again," I murmured and looked away.

"That fucking bastard," Amanda seethed. Her eyes were bright with her fury, her cheeks flushed pink.

I was taken a back at her anger on my behalf. "I suppose it's all worked out. He's not helping my career, but he's not hurting it either, and I get to see Jake all the time, since you've hired me as his nanny."

Amanda's jaw ticked. "We should both get rid of Nelson for good."

"I'll drink to that," I murmured, thinking she must be finally ready to divorce him. It was about time. Maybe if she did, Jake would be more settled. There would be less fighting and stress in his household.

Shortly after that, Amanda made her excuses, saying she had a long drive home and didn't want to be out too late. I couldn't say I minded. I was actually glad she'd left when she did, before Hans finished his set and joined us. Call me crazy, but I didn't want her hitting on him just to piss me off or to try to make me jealous. I might have had it coming, but that didn't mean I wanted to sit by and let her do it. I liked Hans too much to allow that.

"So that barracuda was Jake's mom?" Hans murmured as he kissed my cheek and sat down.

I giggled. "That's a good description of her. She didn't use to be like that. The Amanda prior to the attack would never have dressed like. . ." I paused, searching for the right words.

"A hundred-dollar hooker?" Hans' lips quirked up in a half grin.

I laughed. "Well, yeah. She was always elegant before. There was nothing elegant about that dress. The more I think about it, the more I think Jake could be right. And if he is, then is he in danger? Am I?"

onday evening, as I was fixing dinner for Jake, the doorbell to the townhouse rang. I paused in my veggie chopping, waiting to see if someone answered it.

When no one did and the bell rang again, I set the knife down, wiped my hands and went to the door. Pulling it open, I frowned upon seeing two police officers on the stoop. "May I help you?"

"Ms. Carter?" the heavier officer asked, giving me a strange look.

"No. Let me get her for you. Would you like to come in?"

"Thank you," the same officer replied as the two of them stepped into the entryway.

I strode into the living room and saw Amanda on the sofa, flipping through a magazine. "There are a couple of police officers here to see you," I said softly, catching her gaze.

Amanda pursed her lips, kicked her legs off the sofa and set her magazine down. "Send them in."

I wanted to roll my eyes and tell her I wasn't her servant to order around, but it wasn't really worth it. Instead, I headed back to the foyer and said, "She's through here," gesturing for them to come with me.

Once they entered the room, Amanda was looking for all the world like a queen granting an audience to the peasants. "Officers, what brings you to my door?"

They both took off their hats, but it was once again the heavier officer who spoke. "Ma'am, we wanted to give you an update on the case."

"Have you caught the person who attacked me?" she questioned haughtily, her chin raised and her gaze fierce.

"No, ma'am, not yet."

"Then don't you think you should be out there looking for them?" she demanded.

"I assure you, ma'am, we have been. In fact, we're looking for a particular man we caught on CCTV footage leaving the area shortly before you were found."

Amanda drew in a sharp breath, but that was the only sign that showed she was somewhat rattled. I was beginning to recognize her new tells. Those little quirks and habits of the things she did now, after the attack. "Who is he?" she questioned.

"We don't know. He was a heavyset man with long dark blond hair and a beard, wearing a long, tan coat and a ball cap pulled low. We were hoping you might recognize him."

The second officer held out a grainy photo to her.

"You expect me to recognize anyone from this?" Amanda snorted and turned the photo toward me. She seemed angry. More so than normal.

I glanced at the image, and I understood where she was coming from; the photo was pretty terrible. It was a really fuzzy image of a man that I'd never seen before. I wondered how it was possible for us to have such clear pictures of Jupiter, which is more than four hundred and eighty million miles away, and yet photos from CCTV footage were like this grainy smudge on paper. It didn't make any sense to me.

"It's the best image we could get of him, ma'am. Do you know him?"

Amanda shook her head. "I don't know. Even if I did at one time, I've got amnesia."

"Yes, well, we had hoped seeing the photo might trigger your memory of the event, ma'am."

"Well, it didn't." Her voice was snotty.

"Okay, thank you for your time. We'll see ourselves out."

Amanda just stared at them, seething.

I didn't understand what had her so angry. Maybe it was just frustration that she couldn't identify the guy and she couldn't recall anything of the attack. I walked with the officers to the front hall and opened the door for them before heading back to the kitchen to finish getting dinner ready.

Amanda joined me a few minutes later. "Can you stay the night? Maybe a few nights?"

I pushed the roast into the oven and closed the door with my hip. "Why?" I asked as I turned to rinse the cutting board and knife.

She sighed. "Jake's been having nightmares and to be honest, I'm tired of dealing with them."

I frowned. This was the first I'd heard about him having bad dreams. He never had them at my place. Was he merely overhearing her and Nelson fighting and then saying it was nightmares that woke him?

"Well?" she prompted.

"Sure, I guess I can stay."

"Good. I'm going to go lie down. My head is killing me." She swanned out of the room.

I finished the dinner prep then went upstairs to check on Jake while it cooked. I knocked on the door of his room and poked my head in. He was seated at his desk, his history book open as he filled in blanks on his study guide. "Hey, you, how's it going?"

Jake dropped his head to his book then turned to look at me. "This is dumb. When am I ever going to need to know what Native Americans settled here or which ones sided with the French or English in the French and Indian War?"

I put my hands on my hips and arched a brow at him. "What if one day when you're older, you're on Jeopardy and you get asked that question, but you blew off learning it in fourth grade and lose a hundred thousand dollars?"

Jake stared at me, but then cracked a smile. "Ugh. Fine. This better be worth it."

I laughed. "Sorry, kiddo, but it's actually a good thing to know the history of your state. It helps to understand what the people of the time went through, the hardships, and all of that so that you can enjoy the freedoms you have today."

"So, what tribes were part of the Six Nations? I can only find five." He frowned.

"Probably because the last tribe didn't join until later. You might have to look further into the chapter to find it. Let me help you look," I offered as I pulled an extra chair over and joined him. I scanned the pages of the textbook, and then I pointed to the name. "Tuscarora. See, they came from North Carolina and settled in south-central New York."

Jake wrote the name in on the proper blank. "Now I have to find the group who sided with the French."

We found them—the Algonquian—as well as the rest of

the answers he needed for the guide, and then we put his homework and books away. He seemed happy that he'd gotten it all finished and had time to play video games before dinner.

I was about to leave him to it, but I paused at the door. "Hey, your mom asked me to stay the night. She said you'd been having nightmares," I said softly, looking at him.

Jake scoffed and rolled his eyes, falling over on his side on the bed. "I'm not. Geez. That's just what I tell her when she catches me out of bed trying to watch her."

My lips twisted into a grimace. "Jake, you need your sleep. Are you sure you're not having bad dreams?"

He sat up and looked at me. "Okay, sometimes, but not a lot."

I walked back into the room and sat down next to him. "What are they about?"

He shrugged. "You know, just like... monsters and stuff."

I put an arm around him and hugged him to me. "You don't have to be scared of monsters; they aren't real."

"Some are. The ones who look like people but are really awful," he said, keeping his voice low, barely even a whisper.

"You're thinking of your mom."

"She's not my mom, Carly. I know she's not."

His eyes flashed to mine, and I could see that he really believed that. I was actually pretty convinced of it myself, but I didn't know what to do about it. I needed proof, but how did you prove someone wasn't who they appeared to be?

I hugged him tighter. "We'll figure it out, I promise."

"I'm glad you're staying the night. I wish you could stay every night." He smiled at me.

"Well, I don't know about that. I've got my own place and all."

He nodded. "You're right, it'd be better if I could stay with you there every night. It's better than here."

"I wish it was possible too, kiddo." I smiled and gave him another hug. "All right, I'll let you go play Zelma—"

"Zel*da*, it's Zelda."

"Right, that." I grinned to let him know I was teasing him. I knew the game. Heck, I'd played the original back in the day. "Dinner should be ready in about thirty minutes, so keep an eye on the time, okay?"

"Okay," he answered as he turned the TV on and plugged in his console.

I watched him for a moment, wishing things were different. That he was actually my kid.

With a sigh, I left him to play his video game and headed down to the kitchen to finish up dinner, my mind still contemplating how to prove that Amanda wasn't the real Amanda. But how could I prove it when everyone thought it was impossible?

18

"Jake, dinner," I called up the stairs, then returned to the kitchen.

I fixed two plates, one for Jake and one for myself. I'd made plenty if Amanda or Nelson wanted to eat with us, not that Nelson ever did, thank God. He was always out these days. Judging by his Instagram posts, he was bedding half of the models in NYC.

It didn't bother me.

Much.

Really, what bothered me the most was the fact that he was probably doing all of that shit while he was with me, and I just hadn't noticed it. I had been so stupid to get involved with him, but then if I hadn't, I wouldn't have gotten to know Jake, the sweet little boy who needed me in his life. I was the one adult he could count on through thick and thin and I wasn't about to let him down.

When I didn't hear Jake on the stairs, I went to the bottom step and called up again. "Jake, dinner is getting cold. If you don't come down here right now, I'll eat your dessert," I threatened.

Within a few seconds, Jake was at the top of the stairs. "No, don't do that. I'm coming," he said with a laugh. "What's for dessert anyway?"

"I bought a chocolate pie this morning at the bakery. It looks delicious. I'm sad you decided to join me. I was looking forward to eating your piece," I teased.

"No way. You can't have it." He laughed.

"We'll see about that. You have to finish all your dinner first. I might still get it." I winked at him as we sat down with our plates.

Jake ate his portion of dinner so fast I thought he'd end up with heartburn. "Done. Can I have pie now?" he said through a mouthful of food.

"You need to slow down and chew your food. Did you even taste it?" I shook my head at him. I still had half of a plate left to eat.

"Sure. It was great." He picked up his glass of water and drank three-fourths of it.

When I finished my dinner, I cut him a piece of the pie, added a dollop of whipped cream, and put it in front of him. "Now don't eat it like you're in some kind of race."

Jake sighed as if I'd just told him his favorite show had been cancelled. "Fine." He dug his spoon into the pie, drew the bite up to his mouth and then nibbled on it. Slowly.

This kid. I grinned. I fixed myself a piece and joined him at the table. Instead of a race to be the first one done, it became a race to see who could eat the slowest. Jake won. Every bite, he licked the fork clean, then his lips and his teeth, loudly smacking his lips as he made noises to let me know how delicious the pie was.

I laughed. "Okay, okay, you've savored the pie. Next time try that with your dinner." I tweaked his nose.

"Dinner was good, but not as good as dessert." His grin widened.

"All right, you, finish that last bite and go get washed up for bed."

"Already?" His lower lip jutted out in a pout.

"I said wash up, not that you have to go to sleep right now." I rolled my eyes. "Once all that is done, you can play your game for a while longer."

Jake nodded, jumped up from the table, grabbed his plate and brought it over to the sink. After loading it into the dishwasher, he ran up the stairs and I finished cleaning the kitchen. It dawned on me that I hadn't brought anything to wear to bed, or for tomorrow. Then I remembered the bag I had in the trunk. It was full of clothes I'd planned to give to charity, but I hadn't gotten a chance to drop it off yet.

Once the kitchen was cleaned up, I jogged out to my car, dug through the bag and found a t-shirt and shorts to sleep in, as well as a top for tomorrow. I'd have to re-wear my jeans as well as my undergarments. That part sucked, but it was only for a little while, then I could go home and change clothes.

I took everything upstairs to the guest suite next door to Jake's room. I didn't know what to do with myself for the next couple of hours. I certainly didn't want to track down Amanda and play buddy-buddy with her. Nor did I want to sit and watch Jake play his video game. I sank down on the comfortable mattress and bounced a little. I decided to pull out my phone and read on my Kindle app.

I scrolled through my library, looking for a book I'd downloaded but hadn't read yet. When I'd found one that looked promising, I leaned back against the pillows and began to read. The time flew by and when I glanced at the clock it was almost time to say goodnight to Jake.

After logging out of the app, I sent Hans a text.

> Hey, I'm staying at Amanda's tonight and maybe for the next few. She says Jake's been having nightmares.

He must have had his phone in his hand because his reply was almost immediate.

> Hi, gorgeous. Why is he having nightmares?

> I think he's worried about the Amanda 'not mom' situation.

> I guess that would give any kid nightmares.

> Probably. I wondered if you'd like to grab lunch tomorrow.

> I would love to, but I can't. I'm headed to Philadelphia for the next two days, remember?

> Shoot, I forgot. I'll miss you.

> Me too. We can make plans for when I get back. Dinner and dancing?

> Perfect.

I sent him a kiss emoji and then set my phone aside. It was time to tell Jake goodnight.

I knocked on Jake's door and said, "Lights out, kiddo. If

you have a nightmare, come find me, okay? I'm right next door."

"Okay. Night, Carly."

"Night," I replied, closing the door. I returned to the guest suite, which thankfully had a private bathroom, and got myself ready. However, instead of climbing into bed, I decided to do a bit of spying.

On Amanda.

I had my phone in my hand as I crept forward down the hall. Amanda and Nelson's room was at the opposite end of the hall. I wondered if Nelson had gotten home yet. I could hear Amanda muttering to herself through the partially opened door, but I couldn't make out what she was saying.

I moved closer, keeping to my tip-toes so I wouldn't make the floor squeak. I leaned in toward the door.

"— on, answer the fucking phone," she huffed.

I wondered whom she could be calling. Nelson maybe? Was I about to hear a one-sided fight between them? If that was the case, I was going to run back to the guest room with my hands over my ears. I didn't need to hear that.

"Finally." Amanda sounded exasperated. "Where the hell have you been? I've been trying to get a hold of you all day."

She's probably not talking to Nelson, I thought. I leaned closer.

"Because, you stupid jackass, you let yourself be seen," she hissed.

Did she just say what I think she did? I questioned.

"No, not by a fucking witness; you were seen on the CCTV," Amanda added. "Cops came around here asking questions. They wanted to know if I recognized you."

I gulped. She *was* saying what I thought she was saying. She knew the man on the security video. And if she knew him... did that mean she also knew who attacked her? Was it this guy? And if it was, why didn't she report him?

"Of course I said I didn't. What the fuck do you take me for? I played up the amnesia, but that's not the point, idiot. The camera caught you leaving the area. It's only a matter of time before they put a name to a face."

Amanda's voice grew louder as she moved closer to the bedroom door, the one I was standing just on the other side of, and my blood ran cold. She was berating whoever was on the other end of that call, threatening them with bodily harm. I crept backwards, not taking my eyes off the door, as I tried to be as silent as possible. I couldn't hear her anymore, but that didn't mean I wanted to get caught out here in the hallway.

I let my fingers glide over the hallway wall, directing me toward the guest room door. When I found it, I turned the knob and slipped in, closing the door quietly in front of me. I leaned my forehead against it and took a ragged breath, then I flipped to press my back to the door.

I couldn't believe what I'd just heard. I looked down at my bare arms and then pinched myself to make sure I was actually awake, and this wasn't a dream. It wasn't; that pinch stung. I was pretty sure you couldn't feel pain in a dream.

My mind drifted back to Amanda's words. She had to know the man.

The question was, how was this guy involved and how did she know him? Okay, that was two questions, but they weren't my only ones. I also needed to know who the man was.

I wondered if I should go to the police and tell them that Amanda had lied because she knew the guy on the video. That would have to wait, though, since it would be her word against mine. I had no proof that she was faking this amnesia.

I frowned. But why fake amnesia and pretend you don't know your own son? That didn't make sense to me. There had to be something else going on.

I climbed into the bed and continued to think about it. I'd have to do some more digging. Some more spying. And I needed to get my hands on Amanda's phone.

19

I could barely contain myself as I made Jake's breakfast. I wanted to tell him that he might be right. That the Amanda who was in this house might not be his mom. I didn't know that for certain. She did look like Amanda. It was just that everything else about her was different.

"Carly?"

"Hmmm," I murmured, not really paying attention. My mind was on my discoveries from the evening before.

"The toast is done," Jake said, tugging on my sleeve.

"Oh, sorry. I'll grab it. Go ahead and sit down. Your eggs will be ready in a minute." I pulled the toast from the toaster and slathered it with butter, then set it on the plate. I turned back to the eggs and shoved them around until they fluffed, then added them to the plate too. "Here you go."

"Thanks, Carly." Jake dug into the eggs, scooping a heaping bite into his mouth. "It's good."

I smiled and poured myself a second cup of coffee. I hadn't seen Amanda yet this morning and I was hoping to get out of the house without seeing her. When Jake finished,

I rinsed his plate while he went up to brush his teeth and grab his backpack.

Once we were in the car and headed to his school, I glanced over at Jake. "So, I did a little spying last night."

Jake's eyes widened. "Did you find something out?"

I nodded. "She was on the phone with someone. The person the cops saw on the security cameras leaving the area where she was attacked."

"Do you think she knew her attacker then?"

I glanced over at Jake. His eyes were so huge, I thought they might pop out of his head. "Maybe. I need to get a hold of her phone and see who she called."

"How are we going to do that?" he fretted, his fingers knotting together in his lap.

"I'll come up with a plan." I smiled as I pulled into his school parking lot. "Have a good day, okay? And don't be worrying about Amanda. Listen to your teachers."

"Okay, I will. Bye, Carly." He opened the door and waved as he caught up with a couple of boys entering the building.

I sighed and then pulled away and headed to Brooklyn. I needed to get some work done, and I wanted to pack a bag to take back to the townhouse. If I was going to be staying there for a few days, I wanted my things. Before I got to work, I changed my top and threw the one I had been wearing, along with the shorts and top I'd slept in, into the washer with some other clothes.

Six hours later, I had everything I needed to work on finished, and the laundry done. I packed my bag, and headed back to my car. I stopped at a local deli and picked up a sandwich, then drove across the bridge into Manhattan and to Jake's school to retrieve him.

"How was school?" I asked as I pulled away.

"It was okay. We had a sub."

"Oh? You weren't mean to them, were you?" I eyed him. I remembered we used to give subs a hard time whenever our teacher was absent back when I was in school.

"No. She was nice." Jake turned to me. "Did you come up with an idea on how to get her phone?"

"She leaves it on the counter when she's in the kitchen. Maybe if we distract her, we can get it away from her?"

"Maybe. She's also left it in the living room on the coffee table when she's sitting in there reading magazines."

"True... Okay, we've got a couple of options. Now we just have to figure out how to distract her."

"Make a cake?"

I glanced at him and grinned. "You just want to eat the batter."

"It's so good," he said with a laugh.

"It is. And you're right, she does have a sweet tooth now... so that might work. Do you have homework?"

"Nope."

"Want to help with the cake?"

"Sure."

We headed in, and after he dropped his stuff in his room, I got started on the chocolate cake. Jake helped dump in ingredients and then he licked the beaters after I mixed it all up. While the cake baked, I made the icing and then threw together a chicken casserole to pop in the oven when the cake came out.

"Oh my God, what is that? It smells so fucking good in here." Amanda strolled into the room, her phone in her hand.

I opened the oven door, and a whiff of the cooking chocolate cake filled the room.

Amanda set her phone on the counter and joined me.

I glanced at Jake, who was inching toward the phone. "I thought I'd make a cake for dessert. Do you like triple chocolate?"

"My mouth is watering just smelling it." She grinned and moved toward the bowl of icing on the counter.

Jake drew his hand back just in time. The bowl of icing was near where she'd set her phone. If he hadn't stopped himself, she'd have seen him with his hand hovering over it. He tossed me a look of frustration.

I needed to do something to distract her more. I picked up the bowl and moved it to the opposite counter to pull off the cellophane. "Can you taste this and tell me if it's sweet enough? I think it might need more chocolate."

Amanda's eyes brightened. "Sure."

I dipped a teaspoon in and drew out a little bit as my eyes strayed to Jake. He was once again inching toward her phone. "Here." I held the spoon out toward her.

Amanda took the bite and then turned back toward Jake. "Did you help make this?"

"Uh... yeah," he said, sounding startled as his hands flew down to his sides.

"It's really good. Just the right amount of sweet."

"Great," I replied, giving my head a slight shake at Jake. We weren't going to get the phone at the moment. We'd have to try something else.

Over the next couple of days, the two of us attempted to get hold of the phone in various ways, but it was never very far from Amanda, and we were nearly caught. Once, I got my hands on it, but it was locked and I had no idea what her password was, so I had to put it back. I'd need to keep an eye on her and see if I could figure out the password when she typed it in.

On top of that Nelson had reappeared. He'd slunk in quietly, looking dejected until he realized I was staying at the townhouse. Then he'd lit up like a Christmas tree, which pissed Amanda off.

"Leave her the fuck alone. She's not here for you. She's here for Jake. He's been having nightmares," Amanda declared as Nelson tried to corner me in the kitchen.

I'd been doing my best to avoid him, slipping in and out of rooms as soon as he entered, but I was in the middle of chopping vegetables when he'd walked up behind me and put his hands on my hips. I turned with the knife in my hand and glared at him.

Nelson shrugged and barely spared a glance at Amanda. "No need to be so prickly, babe."

I snorted and turned back to the veggies, slamming the knife into them with a greater force than I had been. I was picturing his junk beneath the knife as I sliced and diced the carrots. I wasn't going to be able to eat them if I kept it up. I set the knife down and took a deep breath, then let it out slowly.

"I'm not fucking around. If you don't leave her alone, you're going to find yourself kicked out of the house," Amanda seethed.

Nelson held his hands up and backed off. It didn't stop him permanently, though. All through dinner, he kept trying to get my attention, but I ignored him. We all did. Jake and I were focused on keeping our eyes on Amanda and her phone. She would pick it up and put in the code to text and then shut it down and set it on the table until it buzzed with a reply. She wasn't trying to hide what she was doing, so I was able to pick up the first two numbers and when I checked with Jake as we cleared the table, he'd got the rest. The only thing left to do was get our hands on her phone.

"I'll try once she falls asleep," I whispered to Jake.

"Okay. Let me know if you get it," Jake replied softly as he loaded the dishwasher.

"Look at you two being so domestic," Nelson said from the doorway. "Get me a beer, would you, babe?"

I glared at him. "Get it yourself, and leave me alone."

Jake moved to the fridge and pulled out a can, then handed it to his dad. "Here."

Nelson ruffled his hair. "Thanks, bud. I'm gonna go watch the game. Wanna join me?"

Jake looked at me and I gave him a slight nod. It was good for him to spend time with Nelson, and it would keep Nelson occupied and away from me.

He shrugged and said, "Sure. Let me finish loading the dishwasher, then I'll meet you in the living room."

Nelson raked his gaze over me once more as he took a sip of his beer. "You can join us too if you want."

I bit my tongue to keep from saying what was really on my mind. "I've got a few things I need to do, so I'll be heading to my room."

It was probably the wrong thing to say, because once Amanda went to bed, Nelson attempted to get into my room. Only I wasn't in my room. I was in Amanda's trying to get hold of her phone. I'd noticed that she slept pretty hard, so I figured I might have a better chance at taking it if I waited until she was asleep.

I heard Nelson in the hallway, his hand on my door, when Jake pulled his own door open and said, "Hey, Dad, can I have a glass of water?"

I glanced at Amanda in the bed, her phone next to her, and sighed. It was so close. I was just inches away. However, I needed to get out of there before she woke up or Nelson made it into my room and discovered I wasn't there. I didn't want him shouting down the house if he found me in Amanda's room. I turned and eased Amanda's bedroom door open wider, then slipped out.

"Uh... what are you doing up, Jake?" he asked, sounding slightly drunk. "Shouldn't you be asleep by now?"

"I got thirsty."

I crept down the hall toward the stairway, then slipped down about halfway without Nelson noticing me. I made a little bit of noise as I turned and headed back up. "Jake, why are you up? Did you have a nightmare?"

"Yeah." He rubbed his eyes and made his lip tremble. "I was just asking Dad for a drink of water. I thought it might help me go back to sleep."

"Nelson? Were you trying to go into my room?" I arched a brow.

"What? No. I was just... checking... screw it, yeah, I was. I don't know why you're being so difficult. Weren't we good together? Don't you love me? Don't you want to be a family with me and Jake? I mean you're here; it would be so easy."

I shook my head and frowned at him, but turned to Jake. "Hey, kiddo, go on back to bed. I'll be in with a cup of water in a minute. I just need to speak to your father first."

"Okay." Jake went back in his room and closed the door.

I glanced back at Nelson. "I told you before, I'm only here for Jake. I want nothing more to do with you. I don't love you and you using Jake like a pawn you can wield to get me to comply with your manipulations is low, even for you. Though I suppose I should expect it; you've done it before.

Still, it surprises me every time you do," I fumed as I stabbed him in the chest with my finger. "You need to leave me alone."

"But—" he pouted.

"No. I'm not doing this." I brushed past him and headed for the bathroom to get Jake a cup of water. Nelson was still standing in the hall looking dumbfounded, but I ignored him and entered Jake's room, closing the door behind me.

"Thanks, Carly," Jake said loud enough to let his dad know he was still awake. Then he whispered, "Did you get it?"

"No, I heard you and your dad in the hall and figured I better leave it. I didn't want to have Amanda wake up and catch me, and I certainly didn't want your dad to find me with it either."

Jake sighed. "How are we going to get it now?"

I was beyond stressed out over the whole thing. "We both need a break. I'll ask Amanda if you can come and stay at my place for a few days."

Jake brightened. "Really?"

"Yes, really. Get some sleep, kiddo."

Jake snuggled down into his bed. "Night."

"Goodnight," I murmured as I leaned down and kissed the top of his head. "Sweet dreams."

When I stepped out of Jake's room, closing the door behind me, Nelson was gone.

As I prepared for bed, I thought about Jake's and my mission to discover what Amanda was up to. It was basically on hold until I could get my hands on her phone, and now that was going to have to wait because Nelson was making things more difficult.

I needed to come up with a new plan.

And fast.

20

After dropping Jake at school, I returned to the townhouse to talk to Amanda about taking Jake to my place for a while. She hadn't been awake prior to us leaving or I'd have asked her then. I doubted that she would say no, so I'd had Jake pack his things before school and leave the bag in his room by his bed. I'd just have to grab it when I grabbed my own things.

"Hey," I said when I entered the house. My gaze slid over the room, looking for Nelson. He didn't seem to be around, for which I was grateful.

"Oh, hi. Did you need something?" Amanda asked, looking up from her coffee. She was sitting at the table, still in her loungewear.

"I was thinking maybe what Jake needs is a change of scenery to help with his nightmares. What if I take him to my place for a bit?"

Amanda shrugged. "Sure. Whatever. I don't care."

I swallowed back a mean retort about it being obvious she didn't care about her own son; she barely even spoke to him. "Great. I'll just grab some of his stuff and we'll go to my place after I pick him up from school."

She nodded but didn't say anything else.

I turned on my heel and went for the stairs. I went to the room I'd been using first, and made sure I had everything. Then I entered his room, picked up his bag, noticing he'd packed half his dresser as well as all of his video games and the console. I added a couple of books from his shelf and a stuffed sea lion I'd gotten him at the zoo. I checked the bag for his toothbrush before heading out to my car with everything. I put it all in the backseat, then drove to Brooklyn.

Back in my apartment, I sorted my things first, then took care of his. I filled the dresser with his clothes, set up his console and set the books on the small desk. I put the sea lion on the pillow and then went to my studio to paint.

An hour into it, I had an idea, but I needed to call my brother to see if he knew whom to call for what I was considering. I cleaned up my brushes and put everything away, then went to the kitchen to make the call.

"Hey, big brother," I said into the phone.

"Carly, what's wrong?" he asked, sounding worried.

"Nothing."

"Don't give me that. You don't call just out of the blue. What's going on?"

"I need your advice." I told him about the cops finding a guy on the security cameras and Amanda's phone call that seemed to indicate she knew the guy. I also told him about trying to get hold of her phone and how unsuccessful that endeavor was. "So, I was thinking I need to hire a private investigator, and since that's what you and Dave do, I thought I'd get your advice."

Blaine whistled. "We're pretty pricy, sis. Can't you just let it go?"

I shook my head, not that he could see me. "No. This is Jake we're talking about. I want to make sure he's safe. Blaine, what if she's not Amanda, but some imposter?"

"I'm not sure how she couldn't be Amanda. I mean, how would she hide that from people who know her? Sure, she's forgotten stuff, but she did get hit on the head hard enough to give her amnesia."

"I know, but something is just off. I don't know how exactly she's done it, but I'm almost positive she's not the real Amanda."

"Okay, let me talk to Dave. I don't think we can take this on for you—we've got a full load of clients at the moment—but maybe Dave knows something I don't."

"I'd pay you guys; I don't have a lot in my savings but—"

"Hey, like I said, let me talk to Dave. If we can, we'll do it. If not, maybe he has a suggestion. I'll text you."

"Okay, thanks," I murmured. "I need to go; I've got to pick up Jake."

"See you." He hung up.

I grabbed my keys and headed out the door.

By the time I reached my car, I had a text from him.

Dave said we're overwhelmed at the moment with clients, but he told me to have you give Marianne Shelton a call. He's contacting her now and letting her know your situation. He says she'll work with you on price.

Thanks, Blaine. Thank Dave too. I'll give her a call. Can you send her number?

My phone beeped a few minutes later with her contact information. I plugged the number into my contacts and then drove into Manhattan. I was afraid of calling her while I was driving, since there was a good chance that the call would cut out while I was on the bridge. That wasn't a good look, so I decided to wait. Besides, I needed to check my account and see exactly how much I even had to put toward hiring her. Just because Dave had said she would work with me on price, it didn't mean I was going to have enough.

With it being Friday, I picked Jake up and headed back to Brooklyn.

"I'm glad we're going to your place. It's at least normal there," Jake said after I told him that Amanda had agreed to let him stay with me.

"Aw, kiddo," I murmured and ruffled his hair. I wished I could give him the world and keep him safe. We were on our own that night, but Saturday afternoon we went out to lunch with Hans. On Sunday, we played some video games and spent the day just hanging out in my apartment.

"Hey," I glanced at him in the passenger seat on the way to drop him at school Monday morning, "I have an appointment this afternoon with a possible new client, so I'm going to call the car company your parents use and have them get you, okay?"

"Okay," Jake agreed. "But I'm going back to your place, right?"

"Yes, I'll have the driver bring you to my place, don't worry." I smiled.

After I dropped Jake off, I dialed Amanda.

"Carly, this is a surprise."

"Hi. I just had a question. I have an appointment this

afternoon and I wondered what car company you use to pick up Jake. I need to call them to set up a ride for him."

"Oh? Well, it's Delta Rides. Just charge it to Nelson."

"Okay, thanks."

"My pleasure." She hung up.

I found the number online and called to set it up. With that taken care of, I decided to put in a call to Marianne as well. I'd checked my funds and I wanted to make an appointment to speak to her as soon as possible.

"You've reached Marianne Shelton, private investigator. I'm sorry, I'm not in right now. If you leave your name and number, I'll get back to you as soon as possible."

I hung up. I didn't want her to get my message and call back while I was meeting with this new client. I figured I would just try again later.

I went to meet with Vivienne, since she was the one who set up the meeting with Jasmine, the author who wanted the zoo images. I pulled into a parking garage, locked my car, and walked the rest of the way to her office.

"Hey, Viv," I greeted her as I unbundled myself from my outerwear.

"Darling, what are you doing here?" she asked as she got up to hug me.

I stopped short. "Aren't we meeting with Jasmine today? I thought you wanted to see me beforehand; isn't that what you said?"

"Oh, never mind that, dear. Something more important has come up for me. You'll need to see Jasmine on your own. She's meeting you in Brooklyn. Didn't I give you the address?"

I gritted my teeth. "Seriously? No, you didn't. And I thought we were meeting at two here in Manhattan."

"Well, I'm sure I texted you the change of plans, but you know these cyberspace things. They go all awry at times. I'll just write down the address." She turned to her desk and scribbled out a note. "There you are. Now, do run along. You don't want to be late, do you?"

I took the note and quickly buttoned back up. "What time am I supposed to meet her?"

"Ten thirty."

It was a little past nine now and it was at minimum a forty-five-minute drive into Brooklyn. "I'll call you later," I murmured as I rushed out of her office and back to the street. I couldn't believe she hadn't called me to make sure I got the message.

Thankfully, there wasn't too much traffic and I pulled into the parking lot of the coffee shop I was meeting Jasmine at with ten minutes to spare. I'd stuck my portfolio in the car that morning, since I'd been planning to stay in Manhattan today and figured I'd need it for this meeting. I grabbed it and headed in. I looked around the shop. I had no idea what Jasmine looked like, but there was only one woman in the shop, so I approached her.

"Excuse me, are you Jasmine Fortune?"

The red-headed woman looked up and smiled. "Hi. Are you Carly Michaelson?"

"Yes. May I?" I asked, indicating the seat.

"Of course. I'm so glad you could make it. Normally, I wouldn't be in Brooklyn, but I have a book signing at a shop here this afternoon. It was a last-minute addition to my calendar, so I needed to rearrange things."

"That's great. Do you often get last-minute book signing engagements?" I was curious to understand how that came about.

She laughed. "Rarely. Vivienne actually set it up. She's not my agent, but she knew we were meeting and thought this would be the perfect opportunity to sway me to her, I think. I'm not going to turn down a book signing that I didn't have to work for."

I frowned. Vivienne was trying to gain her as a client? Did that have anything to do with me being chosen to work on Jasmine's illustrations? "Are you looking for an agent?"

"Not really. My agent retired, but I'm not even sure I want a new one. Do you like Vivienne?"

"Yes, I do," I said hesitantly. "I'm a little confused though. I thought Viv's focus was the art world."

"It's my understanding she's moved into the publishing world. Anyway, I didn't ask you here to discuss agents." She laughed again. "I want to talk about the art you submitted for my new series. You are seriously talented. It's exactly what I was looking for but couldn't put into words."

My cheeks heated and I smiled. "I'm so glad. I brought my portfolio, just in case you wanted to see some more of my work." I held it out to her.

She took it and glanced through it. "These are great, but I really adore the watercolor you submitted. I think that style will be perfect."

"I'm anxious to see what you have in mind for the series. Do you have a storyboard already worked out?"

"I do." Jasmine pulled out a hard copy of her story. "This should get you started. It's book one."

We went over details and agreed that I would send her shots of each image as I finished them so she could make sure it was exactly what she was looking for. Then we discussed a timeline and, while it was doable, it would take up a good bulk of my time. Still, it was a lucrative project, and I didn't want to say no.

"I think that should cover it," she said, glancing across the table at me.

"I'm looking forward to getting started." When I checked the time, I was surprised to discover we'd been talking for three hours. I moved to stand up. "I'll give you a shout when I've got the first image ready for you."

"Thank you so much, Carly. I'm really looking forward to working with you." She shook my hand.

I pulled my coat on, picked up my portfolio and her storyboard and gave her a wave as I left. I headed for my car and realized I was suddenly famished. I pulled my phone from my pocket and dialed Hans.

"Gorgeous, this is an unexpected treat," Hans said when he answered the phone.

His words made me smile. "Hi. I was wondering if you were free to meet me for a late lunch?"

"Aren't you in Manhattan today? I thought you were meeting with that new client."

"We had a change of plans. I just finished meeting with her, and since I ordered a car for Jake, I have some free time. So, what do you say?"

"I would love to."

I PULLED into the parking lot near Delphine's, which was a chic French café. Hans was already inside, seated at a table. I could see him through the large picture window as I made my way toward the door. He rose when he saw me headed toward his table. He greeted me with a kiss and then helped me out of my coat.

After ordering we sat and chatted for a while about his most recent trip and the audience he'd encountered. We also discussed my work, both my commissioned clients as well as the series I was doing in hopes of getting a gallery showing.

"I know I'm not an agent or anything, but I do know a couple of people in the art world. Would you mind if I showed some of your work to them?" Hans asked once the waitress brought our food.

"Absolutely not. That would be wonderful, Hans." I was overwhelmed with gratitude. I knew he liked my work, but for him to offer to show it to people in the art world was beyond anything I could have expected.

"Maybe I could get a few more pictures on my phone to show them?" he suggested.

"Sure. We could head over to my place after we eat." I paused and gave him a teasing look. "Is this just so you can see the series I'm doing of you?"

He chuckled. "You've caught me, love. I'm dying to see more of what you've done."

"Hmm, maybe I should keep those a secret, only reveal them once I've got a gallery date."

His smile fell and he gave me a fake sad face. "You wouldn't do that to me, would you?"

I giggled. "No. You can see them. So far there's only four, but it might be a while before I can do any more of them. Jasmine's going to keep me pretty busy for the foreseeable future with the illustrations for her new series. Doing those on top of my other client work, I'm going to have some long nights ahead of me."

"But that's good, right?"

"It is—" I stopped as my phone shrilled from my pocket. "Hang on, it's Jake."

"Carly?" His voice came across the phone through sobs.

"What's wrong? Are you okay?" I asked, suddenly filled with panic.

"I— someone..." Jake started. His words were muffled and sounded far away. "Someone tried to kill me."

21

"What?" I screeched, rising from my chair.

Hans reached for my hand, standing too. "What's going on?" he whispered.

I shook my head. "Jake?"

Then a woman's voice came across the phone line. "Ms. Michaelson?"

"Yes. What's going on? Where's Jake? Is he okay?"

"This is Principal Schmitt. We've had an incident. Jake was nearly run over. He's shaken up, but he's physically all right. The police are taking statements. We haven't been able to get a hold of his parents. You are our last resort. Could you come?"

"Yes, of course," I replied. "Tell Jake I will be there as soon as humanly possible. I'm coming from Brooklyn, so it may take a bit."

"I'll keep him in the school office."

"Thank you, Ms. Schmitt." I hung up and started pulling on my coat, then glanced at the table of half-eaten food and up to Hans' face. "I have to go. Jake was almost run over."

"Go take care of him. I'll take care of the bill. Call me later and let me know you're both all right." He gripped my arms and stared into my face.

I nodded. "I will."

He kissed my cheek and let me go. "Be careful," he called as I headed out of the restaurant.

I sped out of the parking lot and hit the Brooklyn Bridge in record time. I didn't care if I was speeding. I needed to get to Jake. A million scenarios raced through my mind as I drove, none of them good. My heart was in my throat as I swung the car into the school parking lot. I parked in the loop at the front of the building where car riders were picked up.

Grabbing my purse, I ran into the building, which still had a handful of police officers hanging about. I didn't give any of them a glance as I headed straight for the office. I pushed open the glass door and said, "Jake!"

He rushed into my arms and burst into tears. "Carly! Someone tried to run me over!"

I held him, rubbing his back. "Shhh, shhhh, it's okay, I'm here," I murmured.

Inside I was seething, but I didn't want him to know how upset I was. Who was supposed to be watching these kids so this kind of thing didn't happen? And how was it even possible in the first place? I had so many questions and zero answers.

When his crying subsided, I directed him to one of the chairs in the waiting area. "Are you okay to wait here while I speak to your principal and a few of the officers?"

Jake nodded and wiped his face on his sleeve.

I patted his shoulder and moved to Ms. Schmitt's office. I knocked on the open door and she looked up.

"Come in," she directed.

I did, but closed the door behind me. Jake didn't need to hear any of this. "What happened?" I asked, trying to keep the bite from my tone, but I wasn't sure I succeeded since she winced.

"I'm not exactly sure. Jake was waiting at the edge of the sidewalk, toward the end of the parking lot. Most of the car riders had already been picked up. There were only a handful left when the incident occurred."

"So he wasn't with the other car riders?"

"I'm not sure we knew he was a car rider today. I believe you were supposed to pick Jake up from school?"

"No, I called a car service for him."

She nodded. "He was with some of his friends who were walking. They went on, but he stayed at the end of the sidewalk. Then this dark brown sedan came out of nowhere and it was as though it was aiming right for him. Jake screamed and ran under the metal awning toward the building. I'm sure you noticed the bent metal pole at the end of the entrance awning when you arrived."

I hadn't noticed anything about the building. I was too concerned with getting to Jake. "No, I didn't. So, the driver hit the pole?"

"Yes, but they didn't stop. The police are going over the security footage from the parking lot. They are trying to identify the driver."

I ran a hand down my face. I didn't like it. It sounded to me as though Jake was targeted, but why? Who would want to run him over? He was just a kid.

"Did you get a hold of his parents yet?" I asked, still fuming.

"We did get a call from his father. He... well, he said he'd make sure a car came to get Jake." She looked away.

I bit back a nasty cuss word. "And his mother?"

"She isn't answering the phone. We've left several messages."

"Thank you," I gritted out. I was beyond pissed.

Yanking open the office door, I went to track down one of the officers. "Excuse me. I'm... well, I'm Jake Carter's nanny. Can you tell me if you've found the driver?"

"No ma'am, not yet. The license plate was smeared with thick mud, making it unidentifiable. We do have a pretty good description of the driver though."

I sucked in a breath. "What did they look like?" I wondered if I might recognize them. Maybe that would give me a clue as to who might want to hurt Jake.

"Heavy-set male, dark blond hair with a beard. Witnesses said he was wearing dark glasses and his hair fell past his shoulders."

Something about the general description struck a chord in me. The man sounded like the one on the CCTV footage from Amanda's attack. The one Amanda had been talking to in that whispered conversation on the phone.

A shiver raced over me.

"Do you know anyone who matches that description?"

"I don't," I said hesitantly. "If I think of someone, I'll be sure to let you know. Can I take Jake home now?"

"Sure." He nodded.

As I turned back to the office, I saw that sweet little boy sitting forlornly in the office chair. He looked so lost and miserable. I headed back over to him and hugged him. "You ready to go?"

Jake nodded.

I had half a mind to file neglect charges against his parents for not being here for him, but seeing as they were so rich, I doubted the police would even care. I wrapped my arm around his shoulders and guided him out to my car where I made sure he was buckled it.

I climbed into the driver's seat, but I didn't turn the car on. "You okay?"

"I think so. I keep seeing the car coming at me," he whispered.

I reached for his hand and squeezed it. "Let's get you back to my place, okay?"

He nodded again.

Once we were home, I let him go to his room and play Switch.

I was still so angry about everything, and I wanted to fight someone. I pulled my phone out and headed for my bedroom. I moved into the bathroom and turned on the water as I dialed. I had a feeling the call was going to get loud, and I hoped the water would drown my words out so Jake wouldn't hear them.

"Hey, babe, what's up?"

"Are you fucking for real, Nelson? Your son was almost run over!"

"He's fine, isn't he? It was probably just some drunk. The cops don't need me over there messin' in their investigation."

"You narcissistic asshole! He's your son! He needed you and you ignored him. Some crazy person tried to kill him. They were aiming for him."

"You're exaggerating. Jake probably just stepped into the path of the car. It's not a big deal."

"You are unbelievable! The two of you disgust me! You deserve each other!" I hit end on the call and slammed my phone down on the counter. I probably shouldn't have since it cracked my screen, but I was so angry I didn't even care.

22

Jake screamed from his room.

I glanced at the clock; it was just past two in the morning. I climbed from bed and ran for Jake's room. I hurried to him and cradled him in my arms. "Shhh, it's okay, Jake. You're at my apartment. Nobody is going to hurt you," I murmured as I rocked him.

Jake buried his face in my shoulder and sobbed, his skinny arms wrapped around me as he held on tight. I rocked him for a good while until he finally calmed down. Eventually, he sniffled and drew back. He wiped his eyes and stared up at me, his lip trembling.

"You're safe, Jake."

He nodded, wiping his nose with the back of his hand.

"That's gross, kiddo."

He laughed, which was what I'd meant for him to do. Then he did it again.

"Ewww." I made a face and stood up. There was a tissue box on the small desk, and I grabbed it and offered it to him.

Jake took a couple and blew his nose.

"Feel better?"

He nodded.

"Want to talk about it?"

"I keep seeing that car coming right at me. The driver... he's a big fat guy... I can't see his eyes. He's wearing dark glasses, but he's staring right at me." His voice was so soft I could barely hear him.

I frowned. I didn't want to scare him, but I also didn't want to keep anything from him. "The officer gave me his description. He sounds like the guy the cops saw on the video in the area your mom was attacked."

Jake's eyes widened. "You think it was him?"

I gave him a slight nod. "I do."

"But why is he coming after me? I didn't see him. I wasn't there when Mom was attacked." He paused and his eyes lifted to mine. "If she was attacked."

"Well, something happened to her; the head injury and bruises were obvious. I just wish I knew what she was doing when it happened."

Jake shrugged. "She said it was a reunion before she left. Now she says she doesn't know why she was there."

"Right, but I've checked. There were no class reunions going on, so it wasn't that kind of reunion. What else could it be?" I wondered what Amanda did before she met Nelson. "Do you know if your mom worked before she met your dad?"

"Just a reception job for a hotel. She was in college classes and working part time. That's what she said when I asked how she met Dad."

"So maybe it was a work reunion?" I murmured. My words were full of doubt, though. Who would go to a work reunion for a part-time job? "Do you know what hotel?"

"No, she never said."

"Probably a dead end anyway." I continued thinking but I could only come to one conclusion. "I think we need to tell the cops what we've been doing."

Jake was reluctant but he finally agreed. "Okay. Do you think they'll help?"

"Honestly, I don't know. I hope so. It's their job to help, right?"

Shrugging, Jake said, "They don't always do that though, do they?"

I frowned at him. He was too young to be so cynical. "Where did you get that idea?"

"Movies, TV shows, the news. They let the criminals go free all the time."

"Jake, I know it looks that way, but I think that's the higher-up people. They're the ones who make the policies. The cops are just following what they've been told, but you're right, it's not very helpful." I shook my head as I considered the turmoil of things going on. It was hard to believe in the good of people, let alone the cops, when all this crap was going on. Still, we had to try.

"Maybe they'll help." He reached for my hand.

I smiled at him. "We'll do our best to convince them, yeah?"

"Yeah." He grinned at me. "I'll bring my journal with all my notes and observations of what she's been doing."

"That's a good plan." I leaned in and hugged him. "You ready to go back to sleep?"

He pulled back and wrapped his arms around his knees, his smile gone as he looked down. "I guess."

"Jake, you need sleep."

"Will you stay in here with me?" he whispered.

The bed was a double, so there was plenty of room for me to lie down. "Okay. Let me grab my pillow. I'll be right back." I hurried to my room, grabbed my pillow and the fuzzy blanket I kept at the end of the bed. I moved to the other side of the bed and lay down on top of the comforter, pulling my blanket over me.

Jake lay down and turned to face me. "Carly, do I have to go to school tomorrow?"

"You mean this morning?" I smiled. "No, I'll call in and let them know you're taking a day to recover from almost being killed. I'm sure they'll understand."

Several hours later, after breakfast and a call to the school, we got in the car and made the journey back to Manhattan. I called Hans as we pulled out of my parking garage and apologized for not calling him the night before, which he totally understood. I then explained what was going on and what we were doing. He agreed it was the right thing to do.

"Be safe," he said before hanging up.

"I like him," Jake murmured.

I smiled over at him. "I do too."

We pulled into the precinct and walked up to the front desk. I explained who we were and asked to speak to a detective. A few minutes later we were led back to Detective Abrahms' desk.

"What can I do for you, Ms. Michaelson?"

"Yesterday, my charge, Jake Carter," I indicated Jake who was seated next to me, "was nearly run over at his school."

"I'm sorry to hear that, but why does that have you at *my* desk?"

I went on to explain about our investigation, the grainy photo of the man who might have attacked Amanda, her secretive phone call to the man, and the description of the driver. "So, you see, we think it's all connected."

"I wrote down everything I noticed about the woman who says she's my mom that isn't right," Jake added, holding up his notebook. He slid it across the desk to the detective.

Detective Abrahms picked it up and looked through it. It was merely a cursory glance, and I was sure he was only doing it to pacify us. He set it aside and folded his hands on the desk. "Look, you need to leave this in our hands. I doubt the jerk who was in the car has anything to do with the attack on your mom, Jake. It is very unlikely. Now if you'll excuse me, I have other cases that need my attention."

The detective was dismissing us. It was as though he thought we were making it all up. That was completely aggravating.

"*We* need your attention," I commented, staring at him. "We need you to take this seriously."

"Ma'am, we are too busy to be dealing with kids with overactive imaginations. I'm sure the experience was scary; however, the driver was probably just a drunk who got freaked out when they hit the pole. We do have officers looking for the car. At the moment that's the best we can do."

"Thanks for nothing." I grabbed the journal from the desk corner, took Jake's hand, and said, "Come on, Jake. It's obvious they're not going to help us."

Jake sighed and followed me out of the station. "What now?" he asked, sounding defeated.

"I don't know. Not exactly." I pursed my lips as I thought about it. We were in the parking lot, and I paused next to my car. "Okay, this is what we're going to do. No more car service. I will drive you and pick you up from school every day. I will rearrange my schedule if I have to. You will stay by a teacher's side until this gets solved when you're waiting for me. And when I drop you off, you go straight into the building. No walking off with friends before or after school. Got it?"

"Yeah." He sounded scared. His voice was soft and trembly.

I squatted down next to him. "Jake, it's going to be okay. We'll figure this out. I promise you. You'll be safe." I pulled him into a hug and then handed him back his journal.

"Thanks, Carly."

"Come on, kiddo. Let's go get some lunch." I smiled as I stood back up and opened the car door for him. I didn't want him to know how scared and worried I actually was for him. I was determined that he would be safe, and if the police wouldn't do anything, then I would. I just didn't know what yet.

23

T he next few days were quiet. Jake and I traveled to and from Brooklyn without incident. Driving him was a big part of my day and more stressful than I could have imagined, since I was constantly looking out for the car that had attempted to run over Jake. All I knew was it was a dark brown sedan that was probably battered after having hit the pole at the school. There were a lot of dark brown sedans in NYC. So, I was cautious around every single one I saw.

While he was in school, I spent my days painting the watercolor images for Jasmine or working on various other client projects. My collection for possible gallery work was put on hold, which was disappointing because I had this image in my head that I really wanted to get down on canvas. For now, all I could do was keep pulling it up in my head and filling in the details so I could paint it later when I had time.

I was putting the finishing touches on the eight-by-ten landscape canvas that would be the first full page image of Jasmine's book when my phone rang. "Hello?" I answered.

"Beautiful, how are you this morning?"

I smiled and relaxed my spine. "Hi, Hans, I'm good. How are you?"

"Not bad. Better for talking to you." He chuckled. "I wondered if you were up for lunch."

I glanced at my canvas and the other projects I needed to work on. "Um..."

"You're working, aren't you?"

"Yeah," I said with a sigh.

"How about I pick something up and bring it to you?" he suggested. "That way you don't have to leave your work for very long. After all, you have to eat, right?"

I smiled. "That sounds nice. And you could get some photos to show your friend," I added, hoping he'd really meant what he'd said the other day when we'd been out together.

"I had hoped I could. Desmond is excited to see more of your work. I showed him the one you did that's hanging up at Melodies."

"Desmond?"

"Desmond Dietrich. He and his wife Karla own D&K Art Gallery. It's not a huge venue, but it's popular among the celebrity set. Desmond was a basketball player with the Knicks, but he retired a few years ago. His wife is an art major who has made a career out of giving up-and-coming artists a boost by sharing their work in various galleries around the country. When he retired, they opened the gallery so they could continue to do that."

"Wow, that's amazing. Do you think they might like my work?"

"I think they will love it."

I blushed. "So, what time do you want to come over?"

"When will you be ready for a break?"

I glanced again at the painting I was currently working on. I didn't have too much more to do. "Maybe in forty-five minutes?" That would give me time to clean up a little bit.

"Sounds good. I'll grab food and be there soon."

"See you then," I murmured as we hung up.

I finished making the final touches to the painting of a little girl with curly blonde hair, holding her mother's hand as they entered the zoo. When I was happy with it, I moved it to my drying rack area. Once it was dry, before I put the glossy protective coat on it, I'd take a picture of it on my phone and send it to Jasmine for her to go over and make sure it was exactly right. When it was approved and the glossy protective coat added, I'd use my high-end digital camera to make a high resolution image of it so it could be digitized for her. She would also get the canvases, since she was paying for them.

Most of the authors I worked with enjoyed having the canvases of their book covers to hang in their offices. Doing an entire book was different though. The canvases could add up and sometimes the authors asked me to just destroy them after they were digitized, which I hated doing. It seemed like such a waste. Other times they'd give them away in raffles and auctions for their fans. I loved when they did that. Jasmine had opted to do that with hers, which was another reason I was thrilled to be working with her.

I cleaned up my palette and brushes and moved my next project to my easel, before heading to my room to clean myself up. I wanted to look somewhat presentable when Hans arrived. I washed my face and hands, added a little makeup so I didn't look so pale, and ran a brush through my short hair. I had just pulled on a clean, paint-free t-shirt when the buzzer sounded.

I hurried to the intercom and pushed the button to let him in. Three minutes later there was a knock on my door. I peeked through the peephole and saw Hans, so I opened the door. "Hi," I said, letting him in.

"I brought Thai food. Hope that's okay," he said, holding up the bags.

"Sounds delicious and it smells just as good." I closed the door, and we went to the kitchen.

As we ate, we chatted about the things going on in both of our lives. I talked about Jake and the near miss, as well as the unhelpful police. He commiserated with me about it and said he liked my idea of hiring a private detective, but understood my hesitancy due to expense.

"I called her once, but got her voice mail. I've really hesitated in hiring her, though, because I know it's going to be expensive." I sighed and twisted my fork in my Thai noodles.

"I could lend you the money," he offered.

"No, I couldn't ask that of you. I have some savings I can dip into."

"If you're sure. The offer stands." He reached a hand across the table and laced his fingers with mine.

We moved on from that conversation to discuss his concert schedule and when he'd be back at Melodies. He was leaving after lunch to head to Connecticut for the weekend, and then to New Hampshire. He wouldn't be back until the middle of the following week, which made me sad.

"I'll miss you," I said as I tucked myself against him.

He squeezed me. "I'll miss you too." He kissed my temple.

We cleaned up the kitchen and then headed to the

studio, where he took photos of all the paintings I'd done with galleries in mind. He had seen most of the landscapes before, but he hadn't seen the newer stuff, the several I'd done of him, and the others in a similar style.

"Carly, these are amazing," he murmured.

"I'm glad you think so and aren't freaked out that I used you as my muse."

He winked at me. "I'm glad you did."

He stayed for a little while longer, and then kissed me before he left with promises to call me later, once he reached his hotel in Hartford.

I got back to work, this time on a book cover for a mystery author. I worked right up until my alarm went off, alerting me it was time to go get Jake. I gave myself enough time to clean my brushes and straighten up the studio, then headed out the door.

"Hi, kiddo," I said when he climbed into the passenger seat next to me. "Good day?"

"It was school," he said with a shrug.

"Hey, at least it's Friday." I grinned at him.

"True." He nodded as we pulled onto the street.

I asked a few more questions about his day as I drove, my eyes bouncing around, looking for threats. Unfortunately, I found one. Two cars behind us was a dark brown sedan. It had a large dent on the front right side. My heart began to race as I kept an eye on the rearview mirror. I made a turn, hoping it was my imagination.

"Where are we going?" Jake asked, since the turn wasn't on our normal route.

"Just taking a different way today," I answered, then drew in a sharp breath as I noticed the sedan made the same turn. I glanced at Jake to make sure he was safely buckled in.

"What is it?" He glanced in the side mirror and gasped. "Carly, that's the car!"

I was afraid of that. "Jake, dial 911."

He pulled out his phone, but hesitated. "What do I tell them?"

I opened my mouth to answer but quickly closed it as the sedan sped up and moved around us, coming really close on the driver's side as it went around me. As soon as it was in front of us, the driver slammed on the brakes and I swerved to the left, putting on my own brakes, fishtailing the car. It was lucky that there were no cars there.

"Carly!" Jake screamed.

"Just hang on," I said frantically as I made a turn trying to escape the lunatic.

A block and a half later, the car was back, speeding up to catch up with us. It was coming up fast on my bumper and my hands were shaking. I realized I was only a few blocks from the police station we'd visited less than a week earlier and decided to head for it.

"Should I still call 911?"

I shook my head, and the sedan did the same maneuver, getting in front of us and brake-checking us, hoping we'd rearend them. I gripped the steering wheel tighter. I slowed the car, dropping back. The sedan made a quick turn to the right, and I searched for a way to make us disappear, but before I knew it, the sedan was back, racing toward us again from behind. It must have cut through an alleyway to get up on us so quickly.

The police station was the safest bet, so I pressed the gas and shifted around a slower vehicle, then made the left-hand turn to take us there. The sedan once again tried to get around us, but this time I sped up faster, not letting him get in front of me. He must have realized what I was doing, though, because the sedan quickly started drifting toward us. There was nowhere for us to go but onto the sidewalk, and that would lead to us crashing or hitting a pedestrian. I couldn't do that. Instead, I slammed on the brakes, and the sedan kept its momentum moving to the right, but the driver hadn't been prepared for my actions, so the sedan bumped up onto the sidewalk, and then slammed into a wooden electric pole.

I quickly pulled over, grabbed my purse, and got my phone out to film the car and the driver. I opened the door, tossed my purse strap over my shoulder so it crossed my chest and wouldn't fall, and stood on the opposite sidewalk, so I could get a good view. The hood of the car was crunched, and steam was filling the air, pouring out from under the hood. The driver door creaked open and the driver, who had long stringy blond hair and a beard and was large and heavyset, stumbled from the car holding his head. He saw me filming him and covered his face before turning back to the car.

"He's going to get away," Jake called from the passenger seat.

"I've got him on camera. They can't deny this evidence," I replied as the man turned back toward us. "Oh my God, Jake get out of the car, now!" I said urgently, keeping my eyes on the man with a huge blade in his hand.

Jake scrambled across the seat and toward me just as the man began moving across the street heading right for us.

"Run!" I screamed as I grabbed his hand.

24

Jake and I took off on foot with the menacing man chasing us. "Move! Get out of the way!" I called as we headed down the sidewalk.

I still had my phone in my other hand, and I held it up over my shoulder so it would hopefully pick up this crazy man chasing us. People moved as they saw us coming, but when they noticed the slimeball chasing us, some of them screamed. Then I noticed the sound of sirens racing toward us.

I slowed, pausing to see if we were still being chased, or if the police had arrived. It certainly sounded like there was a bunch of them nearby. I glanced behind us and realized the lunatic wasn't anywhere around. I blew out a breath and stopped.

"Carly, come on," Jake said, tugging on my hand.

"No, it's okay. We need to go back. The cops are there," I directed his attention back the way we'd come.

We walked back, my head on a swivel as I assessed everyone we passed for threats. I didn't see the asshole with the bowie knife anywhere. I headed for the crashed car where a group of cops were standing around.

"Ma'am, you need to stay clear of the accident."

"It wasn't an accident, it was a maniac trying to kill us," I said to the officer.

He gave me a look of disbelief. "Look, there is no one in the car. The driver took off. Probably some drunk who got confused. It happens. We have a tow truck coming. If you have a car in the area, I suggest you return to it and move along."

"But—"

"Ma'am, we have a job to do. Please move along."

I rolled my eyes and took Jake's hand again as we headed for my car. "We'll just go to the station and talk to Detective Abrahms again. I have video evidence this time."

It didn't take long to get there. I marched over to the front desk and demanded to see Detective Abrahms. We had to wait twenty minutes, cooling our heels on the bench with a few criminals who were handcuffed to the back of it. I pulled Jake close to me, not letting him anywhere near them. Finally, we were directed back to the detective's desk.

"Ms. Michaelson, why are you here?"

"That maniac who tried to run Jake over just tried to run me off the road. He crashed his car and then came after us with a knife." I pulled up the video and handed it to him.

The detective reluctantly took the phone and watched the video. "This is all circumstantial evidence. You have no video of the sedan chasing you. All you have is this person who clearly doesn't want to be filmed, which is his right, charging at you to get you to stop. It could all be staged for all I know."

I looked at him with disbelief. "Are you fucking kidding me?" I growled. "He's got a bowie knife!"

The detective shrugged. "They aren't illegal."

I grabbed back my phone and glared at him. "So you're going to do nothing."

He just stared at me and folded his arms across his chest.

I was seething. It was completely outrageous that they weren't going to help us. "Come on, Jake. There's more than one way to get justice," I muttered as we left the station.

"What are you going to do?" he asked as we got back in the car.

I sat in the driver's seat and pulled up my social media accounts. What I was about to do could cause a bit of chaos and I wasn't sure how Amanda was going to react, given I figured she knew this guy, but I had to do something. I only hesitated for a moment before I began posting that video everywhere with the hashtag of PoliceNegligence and CorruptPolice, adding that the police would do nothing to get this menace off the street. In a couple of the posts, I mentioned that the same man attempted to run Jake over less than a week earlier.

"See what they think about that," I said as I put my phone away. I turned the car on and glanced at Jake. "Seatbelt." I waited for him to buckle up before pulling out of the parking space.

By the time we reached Brooklyn, my phone was blowing up, but I didn't answer it. They were mostly unknown callers, but several had left me voicemail messages. I let us into my apartment and directed Jake to put his stuff away.

"Aren't you going to answer those?" he asked, eyeing my phone, which was ringing again.

I sighed. "Eventually."

He gave me a slow nod and then headed for his room while I went into the living room and sank down on the couch. Once the phone stopped ringing, I began listening to my voicemails. There were fifteen of them.

"Hello, Ms. Michaelson? This is Trent Gooding with WSTP. We'd like to interview—"

I deleted the rest of the message.

There were several others just like it from various other small news agencies and I deleted them as well. They'd probably call back either way.

Then there was a message from Detective Abrahms. *"Ms. Michaelson, it has come to our attention that you've posted that video online and it is causing an uproar on social media and in the city. We are asking politely that you take it down."*

I shook my head. Asshole. I deleted it and hung up. I didn't want to listen to any more, but the moment I did, the phone rang again. This time I answered it. "Hello?"

"Ms. Michaelson, this is Detective Abrahms."

"Hello, Detective. What can I do for you?"

"You can take down that blasted video. Do you know what kind of chaos you're causing?"

"I'm causing chaos? I'm just sitting here in my apartment, minding my own business." I was still seething.

"The video is causing the chaos. You knowingly posted it expecting this. You need to take it down."

"How about this, Detective? I'll take it down when you catch the asshole who tried to kill Jake. He's a ten-year-old boy! He's being stalked and had his life threatened twice now and you're sitting on your ass doing nothing, so yeah, I posted the video and I'll keep posting the video until you do something!" I hung up, my chest heaving in my anger.

The phone rang again and once more I answered it. "Yes?"

"Ms. Michaelson? This is Stacy Lawrence with WNYT. I'd like to ask you a few questions about the video you posted."

I knew she was an anchor with the local TV station for NYC. "Sure. What would you like to know?"

She asked a bunch of questions about who the man was and why I was filming, so I told her everything.

"Would you be willing to come in for an on-camera interview?"

I hesitated for a moment, but then decided what the hell. Maybe this would finally get the cops to do something about the man. "I'd love to."

We set up the interview for the next day and then I went to find Jake. As I did, my phone rang again, but this time I recognized the number.

"Hey, Amanda. I guess you heard—"

"How dare you post that video on the internet!" she screamed over the phone.

I pulled it from my ear and frowned at it. "I'm sorry, what? That man was chasing us through the streets of New York City and it's the same guy who tried to run *your son* over. The cops are doing nothing about it," I added.

"Where are you?" she demanded to know.

"We're back in Brooklyn. Why?"

She huffed and then said, "Meet me at that bar we had drinks at in forty minutes," before hanging up.

I stared at my phone with a frown. Why was she coming to Brooklyn to see me? Wouldn't she want to see Jake? Something was weird about all this. I didn't know what to do, but I supposed I needed to meet her. The problem was what to do with Jake. I couldn't leave him home alone. Not with this knife-wielding asshole on the loose. I considered asking one of my neighbors to watch him, but I didn't want to put that responsibility on them. Instead, I called Blaine.

"Hey, sis. What's going on?"

"Did you see the video I posted?" I asked so he'd understand my concern.

"No. Where did you post it?"

I gave him the information and waited while he pulled it up and looked at it.

"Holy shit, are you two okay?"

"Yeah, I guess, but Amanda called, and she wants me to meet her at a bar. I can't take Jake with me, so I was hoping I could bring him over to you. I don't want to leave him on his own."

"Sure. Has he eaten dinner?"

"No, not yet. Thanks, Blaine. We'll be there in a few minutes."

"See you in a bit. Be careful."

"We will." I hung up and knocked on Jake's door. "Hey, kiddo, I have to go meet Amanda, so I'm going to take you over to my brother's, okay?"

"Why can't I go with you?"

"Because they don't let kids in the place we're meeting."

"Can I bring my Switch?"

"Sure."

We headed out and made it to Blaine's ten minutes later. I had to turn my phone ringer off as we made the trip because it wouldn't stop ringing. I still glanced at it every time a call came in, to make sure it wasn't Hans or Vivienne or anyone I knew.

"Blaine, Dave, this is Jake." I smiled and put my hand on

Jake's shoulder. "Jake, this is my brother Blaine and his husband Dave."

"Nice to meet you," Jake said as we entered their apartment.

"Nice to meet you too," Blaine replied.

"Are you hungry?" Dave questioned. "I made burgers and fries."

"That sounds good." Jake moved with Dave toward the kitchen.

"I'll be back as soon as I can to get him. Amanda was pretty pissed at me for posting the video, so I don't know how this is going to go."

"You would think she'd want this guy caught," Blaine replied with a frown.

Now I had to wonder if she was somehow involved in this guy trying to hurt Jake, because as his mother, she should want Jake to be safe. She should be on my side, wanting everyone to see how the cops weren't helping. Instead, she was practically defending the guy who was trying to hurt Jake. That really had me thinking she was complicit.

I met Blaine's gaze and shared my suspicion. "Not if she's somehow involved. I think it's the same guy who supposedly attacked her."

"The one you think she called?"

"Yeah."

"Be careful. I don't want to have to file a missing person's report on you or hear about your dead body on the six o'clock news."

"I'll be okay."

I called out to Jake that I was leaving, gave Blaine a hug and then left. I drove to Melodies and parked in the small lot in the back. Devon was behind the bar and waved as I entered. Hans wasn't there since he was in Connecticut tonight. Instead, there was a young woman seated at the piano. She was merely playing, not singing.

I didn't see Amanda here yet, so I went to the bar and ordered a drink—not my usual, but a club soda, since I was driving and I wanted to keep a clear head for this upcoming conversation.

"Everything okay?" Devon asked, eyeing me.

"Yeah. Just been a bad day."

"I saw that video. Can't even imagine having that guy chasing me, let alone a kid."

I nodded.

"And the cops aren't doing anything?"

"Nope. The detective said we could have staged the video." I rolled my eyes.

Another patron waved to get his attention and he held a hand up to acknowledge them, but then turned back to me. "You be careful, okay? If you need anything, give me a call. I know Hans would want me to keep you safe."

I smiled. "Thanks, Devon." I took my drink and walked over to one of the tables. My normal table was occupied, but I didn't mind since Hans wasn't here.

I settled in to await Amanda. My thoughts were chaotic as I wondered what Amanda was so pissed about. Had she ordered a hit on Jake? Was that even possible? What kind of monster would do such a thing to a kid?

25

I nervously sipped my club soda as I listened to the girl playing the piano. She wasn't as good as Hans, not that I was biased or anything. She really wasn't. She hesitated over notes, so sometimes the song came out stilted. I finished my drink and looked to see who was working tonight.

Melodies had several cocktail waitresses, along with Devon who was tending bar. I noticed Denise and Lauren were waitressing tonight. I'd sat down in Denise's section. It wasn't long before she approached.

"Hey, Carly. It's good to see you. Do you want another?"

I glanced at my glass. "Sure. It's just a club soda."

"I didn't expect to see you in tonight with Hans gone."

"I wasn't planning to be here either, but I'm meeting someone and figured I'd better keep a clear head."

"Does this have to do with that video you posted?" she asked softly.

I was a little surprised. We weren't friends on social media that I knew of. "Yeah. Where did you see it?"

"Devon showed me earlier. It's gotten thousands of views already."

I hadn't even checked it since I'd posted it. "Where at? I posted it in multiple places."

"I think Devon had it on Facebook."

I nodded. "I'll have to look, but mostly I've been ignoring it since I dropped it. My phone has been blowing up with reporters and the cops trying to get me to take it down."

"Probably because it shows that they're being lazy." She snorted.

"Denise," Devon called from the bar.

She looked up and Devon held up a couple of drinks. "I better get those. I'll be back with another drink for you."

"Thanks." I watched her move to the bar, speak to Devon and take the drinks to another table.

A few minutes later she returned with my drink. "Here you go, hon. Can I get you anything else?"

"No, I'm fine. Who's the woman at the piano?" I asked, curiosity getting the better of me.

Denise pursed her lips and wrinkled her nose. "Tiffani Martin. Devon's girlfriend."

"Oh," I replied with a nod.

"I better get back to work. Let me know if you need anything else, okay?"

"Sure." I watched her head for another table.

The bar was pretty steady with customers, but it was not anywhere near as crowded as it was on the nights Hans played. He was a big draw for the bar. I wondered how he'd ended up playing here. I'd have to remember to ask him.

Thoughts of Hans filled my mind and I decided to text him. It was still early, and I was pretty sure he'd said his concert was not until eight.

> Hey, I'm sitting in Melodies, wishing you were here. I miss you.

He texted back almost immediately. I always liked that about him. He rarely left me hanging.

> Why are you there without me? I miss you too.

> Meeting Amanda. Did you see the video I posted today?

> No. What video?

Hans followed me on social media, but I figured he was too busy to have seen the video yet.

> That guy who tried to run Jake over tried to run us off the road. I got him on video, but the cops won't do anything about him.

> Oh my God, are you and Jake okay?

> Yeah, we're okay.

> Do you want me to cancel my concerts and come home?

His offer touched my heart in a way I didn't expect, but I couldn't let him do that. There was nothing he could do, but it was really nice to know that he cared enough to offer.

> No, it's okay. I'm alright. You don't have to come home.

> Okay, but I expect you to keep me updated
> and I'm calling you tonight after the
> concert. I need to hear your voice.

I smiled. This man was everything that Nelson was not. I couldn't believe how lucky I'd gotten when I met him. We'd only known each other for a short period of time and already he was more caring, loving and kind than Nelson ever was. And he understood my feelings about Jake. He didn't think me looking out for him was weird. He'd even said I was the only responsible adult in Jake's life. I felt that way, but it was nice that he saw it like that too.

> I'm looking forward to it. I need to go; she's
> here.

Okay. Be safe.

> I will. Good luck tonight!

Thanks, beautiful.

I watched Amanda swan in like she owned the place. She stood at the entrance and looked around, a look of distaste on her face. Her eyes landed on me, and her expression turned fierce for a moment before she made her way to my table and sank down into the empty chair across from me.

"Waitress," she called, raising her hand to get Denise's attention.

I rolled my eyes as Denise came over. I'd gotten to know most of the staff at Melodies since I'd started coming here. They were all very nice and pleasant, but they didn't put up with shitty customers. Devon generally asked the obnoxious ones to leave. I didn't want to be connected to that kind of toxicity, so I mouthed, "I'm sorry," to her, knowing Amanda was going to be awful.

"Hi. What can I get you?" Denise pasted a smile on her lips as she gave me a slight nod of acknowledgement.

"Gin and tonic, light ice." Amanda stared at her for a moment. "You can go now." She flicked her hand at her.

I could feel the tension and anger rolling off Amanda and I was wary to ask the questions that were burning in my soul. Questions like, 'Why are you so worked up?' or 'Why aren't you concerned about your son?' were top of the list. I held back though. Maybe a drink would calm her and then I could ask her why she wasn't more interested in catching the guy. I'd have to keep my real suspicions of her under wraps, because I didn't want her to know Jake and I were on to her.

Denise had Amanda's drink to her in record time and she gave me a sympathetic look as she moved on.

I turned my gaze back to Amanda, who was now staring at me. I decided that I wasn't going to say a word. She was the one who asked for this 'meeting'; she could be the one to start. I sipped my club soda and waited for her to speak as I listened to the woman at the piano attempt to play something that sounded vaguely like *November Rain* by Guns N' Roses. I was pretty sure she was off by a few chords though.

Amanda set her drink down on the table, jarring me from my thoughts. "How could you do this? You're getting in the way," she hissed across the table.

That was a curious statement. Whom was I getting in the way of? "I don't understand what you mean, Amanda."

She pursed her lips, then picked up her drink and swallowed half of it. "Don't play coy. It doesn't suit you." She continued to stare daggers at me.

"Look, I don't know why you're upset. I posted the video so that crazy man would be caught. I'm the one taking care of your son. I'm the one who is looking out for him after nearly being murdered by that knife-wielding maniac—and from what I could tell, the same man who attacked you."

"You don't know that," she practically screamed, then slammed her hand on the table, making our glasses jump.

People turned toward us to see what was going on.

I glanced around the room, hoping everyone would just go back to their own conversations and ignore us. "Yes, I do. I recognized him from the photo the cops showed us. It was grainy, but you could make out his features. I know it's the same man."

"No, it isn't. You can't know that. It was just some drunk guy with road rage."

I couldn't figure out why she was so adamant that I was wrong. Not if she really was innocent. It was as though she was defending that slimeball with the knife. I kept my voice down and tried to remain calm, though I was feeling anything but that. "It was more than that and I don't think he was drunk at all. He was being deliberate in his actions."

"You're exaggerating. He was just some random crazy person. Stop making this out to be something it's not," Amanda demanded. "You need to take the video down."

I stared at her. Why wouldn't she want this guy caught? Why didn't she care that Jake was nearly killed? Unless she was involved, but I couldn't ask that question.

"I don't understand you at all, Amanda. You and Nelson act completely unconcerned that Jake has nearly been killed twice. Like it's an inconvenience for you to acknowledge that someone is trying to harm your son." I was flabbergasted that she was behaving this way. What mother on the planet acted like their child was an inconvenience?

"It was random," she denied again.

I continued as if she hadn't answered. "I get that Nelson is a man-baby who runs from the slightest hint of responsibility and has empathy for exactly no one, but you've always been the more responsible parent. You have always looked out for Jake... at least you did before the attack. How can you treat this, treat *him* as if he means nothing to you?"

Amanda just lifted her gin and tonic and took a long drink, her expression blank.

"Please, explain to me like I'm five how you are not the least bit upset that the man who hurt you is now after your son? What the hell is going on with you? Are you really such a cold-hearted bitch that you'd let your own son be murdered and not give a fuck?" I was suddenly irate, and my voice rose as I spoke.

The look on Amanda's face was bone-chilling. It was a cold and calculated look. The look of a psychopath. There was nothing in her eyes, no hint of emotion. Her voice, though, was full of fury. "I don't remember the kid, so of course I don't give a fuck what happens to him." Her gaze didn't even flicker as she added, "In fact, I find that he's almost always in my way and I just wish he would disappear."

26

My whole body was shaking as I stared at Amanda with horror. I couldn't believe she'd just said that. Surely I'd misheard her, right? Right?

How could she wish that Jake would disappear? How could anyone look at the kid, know him for even five seconds and not see how amazing he was? How could his own mother wish something like that?

My heart ached for him, and I wished more than anything on the planet that I could take Jake away from her and Nelson. They didn't deserve him at all. My fingers clenched into tight fists, and I had to stop myself from slapping the ever-loving shit out of her for even putting that thought into the universe.

"I can't even—" I started, but I didn't know how to finish that thought. It didn't matter, though, because my phone rang in that exact moment. Grunting in frustration, I pulled it from my purse to see it was my neighbor from across the hall. She never called. "I have to take this," I murmured with barely a glance at Amanda.

"Whatever." Amanda rolled her eyes.

"Hello?"

"Carly? It's Sandra. I was calling because there's a man trying to break down your door. I've called the police," she said quietly, like she didn't want the man to overhear her.

"What does this man look like?" I asked, feeling panic and fear rise in my chest.

"He's a big guy, long stringy blond hair, a scraggly beard. Do you know him?"

He'd found us. My heart was racing, and I flicked my gaze to Amanda, who was now giving me a concerned look, or at least it looked as though that was what she was attempting to do, but I could see there was no real emotion in her eyes.

"He's the guy on the video I posted. The one who tried to run me off the road."

"The guy with the knife?" Sandra squeaked.

"Yeah, that's the guy. Are the cops there yet? Has he broken into my place?"

"Someone's breaking into your apartment? What about Jake?" Amanda widened her eyes and acted like she was panicked.

"Jake's not there," I said with a hard look in her direction.

"Who's Jake?" Sandra asked.

"The boy I take care of sometimes. I took him to a sitter before I went out," I answered.

"Oh, yes, I've seen him with you before," Sandra acknowledged. "The cops are here, and the man is gone. I need to go so I can talk to them."

"I'm on my way. I have a security camera on my door.

Well, it's one of those Amazon Ring things, but maybe it will help convince them that I'm telling the truth."

"I'll let them know," Sandra said before hanging up.

I started pulling on my coat, then shoved my phone in my purse. "I have to go," I muttered.

Amanda looked frustrated as she stared at her empty glass and then back to me. "We aren't done yet. You need to take that video down."

I glared at her and shook my head. "We are done. And if the cops won't get off their asses and find this guy, then I will." I hurried toward the door and out to my car.

It didn't take me long to drive home. I parked in my usual spot and practically ran to the elevators. The cops were still speaking to Sandra when I arrived.

"There you are," Sandra said with relief, then she looked at the officers. "This is the woman who lives there. Carly Michaelson."

"Ms. Michaelson, Mrs. Jefferies says you might have video of the man who tried to break into your apartment?"

"Yeah. See that?" I pointed to the small buzzer next to my door. "It's got a camera in it."

"May we have the footage?"

"I just have to pull it up on my computer and make you a copy," I said as I put the key in the lock. My door looked beat all to hell, but at least it had withstood the lunatic's attack. We went inside and I grabbed my laptop and logged into my account. I pulled up the recent footage and watched the knife-wielding man attack my door.

"Do you recognize the man?" the officer asked.

"He's the same guy who tried to run me off the road and ran after me with a knife. The same man who tried to run over Jake, the ten-year-old boy I take care of. I think he's also the same man who attacked Jake's mom." I glared at the cop. "If you people would have taken me seriously when I brought this to your attention before, we wouldn't be here now."

"I understand your frustration, ma'am—" he started.

"No, you really don't! This man has tried to kill Jake twice and now he's trying to break into my apartment where Jake is staying. You need to put more effort into catching him," I growled as I made a copy of the Ring video and put it on a thumb drive for them. "Here." I shoved the drive at him. "If you want the video from earlier today of him running at us with a knife, then you can find it all over the internet. Just look up my socials."

"We'll do our best, ma'am." The cop turned and jerked his head toward the door for the other cop to leave.

I followed them out since I still had to go get Jake. I locked the door behind me and made a mental note to talk to the Super about upgrading my door to a steel-reinforced one.

I made the drive to Blaine's place and thirty minutes later knocked on the door. I had been so paranoid as I drove, afraid that the asshole was out there watching me, so I took a circuitous route to his place, making sure the man wasn't following me. My hands were still trembling as I knocked again.

"Hey, come in... are you okay?" Blaine asked, eyeing me up and down.

"Yeah, just..." I shook my head. I didn't want to worry Blaine over an aborted break-in. "Just dealing with Amanda," I finished, trying to dismiss my frazzledness.

"That bad, huh?"

I nodded. "How's Jake?"

"He's been having a great time with Dave," Blaine offered as he led me deeper into their place.

"Carly!" Jake jumped up from the couch and ran to me, hugging me.

"Hey, kiddo. Did you have a good time?"

He grinned. "Yeah. Dave made burgers and fries and then we made sundaes."

"And what's going on here?" I waved my hand toward the coffee table where there was a pile of playing cards.

"We were building a house of cards, but it fell. We got it up to five levels," he said, his grin widening, nearly splitting his face in two.

"We would have made it higher if Blaine hadn't sent a gust of wind through the house when he opened door," Dave teased.

Blaine laughed. "You're blaming me? Carly's the one who knocked. What was I going to do? Leave her out on the step?"

I shook my head at the two of them. "I'm glad you didn't. It's cold out there." I shivered for effect. "You ready to go, kiddo?"

"Sure. Let me grab my stuff." He raced around the room grabbing his coat and Switch, then he hugged both Blaine and Dave. "Thanks for letting me stay here," he said before I had to remind him.

"Anytime, squirt. Next time we'll double our card house," Dave commented as he ruffled Jake's hair.

"Cool. I can come back, can't I, Carly?"

"We'll have to play that by ear." I smiled at him. "Come on, we need to head home. Bye, guys. Thanks for watching him."

"Anytime," Dave answered.

Blaine walked us out to my car. "Drive safe."

"I will." I waved and then pulled away from the building.

"Jake, before we get to my place I need to tell you something." I didn't want to scare him, but he'd notice the door, so I needed to let him know.

"What's up?"

"While we were gone, that guy from earlier tried to break in."

Jake looked startled and then his eyes connected with mine for a minute and his mouth gaped. "Carly, you were meeting with her."

"Yeah," I said, trying to figure out what that had to do with anything.

"What if the guy thought I was still there?" His voice quivered as he shared his fear.

My heart dropped to my stomach. "Jake..." I wanted to tell him that this man wasn't after him, that he was safe, but I couldn't. He could be right.

The timing of everything was too coincidental. Amanda lured me away and I'd seen that cold look on her face and heard her say she wished Jake would disappear. She could have set this whole thing up. She had to have thought that I'd left Jake in my apartment by himself, because that was what she would do. She didn't know me. She didn't know that I would never leave Jake on his own like that. This Amanda didn't know I had a brother who lived only a few blocks away. She didn't know that I had a neighbor I was friendly with and who looked out for me.

"Carly, will you lay with me until I fall asleep?" Jake asked later, snuggling into his covers.

"Sure, kiddo. You don't have to worry; the cops are watching for him now. He's not going to get in here."

"Okay," he answered, but I could see the doubtful look in his eyes.

I leaned in and hugged him, then kissed his forehead. "Go to sleep. We'll figure this out. I promise."

He nodded, and then closed his eyes. He was asleep within ten minutes, snoring softly.

I tiptoed out of the room and closed the door. My phone had vibrated with a call five minutes earlier, but I'd let it go to voicemail. I pulled it out and looked at it to see who had called. It was Hans. I quickly called him back.

"Hey. Sorry, I was getting Jake to bed."

"Kind of late for the kid, isn't it?" he asked, concern laced in his voice.

"Yeah. We had another incident." I told him about the latest bizarre installment that had become my life.

"I'm canceling the rest of my trip. I'm coming home right now."

"You don't have to do that... Your fans—"

"Will understand. I'll reschedule. It's not a big deal and I'd feel better if I was closer to you."

"It's after eleven and you have to drive..."

"I'll catch a plane. There are flights to NYC practically every hour," he huffed.

"Hans, no. We're okay. At least stay the night there and drive back tomorrow. You need your car; you can't leave it there."

He sighed. "Are you sure? I feel like I should be there. I'm worried about you."

"I've got the door locked, the chain is on, and so is the video camera. The cops are, I hope, actively looking for this guy now, so we should be safe enough tonight. Tomorrow I'll ask the Super about getting a steel, reinforced door."

"I don't like this. I don't like you being so vulnerable. I'm just glad you and Jake weren't there when this guy showed up."

"Me too."

We spent a few more minutes talking, and then ended our call with him assuring me that he was leaving at first light and would be back in Brooklyn soon. Again, I marveled at how lucky I'd been to meet him. I set the phone down on my nightstand and headed for the bathroom to clean up.

As I lay in bed later, I thought about my conversation with Amanda again. I thought about how she demanded I meet her at the bar, a place she knew I couldn't bring Jake. She'd set this up. She really had hired that lunatic to go after Jake. First at the school, knowing he would be waiting for a car service ride, not me. Then when that didn't work, she sent the maniac to run us off the road and hack us to pieces with that knife.

I shivered under my covers—not from cold, but from fear.

Me posting that video pissed both of them off. I'd shown the world his face. I was demanding that someone do something. To get the police to take this seriously. And now the man had tried to break in, most likely with the intention of hurting Jake.

It had to be Amanda behind it all, but why would she do all of this? Why would she want to hurt Jake? It didn't make sense. Unless she wasn't his mother. Wasn't the real Amanda.

I needed to figure out what was going on and fast.

Jake's life depended on it.

27

I let Jake sleep in, seeing as it was Saturday. He had woken up twice in the middle of the night with nightmares, so I figured he needed the extra zzz's. I set about my usual cleaning routine, and tossed a load of laundry in the wash. I had just pulled out the ingredients to make pancakes when the intercom buzzed. I pushed the button. "Hello?"

"Carly, it's Hans."

I smiled. He must have gotten up at the ass-crack of dawn to get here so fast. "Come on up." I buzzed him in and then frowned. How had the maniac gotten into the building in the first place? I was still frowning when Hans knocked on the door.

"I can't believe that asshole did all this damage. Have they caught him yet?" Hans asked as he stepped in and kissed me.

I shook my head.

"What's the matter? Are you not happy to see me?"

"What?" His words startled me. "Of course I'm happy to see you." I wrapped my arms around his waist. "I was just thinking. That guy had to be buzzed in to even make it to my door."

"Well, not exactly," Hans answered, shifting the box in his hands. "He could have waited for someone else to get buzzed in, or he could have followed behind someone with a key."

"Oh, yeah, I didn't think of that." I shrugged and glanced at the box. "Are those what I think they are?"

"That depends on if you think they're donuts from Death By Chocolate." He grinned as we headed for the kitchen.

"Jake is going to love you for this." I smiled. "I almost don't want to wake him up so I can eat them all myself."

Hans laughed. "There are plenty for all of us. I promise."

"I was teasing," I said as I knocked on Jake's door. "Hey, kiddo, Hans brought donuts."

"I'm up!" Jake shouted and a moment later yanked the door open before racing to the kitchen. "Hi, Hans."

I followed behind him and saw Hans handing him a plate with two donuts on it.

"Thanks," Jake said before sitting down and taking a big bite of a chocolate cake donut with chocolate fudge icing and crumbled bacon on top.

I picked up a donut and took a bite. "This is so good. Thank you." I leaned in and kissed Hans, who wrapped his arms around my waist and smiled.

"Did you call the Super yet about the door?"

"No, but I will."

"Let me know what he says. I want you safe." He caressed my face then looked over at Jake. "Both of you."

Jake looked up and smiled, but didn't say anything.

"So do you have plans for today?" he asked.

"Does hiding here in the apartment count?" I asked sheepishly.

He chuckled. "Would that include a movie marathon and food delivery?"

"Definitely."

"Then count me in," he said as my phone rang.

I quickly picked it up and saw it was Stacy Lawrence, the anchor I'd said I'd meet with from WNYT. "Oh shoot. I forgot about the interview." I hit the answer button and said, "Hello?"

"Ms. Michaelson? This is Stacy Lawrence. I was just calling to confirm our interview at nine a.m.?"

"Uh, yes. Hi. I am heading out the door to meet you right now." I hurried into the bedroom so I could change my clothes to something more appropriate.

"Great. I'll see you soon then."

"You have an interview?" Hans asked as he watched me from the doorway.

I quickly explained and then stopped and looked at him. "Jake."

"Don't worry, I'll stay with him while you go do that, and when you get back, we can have that movie marathon." He smiled.

I hugged him and pressed my face against his chest. "Thank you."

Once the interview was done, with the promise of it airing that evening on the news, I returned home and we spent the rest of the day together with Jake, just hanging out. I opted out of watching the interview because I didn't want to remind Jake of everything when we were having such a good time. And then later that night, after Jake went to bed, Hans reluctantly left. He had offered to stay the night on the couch, but I'd told him we'd be fine and to go home and get some sleep. We weren't at the stage yet where I was comfortable with him staying over.

On Sunday, Jake and I went for brunch with Blaine and Dave. The Super had agreed to get me a new door, and he installed it while we were gone. Overall, he was very concerned about the tenants and took good care of things in the building.

Monday I drove Jake into Manhattan for school, feeling paranoid about every car that got too close to us. I dropped him off without incident and headed back home to get to work. The problem was my mind was still on the crazy events of the previous week and Amanda's behavior. I decided it was time to call the private investigator that Dave had recommended again and actually speak to her this time. I waited until I was home so I could make the call.

"Shelton Investigations. How may I direct your call?"

"Is Ms. Shelton available?" I asked hesitantly, almost shocked that it didn't go directly to her voice mail.

"May I ask who's calling?"

"Carly Michaelson. My brother-in-law Dave Michaelson recommended I call," I replied.

"One moment and I will see if she's available."

I was put on hold with elevator music playing over the line. I debated just hanging up, but I really wanted to get to the bottom of everything and keep Jake safe, so I didn't.

Three minutes later she came on the line. "Ms. Michaelson, hello. This is Marianne Shelton. Your brother-in-law is Dave Michaelson?"

"Yes, ma'am. He recommended I give you a call because he can't look into what I need right now."

"Well, I'll have to thank him for the business. Now, would you like to set up a meeting?"

"I'm not really sure how we do this. I don't have a whole lot of money—"

"The initial consultation is free. How about we meet, you tell me what it is you need, and we'll discuss my fee then?"

"Yes, okay."

We set up a meeting at her office for twelve thirty. I assured her I would be there and then hung up. I headed to my studio to get a couple hours of work in before I had to leave. Her office wasn't too far away, so at noon I cleaned up and left to go meet her.

"Please have a seat," she directed once I arrived.

"Thanks," I murmured.

"Now, can you tell me what's been going on?"

I nodded. "So, it all started with an attack on Jake's mom—"

"Who is Jake?"

I spent a few awkward minutes explaining the whole sordid relationship between me, Nelson, Jake, and Amanda.

"I see. Continue, please."

I explained Amanda's attack, her subsequent amnesia, and what Jake and I suspected. "So, you see, we aren't even sure that she's the real Amanda. That's one of the major things I need you to look into—if this is the real Amanda or some imposter. And if it is an imposter, what happened to the real Amanda."

"That seems easy enough to look into," she agreed with a nod.

"There's more though." I went on to tell her about Jake

almost getting run over, the sedan nearly running us off the road, the maniac with the knife attacking us, and him trying to break into my apartment. I also mentioned the phone call between what seemed to be Amanda and this man. As well as my theory that Amanda had lured me away from my apartment so he could get at Jake.

"Wow, okay, yeah, I'll definitely look into that as well. You said you have video of this man?"

I had made a copy of the Ring video and the camera footage from the road incident and then put them on a new thumb drive for her. I pulled it out of my purse. "Both videos are on here."

"Excellent. I love when my clients come prepared. Let me take a look." She popped the drive into her laptop and tapped on the first video. "Well, doesn't he look like an upstanding citizen," she snarked as she shook her head. She turned it off and pulled up the Ring video. "Pretty good look at his face here. Should make it easy to identify him." She glanced at me. "Who else has these?"

"I posted the first one online when the cops wouldn't help, but just you and the cops have the Ring footage."

"That's probably how he found your address."

"Or Amanda gave him my address," I suggested.

"That is possible," she agreed.

We talked for a few more minutes and she told me her fees and all that would be included in that. My breath caught in my throat at the expense, but I knew it would be worth it. I just needed to find some more money. *Maybe Blaine will help?* I thought as I shook her hand.

On my way out the door, I dialed Blaine.

"What's up, sis? You okay?"

"I just finished meeting with Marianne Shelton. I think

she'll be able to help, but... Blaine, I'm not going to have enough to cover her fees. Is there any way you can help?"

"How much do you need?" he asked.

I explained how much she was charging per day plus expenses and that I only had enough to cover about a week. "So maybe double that? I just don't know how long it's going to take for her to gather all the information."

"Did she say she can start right away?" he asked.

"She said she'd start as soon as I paid for the first three days, but I wanted to make sure I was going to have enough..."

"Go pay her, get her started. I don't know if you'll need that much, but I've got you covered for the rest. And, sis?"

"Yeah?"

"Stay safe, please. I don't want you going out looking for this guy on your own. He's already tried to run you off the road once. Maybe take the video down? I don't want him finding you."

I sighed. "It's a little too late for that."

"What do you mean?" Blaine sounded worried.

"He's already tried to break into my apartment. He knows where I live."

"Carly! This is so dangerous. Did you report him to the cops?"

"Of course I did! I'm not stupid. It was while you were watching Jake," I admitted.

"Holy shit, and you said nothing? Why?" he demanded.

"I didn't want you to worry. My neighbor called the cops before he could get in. I've got him on the Ring camera that you told me to install, and the Super has already installed a new steel-reinforced door, so you don't have to worry, okay?"

"I'm always going to worry," he ground out. "None of this would be taking place if you'd never have gotten involved—"

"Blaine, please, don't do this," I interrupted his favorite rant. "You're right, I never should have gotten involved with Nelson, but it's too late to change things now. And there's a little boy involved, a little boy I care about as if he was my own. I need to keep him safe; do you understand that?"

Blaine huffed. "Yeah, I know. I do. Sorry, I just... I knew it was going to end badly and I didn't want that for you."

I snorted. "You expected some crazed lunatic to come after me?"

Chuckling, he said, "No, I expected something a little more tame than that. I anticipated a broken heart for you, and I just didn't want you to go through that."

"Thanks. And to be honest, I'm pissed off, yeah, but not brokenhearted over it. And I'm with Hans now, so there's that."

"How are things going with him?"

I smiled as I thought about how caring he was. "Great. When he heard about the attempted break-in, he cancelled the rest of his trip and came home so he'd be close by in case I needed him."

"I'm glad to hear it. Okay, I'm going to have to go, sis. Go pay Marianne and I'll get the rest of the money to you this afternoon."

"Thanks, Blaine. I'll pay you back."

"Don't worry about it. I've got plenty and if we weren't so busy, we'd be doing this for you pro-bono. Now I've gotta go."

"Okay, thanks." I hung up then turned around and went back into Marianne's office.

"Back so soon?" her secretary asked, looking surprised.

I smiled. "Yeah. I needed to check on my funding, but I'm all set. I'd like Ms. Shelton to get started as soon as possible, so I figured I'd better get that fee taken care of now." I pulled my wallet from my purse. "Do you take debit cards?"

"Of course. Just one moment." She fiddled with her phone and then took the card, entered the fee, and scanned my account. "There we go, all set. Let me just pop into her office and tell her you've hired her. She may want to talk to you again real quick."

I sat down on one of the chairs to wait for her. She was back in seconds with Marianne following right behind her.

"Lynn said we're all ready to go." Marianne smiled as she joined me in the waiting area. "Today's fee will only be half, since we're getting started late. I'll begin with the computer work. I don't anticipate having to go beyond the days you've paid for, but I might be doing footwork once that's complete. We'll see what we find."

"Okay. So you'll let me know?"

"Of course. I won't do anything without your say-so. That's how this works. Now I'll get started on the deep search into Amanda Carter and I'll see what I can dig up on this guy who's harassing you and trying to kill Jake. I've got a contact at NYPD. I'll see what I can find out about their case as well."

"That sounds great. Thanks, Ms. Shelton."

"Call me Marianne."

"Thanks, Marianne. You can call me Carly. Is there anything I should do in the meantime?" I fretted. I was worried about the monster coming after me or Jake again.

"You might want to share your fears about Amanda with Jake's father. Maybe you can get through to him that she shouldn't be anywhere near Jake."

"I'll do my best." I had no idea how I was going to accomplish that. Nelson and I weren't exactly speaking to each other these days.

"I'll be in touch," Marianne said as I headed for the door.

As I got in my car, I dialed Nelson's number.

He didn't answer, but I left a voicemail. "Hey, it's me. We need to talk. It's important. Please call me back."

28

T wo days later and I still hadn't heard from Nelson. I'd tried him several times, but every time it just went to voicemail.

"You okay, Carly?" Jake asked as we drove to his school.

"Yeah, just frustrated with your dad. And Amanda has called a few times, leaving crazy messages on my voicemail. She's demanding I bring you back home."

"No!" Jake shouted. "I won't go. I don't want to be there with her."

"I know, kiddo. That's why I've been avoiding her." I reached over and hugged him goodbye. "Okay, have a good day. I'll be back to pick you up right after school."

"Bye, Carly." He jumped out of the car and ran for the doors.

That was his new usual. Running as if the maniac was after him all the way to the building. The teachers didn't even say anything to him as he sped past. They all understood his fear after seeing the videos. They were on high alert and even had an armed security guard on the property now, just in case the maniac tried to get into the school.

In the afternoons when I picked him up, they had someone stand with Jake close to the doors as they waited for me to go through the pick-up line. Once I pulled up out front, they rushed him to the door and got him inside and buckled in as quickly as possible. I was really appreciative of their cooperation and vigilance. They probably cared about him more than either of his parents actually did, which was just sad.

I pulled away from the school and my paranoia rose. It always did whenever I was anywhere near the school. It was an easy way for that guy to find me and start his shit again. I always worried I'd get to the bridge and he'd find some way to ram me off it. That was one of my biggest fears. To be sent flying off the bridge into the East River and sinking to the bottom in my car. Just thinking about it made me hesitant to drive across it. Still, it had to be done. It was the way home.

My knuckles clenched tightly on the steering wheel as I eyed every car around me. I swear I didn't take a full breath until I was safely all the way across the suspension bridge. I relaxed a little more as I pulled into my parking garage.

In the hallway, I ran into the Super. "Hi, Mr. Rodgers. Thanks again for the door."

"My pleasure. Is it working okay? You haven't had any more trouble from that guy, have you?"

"Not so far, but the cops haven't picked him up yet. They haven't even identified him as far as I know."

"We're all keeping an eye out. If he comes back, you can be assured we'll call the cops on him."

"Thanks. I appreciate that." I smiled as I headed for the elevators.

"Have a good day, hon."

"You too." I pushed the button for my floor and soon I was back in my apartment behind the steel door, which was a little heavier than my previous door. It made me feel much more secure in my home, for which I was grateful. I went to work on another of Jasmine's book images.

Three hours into it, Nelson called.

"Babe, you've been persistent. Missing me?" he asked when I answered.

I rolled my eyes. "No, I was calling because I have concerns about Amanda."

"What about her?"

"I think she's trying to murder Jake."

Nelson laughed heartily.

"I'm not joking! He's in danger, Nelson. He's your son. Don't you care?"

"Why the hell would his mom try to kill him? Don't be ridiculous. By the way, she wants him home. Says he's been at your place too long and she's done with you watching him."

"Nelson, that's what I'm talking about. She wants to hurt him. I don't even think she's really the real Amanda."

"You're acting crazy. Just take him home after school today. I'll get a new nanny for him. You don't have to worry about him anymore. See ya around."

"But—" I tried again, but he hung up.

Frustrated, I set the phone down. Glancing at the watercolor, I decided to set it aside. I was too pissed off to work on it. I didn't want that coming across in the image. Instead, I put a fresh canvas on my easel, switched from watercolors to acrylics and just began painting out all my frustrations. It came out in the form of a violent storm with the blurred image of the Brooklyn Bridge and East River in the background. Lightning streaks pierced the sky of black and gray swirling clouds, rain pelted the surrounding waterfront area of the foreground.

I was a little calmer by the time I set my brush down when it was time to clean up. I set the image on the drying rack and rinsed my brushes. With that done, I grabbed my keys and headed to go get Jake. I wasn't taking him home. There was no way I would put him in that kind of danger.

As I drove, I got a text from Marianne.

> I'm making some headway on your case, but I had something come up and I won't be able to wrap up this first part of the investigation until tomorrow. No extra charge for you, so no worries there. Just wanted to keep you updated.

When I reached the carpool line and I was parked to wait for school to let out, I replied.

> That's fine. Thanks for letting me know. Does that mean you want to meet with me tomorrow?

> No. I'll need to type up my report and all my notes, so I'll call you the day after if that works for you?

> That's perfect.

The school bell rang, and the car riders began to dribble out of the building. The line moved forward, and I moved along with it. Within minutes, I was in front, and Jake was being hustled into the car and buckled in.

"How was school?" I asked, hoping it had been uneventful.

"Fine—got an A on my history test," he said, pulling the paper out to show me.

"That's great, Jake. I'm proud of you. I think that deserves a treat. What would you like?"

"Cinnamon pretzels," he suggested.

"You're on." I headed for the pretzel shop, and we ordered those with cups of hot chocolate.

Back on the road twenty minutes later, I asked, "Do you have homework?"

"Just math."

When we got back to my place, Jake got started on his homework and I headed back to the studio to work on Jasmine's watercolor again. I finished it within an hour, cleaned up the studio and started dinner.

I decided on a chicken pasta dish and set the chicken to cooking and the water boiling for the pasta. I added a lemon zest to the chicken as I cooked it in some butter, then added the noodles to the bubbling water.

"Jake, five minutes," I called down the hall.

He didn't acknowledge me, but I knew he'd heard me. I could hear him in his room turning his video game off.

A couple of minutes later he came down the hall. "What are we having?"

"Chicken pasta. Did you wash your hands?"

"Yes, ma'am."

"Set the table, would you?"

He pulled the silverware drawer open and got out what we'd need. It was our usual routine these days, so he knew what to do.

I filled our plates and set them on the table.

As we sat down to eat there was a banging on the door. I was startled when someone shouted, "Police! Open up!"

Jake gave me a frightened look as we both jumped up and headed for the door. "Why are the police here?" he asked.

"I don't know." I undid the security chain and the dead bolt, then opened the door. "What's this about? Did you catch the man who tried to break in?"

"Ma'am, we are here to return Jake Carter to his custodial parent. If you do not cooperate, you will be arrested."

I was taken aback. Why would the police be here to get Jake? It didn't make any sense. "Nelson sent you? Why didn't he just come get him? I don't understand," I protested as two officers entered the apartment and stood in the front hall.

"Not Mr. Carter, ma'am. The boy's mother. Amanda Carter. She said you were refusing to return the child." The officer grabbed hold of Jake.

"Hey! Let me go!" Jake screamed. "No! I don't want to go! I don't want to leave Carly! Carly, don't let them take me!"

My heart broke at the tears pouring down his face. "Please, this isn't necessary. You're scaring him. Can you just let him go? Please."

"Ma'am, we have a job to do. Does he have the things he needs?"

"Yes, in his room—" I started but the other officer pushed by me and deeper into the apartment. "Hey... you can't just—"

"We have a warrant, ma'am." He held up a piece of paper.

I was seething. How could Amanda do this to her own child? I was furious with her but there was nothing I could do at the moment unless I wanted to end up in jail. "Fine, I'll go help get his stuff. Can he at least finish his dinner?"

"I'm not hungry. I don't want to go," Jake sobbed as he struggled against the officer holding him.

"Knock it off, kid, or I'll have to handcuff you," the officer threatened.

His words had me fuming—that he would treat a traumatized child that way. I bent down and hugged him. "Calm down, Jake. We don't need you treated like some juvenile delinquent. It's going to be okay. We'll get this figured out, but it looks like we don't have a choice right now. You have to go with them." I held him tightly. "I promise we'll keep you safe. You know what to look for, what to do while you're there, right?"

He sniffled and wiped his eyes as he stared into my face. It took him a few moments to compose himself as he thought about what I was saying. He opened his mouth and started, "Should I—"

I shook my head slightly, my eyes widening. I didn't want him to say anything about watching Amanda in front of the officers. They were not our friends right now. Hell, they hadn't been our friends since this whole thing started. "I'll talk to Marianne, and we'll find out everything we can about the guy and how it's all connected. Don't worry. Just *stay safe*."

"This is all touching and everything, but we have a job to do," the officer injected, but we both ignored him.

Jake frowned up at the officer, but then turned back to me and the look on his face said he got it. He understood that I wanted him to keep an eye on his mom, but not aggravate her. "Okay. Yeah."

"That's my brave boy," I whispered, then kissed his forehead. "Go finish your dinner. I have to pack your stuff."

He nodded, tugged his arm free from the officer's grip and gave him a glare as he headed back to the kitchen.

I followed him and the officer into the kitchen and then continued on to his room. Once inside I noticed the other officer packing his school bag. I got started putting his clothes in the duffle and taking apart his Switch console. I added his sea lion to the bag last.

"That's everything." I could feel my eyes watering. "This isn't right. He's not safe with her," I muttered.

"Ma'am, she is his mother. Not you." The officer sneered.

"Maybe. Maybe not." I shook my head. I had no proof yet, so I needed to bide my time. I'd have that information in two days.

I prayed that Jake had that long.

As soon as they had Jake down the hall, one of the officers handed me some paperwork. "What's this?"

"A restraining order, ma'am. You are to stay away from Jake Carter and the entire Carter family."

29

As soon as the door closed, I scanned the paperwork. It was filed by Amanda. I was so angry that I could have happily strangled her for doing this. The paperwork, which was a temporary restraining order, said I wasn't physically allowed within fifty feet of Jake. It didn't say anything about texting or calling, but even if it did, it wouldn't stop me. I'd find a way to make sure he was okay. In all the time since the attack on Amanda, she hadn't once tried calling or texting him. I wondered if she even knew he had a phone.

I started thinking about the time I'd been in the townhouse with them all. Had Jake ever had his phone out when Amanda was around? I didn't think so. I began to form an idea. I needed to talk to him, but I didn't want anyone to know he was talking to me. I'd have to use Snapchat. We both had different names on there. I went by IllustratorBabe, and he went by Sea-J. We liked to use the filters and send funny pictures to each other, but I knew he also used it with his friends.

I grabbed my phone and pulled up the app, then sent Jake a quick message.

Hey, kiddo, I miss you already. Let me know when you're home and safe.

I knew he'd check it once he got home. He always kept his phone on vibrate, so he'd know he had a notification, but the cops wouldn't know, which was what I wanted.

I sat down and waited for what seemed like forever before I finally got a notification that he'd replied. I opened the app to read it.

I hate her. She was crying fake tears and hugged me in front of those cops. She acted like I'd been stolen from her, which was stupid, but as soon as they were gone, she shoved me into the living room, called me a brat, and went up to her room. It was really weird.

She didn't hurt you, did she?

I'm okay. I locked myself in my room. So, do you want me to spy on her?

Maybe it would be better if you didn't. We don't want her to catch you. It's more important for you to stay safe. Keep your door locked, and stick with your dad when you can.

Okay, but I don't want to be here. I want to stay with you.

I know. I want that too. I'm going to try calling your dad

and get this sorted again. In the meantime, be careful,
okay?

I will.

I was glad he was okay, but I was really worried about what she had planned. I knew she was the one behind this guy attacking me and Jake. I didn't want him anywhere near her. I didn't think she'd do anything that could possibly be traced back to her, but I thought I should warn him.

Be careful about eating and drinking anything she's
made. Maybe just drink from sealed things and eat
already packaged foods.

I will. She doesn't know how to cook. Everything she
makes is always nasty, so I won't eat it anyway.

Good. Get some sleep, kiddo. Love you.

I will. Love you.

I fretted for a while longer as I tried calling Nelson. Again, it went straight to voicemail. I left him a terse message to call me back. I continued to try calling for the next several hours, but by eleven I gave up for the night. I cleaned up the kitchen and then headed to bed.

The next morning, I woke up early and started toward Jake's room, only to remember that the cops had taken him away from me. I wouldn't be driving him in to Manhattan for school. I wouldn't be seeing his sweet little smile, or hear his laugh as we joked, or hug him when he was upset. My heart ached over it all. I tried calling Nelson again, but once more it went straight to his voicemail.

After drinking my coffee, I went to work in my studio, but my heart wasn't really in it. Still, I had four more images to finish for Jasmine. I put on some calming music and got busy.

At eleven, my phone rang, but it was Hans, not Nelson.

"Hey," I murmured, unable to keep the melancholy from my voice.

"What's the matter?" he asked, sounding concerned.

I told him what happened the night before, barely keeping it together. "And she served me with a restraining order."

"Damn, that's harsh. Why didn't you call me?" he asked. "I would have come over to be with you."

"You were working. I didn't want to bother you."

"Sweetheart, I would have come. Devon would have understood. I'm playing at Melodies until nine tonight, but maybe we can do something after."

I sniffled. "That sounds good. I think I need a night out. It's been a while, and I miss you."

"So, meet me there?"

"Sure," I agreed.

"All right, love. I've got to go, but if you need me, call me. I always have time for you."

His words made me smile. He was always so caring and kind. I once again thanked the universe for him being in my life. "Thank you. I will," I answered. "See you tonight."

We hung up and I went back to work. I wanted to have this watercolor done before I left to meet him. I would still have a couple more to do, but I would still be on schedule if I finished this one today. I worked right up until six, then, after cleaning up the studio and setting the watercolor on the drying rack, I went to get ready for an evening out.

I took a quick bath, then got dressed. I paired my black skirt with a silver, shiny tank top, added a long dangly necklace and chunky earrings with a pair of wedge heels. I added a clip that matched the earrings and necklace to my hair, then did up my face.

I grabbed my heavy coat from the closet, switched out my purse for a smaller black one that I wore crossed over my chest under my coat. By seven thirty I was in my car and headed over to the parking lot near Melodies. I didn't have far to go, and I probably could have walked it, but it was cold out and I didn't want to freeze my butt off.

I pulled into the lot, but it was packed. I had to park on the far side, so I still had a bit of a walk to get inside. As I made my way through the parking lot, I felt like someone was watching me, following me. I looked over my shoulder, but I couldn't make anything out with it being so dark. I hated that it got dark so early in the winter time. I pulled my coat tighter around me as I hurried toward the building. There were other people around and I tried to weave into the groups, hoping to get rid of the creepy feeling of eyes on me, but it didn't go away.

My heart was racing as I yanked open the door. I breathed a little easier once I was in and I saw Devon behind the bar. Megan was floating around the floor taking orders. Hans was seated at the piano, playing his heart out. Denise passed me and smiled. I gave her a nod and smiled back as I took a deep breath, trying to ease the panic that had built up in me.

I unbuttoned my coat, but didn't take it off as I strode to my table, which had the reserved card on it. I sat down and removed my coat. A moment later, Denise set a drink in front of me. It was my usual. I smiled. "Thanks."

"Bad day?" she questioned as she studied my face.

"Kinda."

"Anything I can do?" she asked with a frown.

"Bring me another one of these in about ten minutes?" I said with a laugh.

"You've got it. Your man is killin' it tonight. Makes my night so much better. Tips are always higher when he's playin'."

"He is pretty awesome," I said, turning my gaze to Hans, who was belting out an old Bruce Springsteen hit. "Does he have a break coming up?"

"Yeah, he's due in about ten minutes. I'll bring your drink with his." Denise winked and then moved on.

Seven minutes later, Hans began to play "Red Hot & Blue Love" by Rick Springfield as his lusty gaze landed on me. I felt my skin heat at the look in his eyes. When he reached the final stanza of the song, I would have sworn he'd lit me on fire.

"Red hot and blue, hot and blue love. Well, you know that I take it when I want it and I want it tonight. Tonight." He finished with a bang of the keys and the room exploded in applause. He slid his hand through his hair and turned his grin toward me as he thanked everyone. "I'll be back in a few with more. Just gotta take a break and cool down my vocal cords." He gave them all a wave as he stood up. A moment later he sat down next to me.

Denise was there within seconds, setting both our drinks down. "You're smokin' tonight. Keep it up. I wanna see if I can break a thousand in tips." She laughed.

Hans laughed. "Sure." He picked up his drink and took a

sip as she moved on. He turned that heated gaze on me and smiled. "I'm glad you came early." He leaned forward and kissed me.

I melted into him, enjoying the kiss until I once again felt eyes on me. It wasn't like normal, where people in the bar looked at me with envy because I was with Hans. This was that creepy, skeevy feeling again. It was a menacing feeling. I pulled back and slid my gaze around the room, then gasped.

"What's the matter?" Hans asked. His gaze followed mine and landed on the man at the bar who was staring at me. "Who is that?"

"That's the guy," I hissed and tried to look anywhere but at him.

"I can have him thrown out," he offered.

"No, he'll just wait for me outside."

"What do you want to do?" he asked softly. "Do you want to leave?"

My eyes flashed to his and I shook my head. I knew my fear showed in my eyes. "No, no. I want to stay near you. I don't think he'll do anything here. He's just trying to intimidate me. Maybe he's trying to get me to leave." I shivered.

"I've only got an hour left. How about I finish up, then I'll get you out the back and we'll go to my place. I'll let Devon and the girls know what's going on and they'll provide a distraction. Sound good?"

I blew out a breath of relief. "Yes," I agreed as I relaxed a little bit more.

"That's it. Don't let him see that he's affecting you," he murmured as he lifted my hand and kissed my palm. "Just keep that hot gaze of yours on me."

I grinned. "You're going to put on a show, aren't you?" It wasn't really a question. I knew he was.

He winked, finished his drink in a gulp and then stood. He made his way over to Megan for a quick chat and then over to the piano. He began to play "I Go Crazy" by Flesh for Lulu and the bar patrons joined in on the chorus. For the next hour it was nothing but chaos, with people getting up and dancing as he played, but his eyes always flashed over to me with heat.

At about five to nine, Megan came over to the table and said, "In about two minutes, get up and head for the back like you're going to the bathroom, but turn left instead of right once you're back there. Leave your stuff. Denise will grab it and bring it to Hans' car. Devon and I will make sure the guy is distracted just enough to lose you in the crowd. It's a good thing it's so crazy in here right now."

"But once Hans stops playing it will calm down, right?" I fretted as I looked at Hans.

"Devon's planned for that too. He's already called in a favor. Don't worry." She picked up my empty glass and then said, "Get ready to go as soon as Hans starts the next song."

I nodded as she moved away, picking up empty glasses from another table. I turned back toward Hans and noticed a man slide onto the bench next to him, and then another guy with a guitar set up next to the piano.

Hans transitioned into another song that the two of them began playing and the guitarist joined in, which made everyone in the bar go wild. Hans looked over at me and winked, then tilted his head toward the back entrance.

I gave him a slight nod, slid my glance toward the bar where the maniac waited. His view of me was blocked by a group of women as well as Megan and Denise. I got up and slipped through the crowd toward the back. My heart was pounding loudly in my chest as I hurried to the left, which was where the office was, and beyond that the employee door to the back lot. I waited there and a moment later Hans joined me.

"Let's go, beautiful."

He wrapped me in his coat, and we ran for his car. He unlocked it and got me inside, then jogged over to the driver's side as Denise slipped out of the door with my coat and purse. Hans pulled out of his parking place and maneuvered the car next to where Denise stood with my things. He rolled the window down and she handed them over.

"Don't worry, Carly, we've got your back," she said. "Go."

Hans rolled up the window and a moment later he pulled into traffic, and we were away from the bar and headed to his place. I kept glancing in the side mirrors to see if we were being followed but it was dark and all I saw was headlights. Too many to decipher if any were actually the crazy man following me.

"At least he's following me and not Jake," I murmured.

Hans reached for my hand. "That's true, but I don't like that he found you so easily, love."

"Me neither."

"Maybe you should stay with me for a bit?" he suggested.

I smiled. "Well, maybe for tonight. We'll see about tomorrow. I still have work to do."

Hans lifted my hand and kissed my fingers. "Then maybe I should stay with you."

My smile grew to a grin. "Maybe so."

"So this completely threw my plans for the night all out the window." He chuckled.

"Did it?" I gave him a curious look. "What did you have planned?"

"I was planning to take you out for a late, romantic

dinner at Trastevere, and then I thought we'd head to my place for a nightcap and see what happened from there." He grinned. "I'll have to cancel our reservation."

"Well, we could have a late romantic dinner at your place if they deliver," I suggested as I leaned into him.

"Now there's an idea. I'll call." He tapped a button on the steering wheel and told the car to call Trastevere. A moment later, he'd spoken to the manager and made a special request to have our meals delivered. "Excellent, thank you so much," he said, ending the call.

"He was very accommodating; it must be the celebrity thing," I teased.

Hans chuckled. "I'm just a small-time celebrity. Marcus and I go back a ways. It pays to have ins with restaurant managers." He winked at me, giving me a roguish grin.

He parked the car, and we went into his building, which was much swankier than mine. This was the first time I'd been there. For some reason we always ended up meeting at Melodies, visiting at my place, or going out somewhere. He lived on the seventh floor, and when he opened the door to his place and I got my first glimpse, I gasped. His space was gorgeous, with a bank of floor-to-ceiling windows that overlooked the city.

"Wow, this is incredible." I headed for the windows to look out.

Hans walked up behind me and wrapped his arms around my waist, and I leaned back into him. He kissed my neck, and I turned in his arms. He lowered his lips to mine, and I wrapped my arms around his neck. He lifted me to my toes as he devoured my mouth, his tongue tangling with mine in an erotic kiss.

There was a knock on the door and with a sigh he let me

go, but the heat was in his eyes, and I knew that was just a taste of what was to come. He strode to the door, looked through the peep hole, then opened it.

"Thank you so much," he murmured as he pulled his wallet out and paid the delivery person. He gathered everything and, after shutting the door, headed into the open kitchen.

I followed him in, washed my hands, and asked, "Where are the plates?"

He directed me to the right cabinet and soon we had our decadent meals plated and a bottle of expensive wine opened as we sat at the table. Over the meal, Hans' gaze kept moving to mine and I could feel tingles of excitement racing over my skin. After dinner, he turned on the electric fireplace and some soft music and we sat on the couch with some wine.

Heated, passionate kisses turned to lingering strokes of his fingers on my skin and soon we were wrapped around each other making love for the first time. It was everything I could have hoped for. The man made me tingle in places I didn't know could tingle.

I lifted up on my elbow and traced a hand over his smooth chest. "Do this often?"

He chuckled. "Make love in front of the fire? No." He smiled and cupped my cheek. "I've never brought a woman home. Not here, anyway."

I grinned. "And how long have you lived here?"

He paused to think about it. "About eight years."

My smile dropped and I stared at him. "Seriously? In all that time you haven't—"

He laughed. "I didn't say I haven't had sex in eight years. Just haven't brought a woman home. There hasn't been anyone special enough for that." His gaze lingered on me as his thumb traced my bottom lip. "You're beautiful, Carly. Special. I care about you a lot."

My lips curved up. "I think you're pretty special too, and I care about you too." I wasn't ready to say I loved him but if things continued as they were, I knew I would.

He traced my nose, tapped the end, and then leaned in and kissed me. A moment later he was standing with me in his arms, and he carried me to his bedroom where we made love several more times before morning.

I stretched lazily in his arms, feeling the soreness from our ambitious love-making. I knew I needed to get up though. I had work to do, and I still needed to get my car. "I wish we could stay like this all day…"

He sighed. "But you need to go, don't you?" Though it was a question, he had to know the answer to it.

I leaned in and kissed him. "I do. Can you take me to my car?"

"Only if you promise to call me the minute you're home and we can make plans for tonight." He grinned.

"That is a promise I don't mind making." I winked and got out of the bed.

Once we were both dressed, he drove me to Melodies and parked next to my car. "Stay in the car," Hans said, his voice rough as he stared at my car.

I stared too with my mouth agape, because it had been trashed. The tires weren't just flat, they were shredded and flapping in the winter breeze. The windows were busted and so were the headlights. I couldn't see the back of my car, but there were pieces of red plastic on the ground near it and I had to assume they were broken as well.

Hans got out and walked around my car, taking inventory of it, then returned to sink into the driver's seat. "Call the cops. You need to file an incident report."

I did as he asked and then we went into Melodies to wait for them. Devon, who lived above the bar, came down when he heard us enter.

"Hey, what's going on?" he asked, looking sleepy as he rubbed his eyes. He was wearing a pair of sweatpants with no shirt, and he was barefoot.

"Carly's car was trashed. Did you hear anything?"

Devon shook his head. "No, man, sorry. I sleep with a white noise machine to drown out everything outside. I've got surveillance cameras in the parking lot. Maybe they caught something."

"Can you check? The cops are on their way," Hans told him.

"Sure. Let me run up and grab a shirt and some shoes, then I'll check."

When the cops showed up a little bit later, they merely took my report and the copy of the parking lot surveillance video and sneered at my suggestion it was the man who was trying to kill me and Jake, calling me a Delusional Karen. Hans and Devon corroborated my story, but they didn't care. They just said they'd look into it and left.

"Well, that was completely unhelpful," Devon said, his hands on his hips.

"I don't get it. There is overwhelming evidence of this guy trying to kill me and Jake, and they act like I'm some crazy person crying wolf," I huffed.

Hans wrapped his arms around me and kissed the top of my head. "Maybe that private detective you hired will have some answers soon."

"I hope so, because I can't take much more of this." As I

said this, my phone beeped with a Snapchat notification. It could only be Jake. I pulled my phone out and read it.

I hate her. I couldn't stay there. I snuck out and left home. I'm okay and safe, but I've turned off my phone. I don't want them to track me.

30

"Oh my God," I gasped, my eyes widening. "Jake's run away from home. He's out there somewhere on his own." I turned my terrified gaze to Hans. "Anything could happen to him."

"Let me see what he said," Hans said, holding his hand out for my phone. He stared at it for a moment and then said, "He didn't send this from his phone. My guess is he's gone to an internet café or a library so he could get that message to you. He doesn't want you to worry."

"He's ten! Of course I'm going to worry. I'm going to freaking panic," I fretted as my fingers knotted together. "Why didn't he tell me where he was so I could come get him?"

"Probably because he doesn't want the cops to follow you to him. They did take him from you before. You will be the first one they check with."

"Crap. You're right. I need to head home." I bit my lip as I considered what could happen to him while he was out there on his own. Not only was that maniac after him, but now the cops would be too. How was he going to avoid them? And how was he going to get from Manhattan to Brooklyn? I knew without a doubt he would be heading to me. I was terrified of what could happen to a kid his age on his own.

"Jake isn't without resources," Hans reassured. "And he's a smart kid. He's probably trying to get to Brooklyn, and might already be on his way here. I don't think he's going to do anything stupid like asking a stranger for a ride. He might take a taxi or an Uber, but I doubt he'd ask a friend's parent to help because they'd return him to Amanda."

I nodded. "You're right. But what if he comes to me and the cops show up looking for him?"

"We'll figure it out. Let me get you home. If he does end up there, call me. We'll keep him safe. I promise." He kissed my forehead.

Hans took me home and walked me up to my apartment. He had to go, but promised to check in with me soon. I kept my phone on as I went to my room and changed clothes. I had just walked into my studio when there was a banging on my door.

When I looked through the peephole, I saw a swarm of cops in the hallway. I opened the door.

"What's going on? Is the building on fire?" I asked, trying to keep my nervousness from my voice.

"Ma'am, Jake Carter is missing, and his mother suggested that you might have him. We have a warrant to search your apartment."

I stepped back and widened my eyes. "Jake's missing?" I gasped. "Come in. You can look, but he's not here. How did he go missing? When?" I asked as the group moved in and began walking through my apartment.

"He slipped out of their house sometime last night. Can you account for your whereabouts?"

"Yes, of course. I was at Melodies last night and then I went with my boyfriend to his place. My car was vandalized in their parking lot. There's video of it happening at about one a.m. You can check with the owner of the bar, and with my boyfriend, Hans Wohlers."

"We will, ma'am," the lead officer said.

"It's all clear. Nothing to indicate the kid has been here since we picked him up."

"Okay." The lead officer turned to stare at me. "Do you know where he might go? Any particular friends he would have gone to? His mother doesn't know who his friends are."

Yeah, she wouldn't—because she's not his mother, I thought. "He's got a couple of good friends—Max Hamilton, and Charlie Barton. They're both in his class at school. Have you checked with the school to see if he was there?"

"Yes, we did. He isn't in attendance."

"Are any of his friends missing too?"

"We didn't check on that, ma'am, but we haven't had reports of any other children missing." He rubbed a hand down his face. "Can you think of anywhere else Jake would go?"

I frowned. They were the ones who took him from me, where he was safe and loved. I didn't want to help them, but I couldn't not answer, and I wanted them to know this was their fault. "Well, considering he is being targeted by the same man who attacked the woman claiming to be his mother, and you dragged him away from the one safe place he knew of, my guess is he's trying to find another safe place where that guy won't get to him. He's a ten-year-old who knows NYC like the back of his hand, having gone just about everywhere with his dad. So, he could be anywhere."

He sighed. "If you hear from him or he shows up here, please contact us immediately."

"Sure," I said, but I didn't mean it. I blamed them for this. For not keeping Jake safe. For not keeping me safe. "Maybe if you people would do your damn job and catch the asshole who is trying to kill us, Jake would go home on his own."

"Thank you for your time, ma'am." He let himself and his team out.

I slammed the door with a huff. I was so mad that they weren't even acknowledging the fact there was a maniac after us. I headed to my studio and sat down in front of my easel, but I was so worried and angry at the same time that there was no way I could work on Jasmine's watercolors. I got back up and went to the kitchen to make some coffee. Maybe that would calm me down.

I'd just started the percolator when there was a timid knock on my door. I wondered if the cops were back, but it didn't sound like them. This knock was much softer. I peeked through the security hole and saw a hooded head tilted downward, but it was the height of the person on the other side of the door that had me yanking it open.

"Jake!" I sighed as I pulled him into my arms. "How did you get here? How did you get by all the cops looking for you?"

He laughed as he pulled his thick coat hood off. "I knew this would be the first place they'd check. That woman would have sent them here immediately. I've been in Brooklyn since last night. I took a taxi and paid in cash. I went to the all-night diner that's down the street and hung out there for a while. They were busy and didn't care. Then I waited for the cops to leave here. I caught the door when Mr. Stevens went to work."

I hugged him tight. "You scared the hell out of me, kiddo."

"I'm sorry. That's why I sent the message this morning. I didn't want you to worry for too long." He hugged me back.

"I'm not sure what to do with you now though. I'm betting the cops will be back when they can't find you." I sighed and we headed for the living room to sit down.

"You're not going to make me go back, are you?"

"Hell no." I gave him a look. "Still—" I stopped as my phone rang in the kitchen. "One sec. Stay quiet, okay?"

"Okay."

I went into the kitchen and picked up my phone. "Amanda, what can I do for you?"

"You can give me my fucking brat back! I know you have him!" she screeched.

"I don't. The cops you sent here searched my place. Have you checked the school? It is the middle of the morning on a school day. Maybe he showed up there," I suggested as my eyes landed on Jake, who was sitting on my couch trying not to laugh.

"I am going to fucking kill you, you fucking busybody. Sticking your nose into my business. You are dead. I will rip you apart with my bare hands. You and that fucking brat when I get my hands on him."

I gritted my teeth. "I'm recording this call, Amanda... I'll be sure to give it to the cops—"

Amanda hung up.

Sighing, I set the phone down. I wished I had been recording. That last comment she made would have made the cops listen to me. At least it should have. If I had been smart enough to turn on the recorder when I answered the phone. Stupid hindsight. I shook my head at how dumb I'd been to answer it without being prepared. I headed back into the living room and stood just behind the couch where Jake was sitting.

He turned to look at me. "Now what?"

I honestly didn't know. I was afraid of keeping Jake here and having the cops show up to return him to the fake Amanda. The problem was I didn't know where to take him. I needed to call Nelson and get him to understand that Amanda was a threat to Jake, but he still wasn't answering my calls.

"How about lunch? Have you eaten?"

"I'm starved." He grinned.

I made us a couple of turkey and cheese sandwiches with chips, and we ate together at the table. "So, how did you manage to catch a taxi and pay for them to drive you all the way to Brooklyn?"

Jake shrugged. "I walked a few blocks and waved one down. I have a bunch of savings. Birthday money, Christmas money... I just brought it all with me."

"Do you know how lucky you were not to be picked up by some human trafficking group? Kids go missing all the time, Jake. Please, don't do that again, okay?"

"Yeah, okay. But I was fine."

"Did you bring everything you'd need for a while?"

Jake snickered. "I didn't even unpack from before."

"I noticed you didn't bring your school bag though," I said, eyeing him.

Grinning, he said, "Oops, knew I forgot something."

This kid cracked me up. "Sure, you forgot." I laughed.

He shrugged. "Well, it's not like I can go to school when the cops are looking for me to send me back to that woman."

He had a point. I supposed we'd deal with the school issue once this was all over.

When we finished eating, I called Hans to tell him what was going on. He offered to bring over dinner later. Once I got off the phone, I let Jake watch some TV while I went to work in my studio. I was finally calm enough to work on the next watercolor for Jasmine's children's book.

I was pretty satisfied with how it came out and I moved on to the next image. Despite everything going on, I was making good headway on the project, and I'd be happy when I had it finished. Jasmine had been thrilled with the group I'd sent to her, and she'd only asked for one minor addition.

I cleaned up my studio and set everything aside to dry at four thirty. I knew Hans would be coming by soon with dinner and I wanted to look nice when he got here. Just after five, my phone rang again, and I headed for the kitchen to grab it.

"Marianne, hi." I prayed she had something for me.

"Hey, Carly. I wanted to call with an update on everything I've uncovered. I'm afraid it's not the best news."

I sank down into one of my kitchen chairs. "What did you find?"

"So, let's start with Amanda Carter. She has an identical twin sister named Selina."

31

"Oh wow," I murmured as my mind raced. "So then it's possible that Amanda isn't really Amanda, but her sister Selina?"

It made sense that the Amanda who'd come back from the attack wasn't the real Amanda. I felt vindicated for both me and Jake. Jake especially, since he had known almost immediately that she wasn't his mom. People needed to listen to kids more often. Kids had some sort of instinctual intuition that adults often ignored or lost as they aged.

"Yes, but let me continue. As young girls, their mother disappeared. I did find her death certificate saying she died of a drug overdose. After she left, they lived with their alcoholic father, who abused them. There were numerous reports of the abuse, but somehow CPS kept sending them back to him. Eventually, at the age of thirteen they ended up murdering their father in what they claimed was self-defense, but it was a particularly violent event, as they bludgeoned him to death with a hammer.

I couldn't speak. I was shell-shocked.

"They spent their early to late teens in an institution for troubled and violent teens. Notes on the two of them say that Amanda was the more sane of the two, mild mannered and stable while Selina was known to bully her sister into doing things and was often in trouble for flouting the rules. She got into a number of fights, even one where she stabbed a boy with a knife. He survived, but she left him with a massive scar from his eyebrow down to his chin.

"Amanda and Selina were released at eighteen, no longer wards of the state. Selina went on to marry at nineteen, but it was to a man like her father, alcoholic and both physically and sexually abusive, and she murdered him. The murder was incredibly vicious, which landed her in a prison psych ward for violent criminals. A few months ago, she escaped."

"What?" I was breathing hard. I knew there was something seriously wrong with Amanda, or rather Selina, but I didn't think she was this insane. "How did she escape?"

"She had help. Her cousin Danny, who has also served time for violent, criminal behavior, helped her break out. He matches the person in the video on your Ring camera as well as the video you took on your phone. He's murdered people, but got off on a technicality and only served time for assault and battery as well as armed robbery."

"Oh my God," I murmured, feeling completely overwhelmed.

"Both of them are wanted in connection with the murder of one of the guards at the asylum, which is upstate, but because of jurisdiction and probably incompetence, the cops here haven't made the connection yet."

"Oh my God," I repeated.

"And, I am fairly certain that if you *are* dealing with Selina, then Amanda is most likely dead."

"Why would she kill her own sister?" I asked.

"I spoke with some of the staff at the institution where she was being kept. From what they shared, Selina had anger issues to go along with her violent temper and much of that anger was directed at her sister for achieving the life she wanted. Meaning Amanda married a rich man and was living in the lap of luxury, which Selina felt she deserved. In many of her group sessions she spoke about how unfair it was that Amanda hadn't helped her when she'd needed her and had chosen to ignore her in favor of her new life living like a socialite with a wealthy, famous husband."

I let her words sink in. Selina had stolen Amanda's life because she'd turned her back on her, and because she'd married well. "So, you think her plan was to kill Amanda and take over her life?"

"I do think that was the beginning of her plan. Considering she and Danny have been going after Jake, though, I now think she is trying to kill off anyone who might be a threat to her taking all the wealth for herself. So I believe Nelson may also be in danger."

I couldn't help but agree. "I'll keep trying to get a hold of him."

"And you and Jake need to be careful until Selina and Danny are caught. I'll share my information with the authorities once I get it all organized. I'll send you copies of everything too."

"Thanks, I appreciate that." I really did. Marianne had found an incredible amount of information in just three and a half days. I was lucky that she was available to work on this case for me. I needed to thank Dave for giving me her name.

"If you need anything else, just give me a call."

"Okay. Thanks, Marianne, I will."

I hung up the phone, walked into the living room and said, "Jake, you aren't going to believe this…"

As I was telling Jake about Marianne's call, Hans arrived, and I had to start over. I put the conversation on hold as we went into the kitchen and got plates for the pizza he'd brought. Once we were all seated, I began again. We'd devoured more than half of the pizza by the time I finished.

"So now I have to try and get a hold of Nelson and convince him that the woman he thinks is his wife is really his sister-in-law who he didn't even know existed. And not only that but that she most likely murdered Amanda and is planning to murder him." I sighed and dropped my head to my hands.

Hans reached over and rubbed my back. "We could just go to the cops," he suggested.

I looked up at him. "Because they've been super-helpful so far?"

He chuckled. "Good point." He ate another slice. "Maybe you could be sneaky in getting him to come over so you can talk to him."

"What do you mean?" I asked.

Hans glanced at Jake and then back to me, obviously choosing his words carefully. "Well, from what you've told me, Nelson is a bit of a player."

I snorted. "That's an understatement."

"But he's always had a thing for you. Of all the women, aside from Amanda, that he's been with, he always comes back to you…" He said it matter-of-factly, without a hint of jealousy, but there was something in his eyes that belied his true feelings.

I reached a hand over to him and smiled. "You have

nothing to worry about. I'm no longer interested in taking him back."

His lips quirked up in a smile. "I didn't think so. However, that's not my point. Nelson doesn't know that you won't."

It dawned on me what he was suggesting. "It could work, if I text him instead of call. If he hears my voice, he'll know."

"So text him. Get him to come over here."

I reached for my phone and then eyed Hans. "You'll stay, right? You're not going to leave me here to deal with his whining, are you?"

Hans chuckled. "I'll stay, love."

I nodded and typed out the text.

> Are you free? I miss you so much, and I'm horny. Come visit?

I showed Hans before I hit send.

He laughed. "Well, if that doesn't do it, I don't know what will."

"What did you say?" Jake asked, full of curiosity.

"Never you mind, kiddo." I ruffled his hair.

Jake looked at me suspiciously, but then nodded and took another slice of pizza.

My phone pinged less than a minute later.

> Babe, I knew you would come around. I'll be there in ten.

"He'll be here in ten minutes," I said with a shake of my head. "Should have thought of doing that sooner." I glanced at the near-empty pizza box. "You guys finished?"

Both of them nodded.

"Let us help you clean up," Hans offered.

It took less than three minutes to get the leftovers put

away and the dishes into the dishwasher. We were all in the living room when Nelson buzzed the apartment. Instead of answering, I just hit the button to let him in. A few minutes later he knocked on the door.

I opened it with Jake and Hans right behind me.

"Babe, I've mi—" he stopped short, his eyes landing on Jake and then Hans. "What's going on? Who are you?"

I yanked him in and closed the door. "Nelson, meet Hans, my demanding and sensational lover. Hans, my douchebag ex."

"I thought you missed me," Nelson pouted. "I thought you wanted to get back together."

"That is never going to happen. I needed to talk to you, and you wouldn't answer your phone."

He ignored that and looked at Jake. "Why am I getting calls from the cops saying you're missing?"

Jake shook his head. "Dad, it's important! You need to listen to Carly."

Nelson sighed. "Fine. What?"

We all went into the living room, and I sat with Hans on the couch. Jake sat down on my other side and then Nelson took one of the chairs. I took a breath and said, "Did you know that Amanda has a twin sister? An identical twin sister?"

He frowned. "No, she was an only child."

I shook my head. "She lied." I told him everything that Marianne had discovered about Selina and Danny and how it was all connected.

"That's crazy. You're just mad that we're back together."

I rolled my eyes. "Are you freaking kidding me? You're telling me that the Amanda after the attack is the same woman she was before the attack? No. I've seen how she talks to you, how you act around her. This woman says jump and you do because you're scared of her."

"Okay, maybe," he conceded. "Still, that doesn't mean she's trying to kill you or Jake."

"Have you seen the videos?" Hans asked.

Nelson shook his head. "What videos?"

I pulled my phone out and handed it to him. Nelson watched them and then Hans showed him the pictures of my car. "Do you believe us now?"

Nelson reached behind him and rubbed his neck, looking awkward. "Yeah, I guess, but what do you want me to do about it?"

I breathed a sigh of relief. "I want you to talk to the cops. Tell them what I told you. Maybe they'll actually listen to you."

"Why would they listen to me?"

"Because she's your wife. Jake's mom. Maybe if you both go and talk to them, tell them everything about Selina and her escape, and your suspicions that she murdered Amanda and took her identity, they will get off their asses and arrest her."

Nelson nodded. "Yeah, okay. But why can't Jake stay here with you?"

"If the cops find out he's here, I could be arrested. Selina acting as Amanda took out a restraining order against me. The cops forcibly removed Jake from my apartment two days ago— Geez, was that just two days ago?" I looked to Hans.

"It was. A lot has happened in the last forty-eight hours." He winked at me.

I felt a blush heat my cheeks.

"Why didn't you call me then?" Nelson asked.

I wanted to hit him. "I did!"

"Oh, right." He looked down. "Sorry."

"So will you do it?"

"Yeah." Nelson sighed. "Come on, Jake, let's go try to convince the cops."

I blew out a breath of relief that everything was about to be resolved. That Jake was finally going to be safe.

"Do I really have to go?" Jake asked.

I nodded. "Go with your dad so he can straighten this out, then he can bring you back here, okay?"

"Okay." He stood up reluctantly.

We all went to the apartment door, and I hugged Jake goodbye. "I'll see you in a little while. It's going to be okay."

I finally felt relaxed once they were on their way, and I sank down on the couch with Hans. I leaned my head on his shoulder.

He kissed my forehead. "It's almost over."

"I'm still worried about what will happen with Jake. He'll be safer with Selina back in the asylum, but with his mom gone and Nelson so neglectful, I still worry."

"He's always got you."

I smiled. I was glad that Hans understood that I would always have Jake in my life. "I'm glad you aren't jealous of my relationship with him. A lot of men wouldn't be so understanding."

"I'm not a lot of men, and you've raised that kid, not his parents. He's lucky he's turned out as well as he has with them."

"The real Amanda wasn't so bad. She was always caring about Jake, but she really liked playing the socialite and left things with him to me or other caretakers."

"I wish I could stay," Hans murmured.

"Can't you?"

"I promised Devon I would play tonight. At least for a little while."

I sighed. "Can you come back after?"

He smiled. "I was hoping you'd ask." He leaned in and kissed me again.

We stood up and I walked him to the door. We lingered there, kissing some more.

I giggled. "You're going to be late."

Laughing, he nodded. "I know, but Devon will understand. I'll see you later, love."

"Bye." I watched him walk down the hall to the elevators.

An hour and a half later, my phone rang. It was Jake's ringtone and I wondered if he was calling to tell me the cops were on their way to pick up Selina and Danny.

"Jake?"

"Carly," he whispered, but I could tell he was sobbing. "Dad's dead."

32

I nearly dropped the phone. "Jake? What happened?"

"Dad didn't go to the police station. He wanted to confront Selina. I tried to tell him no, but he wouldn't listen. They killed him."

"Oh my God. Where are you now?"

"Hiding. I'm in the guest bathroom linen closet." His voice was barely a whisper, more of a breath.

"Okay, Jake, I'm on my way. I—" I suddenly remembered I didn't have a car. "I'll borrow Hans' car and be there as soon as I can. I'll call the cops on my way. Stay hidden unless you can get out of there."

"Hurry, Carly."

"I will. Be safe. Love you, Jake," I choked out.

I grabbed my purse and ran for the door, not caring that I didn't have a coat on. I tore out of the building and ran the several blocks to Melodies. I was breathing hard when I made it inside. I didn't care that I was interrupting him playing. "Hans, I need to borrow your car, Jake's in trouble," I gasped.

"What's happened?" He reached in his pocket for his keys.

"Nelson's dead. He didn't go to the cops; he went after them on his own with Jake. Jake's hiding."

Hans stood, pushing away from the piano, and grabbed my hand. "Devon, emergency!" he called as we ran for the back door.

"Go!" Devon shouted.

We were in the car and headed for Manhattan within seconds. I dialed 911 and sent the cops to Nelson's place. "Please hurry."

"Officers are on their way, ma'am. What is your name and contact number?"

"Carly Michaelson. I'm a friend of the family." I gave her my number and then hung up. "Can you go any faster?" I asked, my heart in my throat.

"Not across the bridge, but I'll go as fast as possible after."

We were nearly there when my phone rang. "Hello?"

"Ms. Michaelson, where are you? The NYPD do not appreciate prank calls—"

"What? This isn't a prank call! Jake said his dad was dead and that his aunt had killed him! Haven't you gotten there yet? He's hiding in the linen closet," I said, panicked.

"Ma'am there is no one at the address."

"Shit, they must be at the penthouse. I gave you the wrong address. I'm sorry. They have more than one home and I just assumed they were at the townhouse. Please, you have to go over there."

"We'll check it out. What is that address?"

I gave it to them and hung up.

"Where to?" Hans stopped at a stop sign.

I looked around and realized we were only a block from the apartment building with the penthouse that Amanda liked to use. "One more block up, it's the building on the right. There's only fifteen-minute parking on the street though. You'll have to park in the garage on the next block, but let me out in front."

Hans frowned. "I don't like it; they've already killed people... I don't want to lose you." He grabbed my hand and brought it to his lips.

"Please, Hans, I have to get Jake. I have to," I pleaded with him to understand. "I'll be careful."

Hans sighed, and let my hand go. "I'll be right behind you. Don't confront them, okay?"

I nodded and climbed out of the car. I ran inside, expecting to have to explain everything to the doorman, but in a stroke of luck he wasn't there, and while the reception person was occupied at their computer, I headed for the elevators and pushed the button for the penthouse. I had no idea how I was going to get in, but I was going to rescue Jake no matter what.

When the elevator dinged, I cautiously got off. I knew which door was Amanda's. I'd been here before with Jake to get his stuff. I crept closer and pressed my ear to the door. I couldn't hear anything going on inside. I touched the knob and it turned with ease. I should have known it was too easy.

The door was yanked from my hand and the maniac was there, reaching for me. I screamed, hoping that someone would hear me. That they'd hurry the cops along. I knew they were on the way. So was Hans, but I was in trouble in that moment.

Danny dragged me into the living room where Jake was

seated on a chair with Selina holding a gun on him. He looked terrified and my heart broke.

"It's about damn time you fucking got here," Selina complained, looking at me.

"Carly!" Jake sobbed. "I tried to run... I tried..."

"Shhh, it's okay, Jake. It's going to be okay." I pulled my arm from Danny and rushed over to Jake. I had no idea how it was going to be okay, but I had to stay positive for him.

Selina laughed hysterically. "You're delusional if you think either one of you is making it out of here alive."

I glared at her. "Look, you psycho bitch, you're not going to get away with this. Too many people already know what you've done and who you are."

She turned to Danny and handed him the gun. "Kill the kid first. Make her watch, then kill her. I'm so sick of her holier than thou attitude. She's a sanctimonious bitch and I'm done dealing with her."

I couldn't say I regretted coming in here without Hans. That was the one thing I'd done right. I prayed that he'd take so long getting up here that the cops would arrive before he got himself killed. A world without him would be a sad world. A world without Jake would be too, and I'd do everything in my power to keep him alive. I'd even give my own to save him. I prayed it wouldn't come to that.

"But, Selina, I can't kill the kid... not like this."

Selina turned on him, her face a mirror of fury. "What the fuck are you talking about? You've already tried to kill him twice."

"That was different. Those could be written off as accidents. This is outright murder," he argued.

"You're a fucking idiot. It's the same fucking thing. The only difference is the method."

"I ain't killin' no kid like this."

"Why are you doing all this?" I interjected as I stood next to Jake.

Selina turned her gaze back to me; her expression was one of hatred and it made me shiver with the depths of it. I couldn't understand her at all, but then I wasn't crazy like she was. And she was definitely insane.

"Do you know what I've been through?" she asked, her voice full of anger. "While I suffered in that hell hole, my sister got to live it up in the lap of luxury. She wasn't better than me. We were twins. We were supposed to have this together and she fucking turned her back on me. When my asshole husband started hitting me and abusing me, she turned away. She ignored my pleas for help. She could have helped, and she cut me off like I was nothing!" Selina fumed. Her shoulders were heaving, and her breathing was hard.

"You violently murdered him," I commented.

"Yeah, I murdered the bastard. But he deserved it. He raped me and beat the shit out of me all the fucking time. So I cut his wanker off and shoved it down his throat. I cut out his heart and stomped on it. I wish I could have made him suffer more."

"What did you expect Amanda to do? She had a child and a husband to think about. She couldn't—" I tried to reason with her.

"She was my fucking twin! She was supposed to care about me first. But she was too caught up in living like a fucking princess to help me. So she got what she deserved too." She sneered at me. "That bitch wanted to be cold to me, so I made her cold for real. She's frozen in a freezer in a storage unit."

I looked at her with horror.

Jake sobbed and I wished he wasn't listening to all this. He was going to need therapy for life to even be a little bit okay. That was better than dead though.

I needed to keep her talking but I had no idea how to do that. How did you deal with someone so insane they murdered their own twin? Not to mention her husband and father and who knew how many other people. "You froze your own sister to death?"

Selina cackled. "It was so easy. That stupid trusting bitch didn't even see it coming. She thought they released me. That I was out on parole and wanted a happy sister reunion. What she got was a whack on the head and then dumped in the freezer. I took her clothes and purse and left her with mine."

"Why?" I asked.

"It's high time I get to be the one living like a fucking princess with my own prince. Not that sack of cheating shit she married. I deserve every fucking penny of what they have. I've fought for it. It's mine."

"So you think you can just take her life? What about Jake? He's your nephew, your blood—"

"He's nothing to me. He's just in the way. The insurance, the will, everything will go to me once the kid is gone." Selina smiled, but it was dark, evil.

I shivered.

"I'm done with you. I'm so sick of looking at you." Selina stared at me with so much hatred that I felt it all the way down to my toes. "I have no idea what Nelson or that Hans guy sees in you. You're pathetic. Hanging around, playing mommy to some other woman's kid. You're a fucking joke. He only fucked you because you watched the kid. He didn't care about you."

She wasn't saying anything I hadn't thought about myself until recently. It didn't matter though. I loved Jake. He loved me back. I was like a mother to him, more of a mother than Selina had ever been and probably more of a mom than Amanda had been too. I hated to speak ill of the dead, but being a mom wasn't high on her list of things to do.

"I guess the piano player is more your speed," Selina continued. "Some loser with a hot body who's dumber than a box of rocks. Probably cheating on you too with any slut that walks into that place," she added, her eyes bright with her delight in trying to hurt me.

I didn't dissuade her from her thoughts on Hans. I knew better. He was amazing, and smart, and sexy. The only true thing she said was that he had a hot body, and she didn't even know the half of it. Hans was perfectly sculpted. Despite everything that Nelson put me though, I had no concerns that Hans would do the same. He was too ethical for that. Besides, the women there would have warned me away if Hans was a player. No, I didn't have to worry about him cheating.

"What? You've got nothing to say about that? Awww, you believe he's a good guy." She smirked. "Maybe I'll give him a try once you're gone. I can comfort him over your death."

"You leave Hans alone," I said vehemently.

Selina guffawed, her evil smile back on her face. "If I want to fuck him I will, and I'll do it with pleasure." She gave me a look of triumph, then turned her gaze to her cousin. "Take care of them."

33

I watched Selina leave the room and enter the kitchen on the other side of the open dining room. She acted as if she didn't want to hear what Danny was about to do. She probably didn't. In the end, all I could think was that she was a coward who couldn't do her own dirty work.

I refocused on Danny. He didn't want to kill Jake. Not like this. This was too personal. Too hands-on. My bet was that he didn't want to kill me either. He'd even said it—a car accident was one thing; this was cold-blooded murder. I needed him to keep thinking that way.

"You don't want to do this, Danny. He's a little kid. He's only ten," I started, as I tried to appeal to what little moral sense he seemed to have. "Selina doesn't care about you. She doesn't care about the nightmares you'll have if you kill Jake. You already look like you aren't sleeping well. What's going to happen when you use that gun to splatter a little kid's brains all over this room?"

Jake's eyes turned to me with horror, and I reached for his hand, squeezing it, hoping he'd realize that I was trying to save his life. I needed him to understand that I had to talk in visuals for Danny to understand what he'd be doing. I wasn't trying to scar Jake for life with my words and I prayed that he'd get that. That he'd not hate me when this was all over.

"I understand, Danny. I mean, killing a little kid is a bridge too far for anyone. Even Selina won't do it. Why should you be the one committing murder? Why should you be the one taking a little boy's life?" I added.

Danny looked uncertain and his gun hand wavered. He looked toward the kitchen and called out, "Selina! Why won't you do it? Why should I be the one to kill the kid?"

Selina stormed out of the kitchen but stopped just short of the doorway. The look on her face said she was beyond furious.

I could feel her anger from where I stood. I was hoping this would be the distraction I'd need to get Jake out of here, but it didn't go as I'd hoped.

"Don't bother me with this fucking shit. He's just a terrified kid. You do what I pay you to do and don't fucking interrupt me again until it's done!" She spun on her heel and returned to the kitchen, this time slamming the door.

From the kitchen I could hear the blender kick on and I wondered if she'd turned it on to drown us out more, or if she was in there making herself a drink. Probably the latter. She was most likely making daiquiris or margaritas. I turned my eyes back to Danny, who had only taken a couple of steps away from us.

Danny turned and aimed the gun right at my chest. His eyes traveled over my frame with lust.

I knew if he had his way, he'd be doing more than just killing me. I didn't want him anywhere near me. He was disgusting. The idea of him touching me, his fat hands on my body, made me break out in hives. I didn't want him even thinking of doing that kind of thing to me. I needed to keep pushing him to realize killing me and Jake was a bad idea. That doing anything to us was a bad idea.

Maybe pushing him to realize that he'll be next would be the way to go, I thought.

"You know what's going to happen after you kill us, right?" I said, drawing his attention back to my face.

He sneered. "I get so much fucking money I can do whatever the fuck I want."

I laughed. "Really? That's what you think? No... you're a loose end. How do *you* think this is going to end? Nelson, me, and Jake all dead in this penthouse and Selina pretending to be Amanda. Where do you fit, Danny?"

He frowned at me and looked confused. I wondered if he wasn't very bright and that was part of the reason that he was so easily manipulated by Selina, but then I'd allowed Nelson to manipulate me for years, so I supposed I wasn't one to talk.

"I'm her cousin," he muttered.

"No, you're her patsy. You're the violent intruder who murdered her family and the babysitter. You're the only one who can out her as not being Amanda. You're the only one who knows she's Selina. That she's wanted for murder. That she's insane and belongs back in the prison psych ward."

He shook his head, but he looked completely unsure now.

"You really believe she's going to let you walk out of here alive? That's not going to happen. Selina only cares about herself. She murdered her own twin; you don't think she won't do the same to you? She wants this life; she doesn't want to share. Not with Jake, not with you."

I could tell that he was almost there, almost seeing it. I just needed to push a little harder.

"The cops already have you on surveillance video leaving the area where she was attacked, Danny. I've seen it. The cops showed it to us so we could ID you. Selina even yelled at you for being caught on camera, remember? Not to mention the video of you trying to kill Jake at the school. There were cameras in that parking lot. The cops know it was you. And then there's the very nice video I captured of you after you tried to run me and Jake off the road. As well as the Ring video of you trying to break into my apartment. And of you at Melodies demolishing my car... It will be so easy for Selina to place all the blame on you. So easy for her to kill you after you take care of us for her. The cops are going to believe her. She's Amanda, after all. The wealthy socialite, not the murderous Selina. She'll have everything and you'll have nothing. The minute you pull that trigger to kill me and Jake, you've signed your death certificate."

Jake was breathing hard next to me, and I was ready to push him toward the door the moment Danny was distracted enough. I didn't matter. Jake was what mattered. Jake needed to live. He had to live. I couldn't imagine a world without him. I wouldn't. No matter what, Jake was getting out of here.

Danny looked toward the kitchen; I could see the anger settling over him. His back was rigid, his muscles flexed, his jaw locked. He was nearly over the edge with anger toward Selina. He took a couple steps away from us, moving closer to the kitchen.

I figured a few more words, a few more harsh truths and

he'd go after Selina and leave us. "You know that's her end game. She practically told us that a few minutes ago. She's not going to share shit with you, Danny. She's going to kill you too. I guarantee it."

He glanced from us to the kitchen door. "Stay there," he growled as he moved through the dining room toward the kitchen and a moment later the door slammed open as he went in. "What the fuck, Selina?" he shouted. "Is it true?"

This was it. My chance to get Jake out. I tightened my grip on his hand and jerked him toward the door. I pushed him in front of me so I could protect him if any bullets came our way. I could hear Danny and Selina yelling in the kitchen.

"Is what true, you idiot? Did you leave them alone? Are you fucking stupid?"

"I'm not stupid. Don't call me stupid!"

"What did that bitch say to you?" Selina demanded. "Why haven't you taken care of them yet?"

We needed to hurry. My heart was pounding as I listened to them bicker. We had seconds before they spilled into the dining room and noticed we weren't where they'd left us.

"Run!"

34

The kitchen had two entrances. One through the dining room and one through the front hall. I heard a crash as we headed for the front hall via the living room. The crash had come from the front hall, and the walls banged as Selina and Danny struggled against each other.

"Carly!" Jake cried out. Panic was clear in his voice as we entered the hall. His eyes were wide as he watched Danny slam Selina down to the ground, his knee on her torso.

Selina was struggling beneath him, trying to get control of his gun hand. "They're going to get away, you fucking moron!" she screeched.

I yanked on the door and shoved Jake through it.

A second later, a bullet ripped into the door just above my head and I gasped, jumping back. I looked back toward Selina and Danny. Danny had his fat hands wrapped around her throat. Selina had pulled her purse from the hallway table and gotten her hands on another gun. She had been aiming for my head when she'd let off that shot.

I prayed that Jake was okay, that he'd run and not wait for me.

Another loud shot reverberated through the front hall, and I watched Danny drop down on top of Selina, dead. She'd shot him in the temple. His blood and brain matter were splattered all over the hallway wall and on Selina's face. She turned her evil eyes on me and aimed the gun.

I screamed and ran back toward the living room. I needed to find somewhere to hide, I thought as she squeezed the trigger. I swear I felt the bullet zip past me, barely missing me as I got out of her sight range. I didn't know where to go. The penthouse was huge, but it was still just a prison. There was nowhere to really go. I could hide, but I couldn't get out. Not with her blocking the door. There was the balcony, but there was no way down from there.

I thought about it for a second, wondering if I could leap from her balcony to the one next door or below her and get away that way.

"Come back here, you fucking bitch! You're dead! You've ruined everything," Selina screamed from the hall.

I could hear her fighting for breath as she struggled under Danny's dead weight. She was pretty slight in stature and size. It might take her a little bit to get free. I needed to use that time to find a place to hide.

I could hear police sirens, but it was hard to tell if they were coming here or going elsewhere. They still sounded some distance away and I was terrified that they'd be too late to save me. Jake was safe though. That was the important thing. I hoped he'd found Hans downstairs somewhere. Had he even found a place to park yet? How long had I been up here?

It seemed as though I'd been here for hours, but it was

probably only fifteen minutes at the most. It would have taken Hans at least that long to find a parking spot in the public garage down the street. Then he'd have had to find his way here again.

"You can't... fucking hide... from me! I know every... damn hiding spot... You aren't... getting out of here alive... Carly!" Her breath was stilted, and she seemed to be gasping her words now. Her voice sounded gravelly, as if her vocal cords had been damaged with Danny crushing her neck earlier.

I was standing perfectly still in the middle of the living room trying to decide where to go.

"Car—" Her voice just stopped on a gasp of air.

I took a chance and cautiously moved back toward the front hall. Pressing myself to the side wall, I tipped my face around the corner to see if she'd managed to get free and that was why she was quiet. However, when I looked, her eyes were closed and her hand with the gun was slack.

I crept forward on my tiptoes, terrified that she was faking it. When I got close enough, I kicked the gun free of her hand, but she didn't move. She didn't make a sound. I noticed that Danny still had the other gun in his hand, and I kicked that away too.

I bent down to look at her, to see if she was still alive. I didn't want to touch her. I was afraid I would wake her if I did. Instead, I held a hand in front of her nose and mouth to feel for her breath. There was just the slightest air movement coming from her.

I wasn't sure if I should be relieved that she was alive, or not, but I wasn't going to stick around to wait for her to wake up. I turned and practically ran for the door, pushing it open as I fled. I didn't see Jake or anyone in the outer hall as I headed for the elevator, and I hoped that he made it all the way downstairs. I pushed the button for the elevator car and waited impatiently as it made it up the twenty flights to the penthouse floor.

Finally, the doors dinged open, and I pressed the close door button twenty times then hit the button for the lobby. I breathed a sigh of relief as the car started descending.

When the doors opened again and I stepped out, Jake's small body flew at me.

"Carly! You're okay!" he cried as he wrapped his arms around me.

I looked up and saw Hans coming toward me and suddenly I was wrapped in two hugs. I didn't want to break down, but the adrenaline was wearing off and my eyes began to leak as wracking sobs filled my chest.

"I've got you, love." Hans rubbed my back. "You're okay. Everything is going to be okay."

And I believed him.

When I quieted, they both let me go and we moved to the seating area in the lobby to wait for the cops.

I wiped my eyes and then pulled Jake from his chair and into my arms. "Do you know how brave you were?" I asked, looking into his face. "All those things I said... you know I was just trying to make Danny angry at Selina so he wouldn't kill you, right? I wasn't trying to give you nightmares or terrify you." I pressed my forehead to his.

He nodded. "I know," he whispered. "You didn't scare me, but they did."

I hugged Jake close, then met Hans' eyes. "Thank you. Thank you for watching out for him down here and not coming upstairs. I don't know what I would have done if you had."

Hans reached for my hand. "When Jake came tearing out of that elevator screaming about his dad being murdered and you being up there, I about had a heart attack. I wasn't about to leave him, but I was terrified for you."

"I was terrified for me too," I admitted.

Suddenly the sirens were right outside the building and were so loud I couldn't think. I glanced to the doors as a swarm of officers entered the building, weapons drawn. The three of us, as well as the staff at the reception area, froze.

"We're evacuating the building. We've had a call about an active shooter," one of the officers shouted as he started making waving motions to the doors.

"They're incapacitated now!" I shouted back. "Where the hell have you been?" I demanded, suddenly angry. "I called you more than an hour ago. I told you they'd murdered Nelson. I told you they had Jake."

"Ma'am, I am unaware of any of that. We need to clear the building. We've had calls of shots fired."

I shook my head as we were escorted outside. "Look, this is Jake..." I indicated him. "We were the ones being held hostage up there. Selina is unconscious and her cousin Danny is dead. She's pinned down and I kicked the weapons away. She's not a threat anymore."

The cop kept escorting us through the door as the rest of the officers continued heading up the stairs and into the elevators. "This way, ma'am. One of these officers will take your statements."

I groaned in frustration. He wasn't listening. He was sending me to someone else to deal with me. More vehicles with sirens showed up, making everything extremely loud outside. It was hard to think out here. Still, I hesitated in moving where the cop was directing me.

"Come on, love, let's do as he asks. They'll figure it out once they're upstairs," Hans murmured as he put a hand on the small of my back.

I couldn't deny how welcome his touch was. It was both comforting and made me feel cared for. In that moment, I knew everything would be all right. I nodded and let the officer finish dragging us to the cops standing around outside. I was so angry at them and how lackadaisical they were about all of this, and I was ready to read them the riot act for almost getting Jake killed. If they were lucky, I might just stop short of taking my complaints to City Hall and getting them all fired.

35

"They were apparently involved in the altercation," the cop said as he spoke to two of the plain clothes cops standing on the sidewalk in front of us.

"We'll take it from here," one of them said then turned to us. "I'm Detective Brian and this is Detective Ferris. Can you tell me who you are and how you're involved in this?" He gestured toward the building.

I nodded. Finally, someone who was willing to listen. "My name is Carly Michaelson. This is Jake Carter and Hans Wohlers."

Detective Brian's eyes went from me down to Jake and back up to Hans, then back to me. "You were the one who called this in?"

I was surprised he knew that much. The other officer hadn't. "Yes. What took so long to get you all here?" It was all I could do to keep my tone civil.

The detective sighed. "Until multiple shots were fired, dispatch thought it wasn't urgent. The officers who checked out the townhouse didn't find anything and had word that the boy and his father were fine. Wires were crossed."

I was so angry I got in his face. "Jake was almost murdered thanks to you all!"

Hans gently pulled me back against his chest. "Don't shoot the messenger," he murmured in my ear.

I relaxed against him and glanced at the detective. "Sorry. Things have been intense."

"No problem, ma'am. I understand your anger. Can you tell me what happened?"

I took a breath. "Let me start at the beginning." I told him all about what we thought was the attack on Amanda. I moved on to the attack on Jake and then the rest of it leading up to this point. I mentioned finding out about Selina and Danny from Marianne.

"Marianne Shelton? I know of her," Detective Ferris said with a nod. "She's thorough."

"She is," I agreed. I continued my story with asking Nelson to go to the police since they weren't listening to me.

"I can only apologize for the way you were treated. I'll be looking into it, I promise you," Detective Brian said.

For the first time since all this started, I finally felt as though someone in authority was actually listening to me. "Thank you." I blew out a breath and continued. "So I only know this part from Jake calling me. His dad for some reason decided to confront Selina."

Detective Ferris looked down at Jake. "Wait." He held a hand up for me to stop. "Jake, can you tell us what occurred after you and your father left Ms. Michaelson's apartment?"

"We got in the car and started heading into Manhattan. I thought he'd go to the station in Brooklyn, but he didn't. I asked him why, and he said he was going to find out if we were telling the truth. I tried to talk him out of it. I told him that Carly had proof from the private detective, but he was —" Jake shook his head and wiped his eyes. "When we got to the townhouse and she wasn't there, I was relieved. I thought maybe then he'd go to the police, but he didn't. He texted her."

"You didn't tell me that," I murmured.

Jake's eyes flashed up to me, then back to the detective. "He asked her where she was and said that they needed to talk. She told him she was at the penthouse. So we went there." He grew quiet and he started to silently cry.

I took his hand in mine and held it. "Jake, if you don't want to say any more, I can tell them," I said, getting down on his level.

He swallowed hard and then shook his head. He wiped his eyes again. "We walked in, and Selina was standing in the living room drinking. She turned and said, 'About damn time,' and then I heard a noise behind us. I turned to see that man who's been trying to kill me behind us. He pointed a gun at the back of Dad's head and shot him." His words came out choked.

My heart broke that he'd seen that. That he'd been there.

"How did you get away?" Detective Ferris asked. His voice remained neutral, free of emotion.

I had to glance at him to see if he was really unmoved by Jake's words, by what he'd just been through. He wasn't. His eyes held compassion, but also, there was a little bit of fury too. I was glad to see it. No kid should witness what Jake did and it was infuriating that he had.

"Selina started laughing and I just ran. They were paying too much attention to Dad on the floor to watch me. I made it to the guest bathroom and hid in the linen closet. That's when I called Carly."

I picked up the story from there. I explained everything from the phone call to racing up to try and help Jake, to baiting Danny, to getting Jake out and then finally what happened after he was out. "She was unconscious when I escaped. I managed to kick the gun from her hand and Danny's too before I left. I didn't want her shooting anyone else and she was pinned under Danny's massive weight."

"You took a real chance going in there like that, Ms. Michaelson. You could have been killed."

"I had to help Jake. He's just a little boy. He'd just watched them murder his dad. I couldn't let them murder him too. I couldn't." I shook my head and my hands held tighter to Jake's shoulders.

Jake leaned into me. "I'm glad you came for me," he whispered.

Detective Ferris flicked his gaze to Hans. "Why didn't you go with her?"

"She promised me she wasn't going to confront them, and I was going to be right behind her. By the time I parked the car and made it to the lobby, Jake was coming out of the elevator screaming bloody murder. I wasn't going to leave him on his own. Carly cares about him more than anything in this world. She'd have killed me if I'd gone up there and left Jake."

I nodded. "He's telling the truth. I wouldn't have literally, of course, but he'd have been on my shit list forever." I smiled at him then turned my gaze back to the cops. I didn't want them thinking I was some crazed murderer too.

"I suppose that was a poor choice of words, considering

the situation, but you understand, it was just a turn of phrase," Hans added with a shrug.

Detective Brian grinned. "I do. I want you both to get checked out by the paramedics. You've been through a lot this evening."

"I'll escort them over. It looks like they're sending a couple stretchers up now," Detective Ferris said with a glance toward the building.

A few minutes later, Jake and I were being examined by Jason and Brenda, the paramedics, and sitting in the back of an ambulance while Hans stood just outside the doors.

"Looks like you're pretty bruised and banged up, little man," Jason said as he looked over Jake.

"You do as well, ma'am," Brenda added. "I think we need to take the two of you in for X-rays and observation."

"What? No... I'm fine," I argued.

"I want to go home, Carly." Jake looked at me with tears in his eyes.

I pressed my lips together and really looked at him. His arms were covered in huge bruises that were just starting to darken in color. I knew he needed to go, so I'd just have to suck it up and go too. I sighed. "I know, kiddo. I do too, but maybe we should get checked out. I don't want to get home and then realize you're hurt more than we thought."

"You'll go too?" he asked softly.

"Yeah. I'll go too." I squeezed his hand gently, then looked at Hans. "Looks like we're heading to the hospital."

"I'll follow you there, love." He didn't break his gaze with me until the doors were fully closed.

"You'll need to lie down, ma'am."

I rolled my eyes as I lay down on the stretcher and they buckled me in. Jake did the same. The siren turned on and then we were moving. It didn't take long to get to the hospital.

Two hours later, Jake and I were settled in a room together because he freaked out when they tried to take him to a different room. Hans was seated in a chair between us. Jake had fallen asleep and was softly snoring in the second bed in the room when Blaine and Dave showed up.

"What are you two doing here? How did you even know —" I looked from them to Hans. "Did you call them?"

Hans shrugged. "You left your phone in the car. I figured you'd want your brother to know."

I reached a hand out to him and smiled. He took my hand and kissed it. "Thank you." I turned back to Blaine and Dave, who'd watched the interaction with interest. "You didn't have to come. I'm fine. We both are." I glanced over to Jake's bed.

"You have no idea how worried I was when Hans called and told me what happened."

"He's not kidding. He was so worried for you that he let *me* drive," Dave deadpanned.

I laughed. Blaine hated Dave's driving because he always drove ten to fifteen miles over the speed limit.

"You're sure you're okay?" Blaine asked as he gave me a hug.

I nodded. "I'm good. Promise."

"So, what happened? Hans didn't give any details. Just said you were here after an attack."

I went through the story once again and Blaine looked as if he was ready to throttle me when I told him I went up to the penthouse on my own and got caught by Selina and Danny.

"Don't you ever do anything like that again, do you hear me? You could have died," he growled.

"Let her finish, honey. I'm sure there's more to this story." Dave put a hand on Blaine's arm, stroking it in a calming manner.

I nodded and continued. Blaine looked almost apoplectic when I got to the part of me taunting Danny, trying to get him to go fight with Selina, but he kept his mouth shut without blowing a gasket.

"For the love of God, Carly," he muttered when I finished. He grabbed me in a tight hug. "I could have lost you."

I hugged him back. "I'm sorry you're upset. You understand why I had to go up there, though, don't you?" I pulled back and looked him in the face. "If it were Dave in there, you'd have done the same."

He drew a sharp breath. "Yeah, I get it. I'm not happy about it, but I get it."

We chatted for a little bit longer and then he and Dave decided to leave. They still had work in the morning, but they promised to come check on me once I was back home.

Ten minutes after they left, Detective Ferris and Detective Brian showed up.

"Ms. Michaelson, would you mind if we come in?" They were standing in the doorway, hesitating before crossing the threshold.

"It's fine, come in."

"We wanted to let you know what was going on," Detective Brian explained.

"Okay..." I didn't know why they felt the need to tell me unless there was something wrong.

"When our officers arrived upstairs, they found Danny

Andrews dead, as you mentioned. Selina Andrews was unconscious, pinned beneath him. They've brought her here and it looks like she's going to pull through."

I frowned. I'd secretly been hoping she'd die, but I quickly regretted it. I didn't want to be the kind of person who hoped for someone else's death.

"She's not awake yet, but she is under arrest, and we have a guard on her room," Detective Ferris shared.

"We went back to the original video from when she claimed to be attacked, and found the storage facility where she was keeping her sister's body. She was exactly how you said she described."

I felt tears well up in my eyes. I hadn't really liked Amanda, but she didn't deserve to die like that. I used my palm to wipe the tears away and sniffled.

"With both of his parents deceased, we've got child protective services coming—"

I sat up like a shot and said, "No, you can't! I'm the only adult he trusts. He's been through a traumatic experience, and he doesn't need to go through more!"

"Ma'am, I understand your concern, but with no other relatives or caregivers—"

"I'm his caregiver. I've taken care of him since he was four," I said vehemently. "He has been in my care more than he's been in his parents' care. You can't have him."

Detective Ferris reached a hand out to my shoulder and looked at me with sincerity. "I'll see what we can do. We may be able to get you temporary custody."

I was breathing hard but gave him a sharp nod. "Thank you."

"We'll leave you in peace for now. Get some rest, Ms. Michaelson."

With that, they left, and I breathed a sigh of relief.

I was still worried that they'd take Jake from me. Put him into foster care or something and that would create another whole host of issues. Jake was the heir to his father's fortune. Putting him into foster care would turn into a shit show. One I wasn't going to allow.

I would fight it with every ounce of my being.

"Love, it's going to be all right," Hans whispered.

I turned to look at him. I prayed he was right.

36

"Ma'am, I'm Cynthia Goodwin with CPS."

I stared at the petite woman standing in the hospital room doorway an hour after the detectives had left. She had long blonde hair that was braided down her back. She wore a black business suit with a skirt and a white blouse. Her heels were sensible and matched her outfit.

"You can't take him." I gave her a mulish look, crossing my arms over my chest.

"I understand that you and Jake have a bond and I don't want to take him. I do need to speak to him, though, before I can release him into your custody."

"Love, listen to her. Let her talk to Jake," Hans murmured as he reached for my hand.

"Okay." I looked around the room and wondered if I was supposed to stay or not. "Can we stay?"

She smiled. "I don't expect you to leave your hospital bed, ma'am. This really won't take long." She moved toward Jake, who was now awake and watching TV.

She spent ten minutes questioning him about his relationship with me, and when she was done she agreed it was best that he stay with me. I didn't realize how nervous I was until she said that the state was granting me temporary custody of him.

"This is only temporary, until after the reading of his parents' wills and the trial. Though I have to amend that if his parents made accommodations for his guardianship in their wills, then those will be honored. If not, then you can apply to have permanent guardianship granted to you."

I nodded. I had no idea what was in Nelson and Amanda's wills regarding Jake. I hadn't even known they had wills. It wasn't something we'd ever discussed. "Thank you."

Hours later, we were released from the hospital and Hans drove us home. Blaine and Dave showed up about twenty minutes later with pizza and the five of us sat down to eat. Jake was exhausted and hadn't fully processed the fact that his parents were murdered by his aunt and her cousin. He was acting as if everything was normal, and that worried me.

I wasn't sure how to deal with it and I didn't know what to do about getting him to therapy. The only thing I could think to do was to call Nelson's agent in the morning and find out who his lawyer was. I needed to know what kind of access Jake had to money. Therapy was expensive and I wanted to find him a really good therapist who had dealt with this kind of trauma.

"Lock up after we leave," Blaine said as he hugged me.

"I will."

"Take care of her," Dave said, shaking Hans' hand.

"I plan to," he replied with a smile.

I glanced at him but didn't say anything. We'd only spent

one night together and that was at his place when I was on my own. Now I had Jake with me. I wasn't sure if him staying was a good idea or not, so I was fretting about it. I didn't say anything as I closed and locked the door behind my brother and Dave.

Hans drew me into his arms and hugged me. "If you're worried about me being here and Jake seeing us, I could stay on the couch."

I looked up at him and smiled. "How did you know I was concerned about that?"

He chuckled. "You always think of how things will affect him. He's been through a lot, so I get it. If you need me to stay on the couch, I will, but I'm not leaving you alone."

I held him tighter. "No, I think I would rather have you in my bed. I think he knows I trust you and that we're in a relationship. I don't think it will mess with him, but if he has nightmares, I might have to go in there with him."

"I can handle that." He smiled. "Come on, let's clean up and head to bed."

We spent the weekend barricaded in my apartment, ordering take-out and trying to rest, though I did get a little painting in so I could stay on schedule. Jake woke up a couple of times after having nightmares, but I was able to soothe him back to sleep.

On Monday morning, Hans left after breakfast to meet with his manager and work out new dates for the concerts he missed and see what else had been set up for him.

I spent the morning painting, finished up the project for Jasmine, who freaked out when I got her all the images on time after what I'd been through. She had been prepared to put everything on hold until I was up for it, but I just wanted the project done.

Jake was in his room playing Switch when I called Glenn Coburn, Nelson's agent.

"May I speak to Glenn, please?" I asked his secretary.

"Can I tell him who is calling?"

"Carly Michaelson, I'm... I was a friend of Nelson Carter's... I—"

"Oh golly, yes, of course!" she exclaimed, sounding flustered. "Just stay on the line, Ms. Michaelson, I will get him right on for you."

A moment later, Glenn got on the phone. "Ms. Michaelson... Carly, how are you? How is Jake? I can't believe what's happened. Murdered! It's crazy. His work has already tripled in price," Glenn said, speaking fast.

"I'm numb if I'm honest. I don't think I've really processed everything. Jake either. Um, I need the number for Nelson's lawyer. I've got temporary custody of Jake, with both his parents just... gone—"

"Of course, of course. Poor kid, I didn't even consider what that might do to him... Yeah, let me get that for you." A moment later he rattled off a number. "Be sure to tell Melanie who you are and that you're Jake's temporary guardian. You know they don't have any other family. Are you going to ask for permanent guardianship?"

"Yes, I'm hoping his lawyer can help with that."

"If he doesn't agree, you let me know and I'll give him a call. Nelson always spoke highly of you."

That made my lips curve up in a temporary smile. "Did he?"

"Yeah. He didn't trust many people with his boy, you know."

I wasn't too sure about that, but I wasn't going to argue the point with him. "Thanks for that. And for the number."

"Anytime, and Carly, when things settle down, I have some things I'd like to discuss with you about your work. If you're interested, that is."

His words took me aback. Nelson had always said that Glenn didn't have time for me, didn't think my work was good enough. "Sure. It might have to wait until after the trial. I have a feeling things are going to be crazy for a while."

"Of course. You just give me a call when you're ready."

"Thanks, Glenn. I will." I hung up and dialed the lawyer's office.

"Mr. Durham's Office. This is Melanie. How may I help you?"

"Hi. I'm Carly Michaelson, Jake Carter's temporary guardian. I was calling to talk to Mr. Durham about Nelson and Amanda Carter's will."

"Yes, Ms. Michaelson, we've been expecting your call. Such sad news about the Carters. Let me patch you through to Mr. Durham."

"Thank you." I blew out an uneasy breath and waited.

"Ms. Michaelson? Jeff Durham. I am so sorry to hear about Nelson and Amanda. How is Jake?"

"He's acting like everything is normal. I don't think he's processing anything. I want to get him some help. He witnessed his father's..."

"Good Lord." He exhaled loudly. "That poor kid. Of course, we can make arrangements for that. I'd like you both to come in for the reading of the will. There are many factors we need to consider. Would you be able to come into the city today?"

"We can be there when you need us. We've got about an hour's drive, though, and I'll have to call for an Uber. My car was destroyed by the..." I broke down in tears. Gasping for breaths after a moment to calm myself, I said, "I'm sorry. It's been a long bunch of weeks that all cumulated in Friday night and I'm still trying to process it all."

"I understand. Why don't I send a car for you?"

"That will be fine. We'll be ready in ten minutes," I said with a sniffle. I needed to wash my face and get Jake prepared to go.

"Excellent. I'll have a car there soon."

"Thank you, Mr. Durham."

When we hung up, I called, "Jake, get dressed and turn off the game. We are headed into the city."

I heard his game pause, and he popped his head out of his room. "Why?" he asked suspiciously.

"We have to go see your dad's lawyer."

He stuck his lower lip out and his eyes began to water. "Are you getting rid of me?"

"What? No! Never. I'm going to talk to him about getting permanent custody, Jake. And we have to make arrangements for... everything." I didn't want to bring up funerals. If I could, I would do all of that without him in the room with the lawyer.

Jake wrapped his arms around me and hugged me. I rubbed his back and his sobs subsided. He wiped his face on my shirt and then laughed a little.

"Gross, Jake," I said, laughing too. "Now we've both got to change."

He grinned.

"Go on. The car will be here in a few minutes."

FOUR HOURS LATER, I was shaking Mr. Durham's hand. "Thank you so much."

I was blown away at what I'd learned. Nelson and Amanda's net worth was close to fifty million, not including the two properties here in New York or the condo down in the Florida Keys. They also had a bungalow on the coast of California. Now everything belonged to Jake. We set up a trust and made a plan to sell off the properties. I had a feeling Jake wouldn't want to live in any of those places. And when I asked, Jake said no, he wanted to stay with me at my place.

Mr. Durham agreed to have anything belonging to Jake, any mementos and the like, packed up and delivered to my place. After that he'd arrange for the furnishings to be sold off and the properties sold.

We also hired someone to arrange the funerals for both Nelson and Amanda once their bodies were released from the city morgue. And Mr. Durham cut me a generous check to cover Jake's living expenses as well as helped me find him a good therapist who dealt with the trauma Jake had been through. He'd have his first appointment tomorrow.

"It's my pleasure, Ms. Michaelson. And we'll get the ball rolling on setting up permanent guardianship. You've been his caretaker for most of his life, and he's got no close relatives. The courts aren't going to fight it. You may have to submit to a visit from Social Services, but I'm sure you'll pass with no worries."

"Thanks."

He led me to the outer office door with Jake. "Call me if you need anything. If the check isn't enough to cover his expenses, just let me know. Raising a kid is expensive. I want to be sure you have everything you need. And if you feel a change of residence would be better for you both, we can make that happen."

I nodded. "I'll keep that in mind."

We headed out to the car that was waiting for us.

After settling in the back, Jake asked, "What did he mean? If you want to move? I want to stay at your place."

I smiled. "I think he's considering the fact that your school is in Manhattan and we're living in Brooklyn now. It's a long drive."

"I don't have to go to school." He folded his arms over his chest and stared at me.

I shook my head and smiled at him. "Nice try, kiddo. You've got some time off because of everything, but you're going back to school."

He looked down at his shoes. "Do I have to go back to that school?"

"Aren't your friends there?" I asked, searching his face.

He shrugged. "I guess, but everyone there will know what happened."

I felt like I'd been sucker-punched. I pulled him into my side and hugged him close, well, as close as the seat belts would allow. "You think they'll treat you differently?"

"Not my friends, but the teachers... the principal... they already were after that man tried to run me over. Now it will be worse."

"We'll figure it out, even if that means enrolling you in a new school."

37

Six weeks later

I'd enrolled Jake in a private school here in Brooklyn. The school was secured behind a gate and the staff treated Jake like just another student. Granted, their students all came from wealthy families, but the point was Jake didn't feel like they pitied him or that they treated him any differently than anyone else.

His therapy sessions had been going on three times a week for a month now. Jake had acted out for a little while, throwing temper tantrums and the like when he didn't get his own way. He'd also had nightmares nearly every night for weeks, but finally things were starting to sort themselves out. His therapist had warned me that his behavior would get worse before it got better as they worked through the trauma, so I'd been somewhat prepared.

After a week of Jake's horrid behavior, I'd thought Hans

was going to give up on us. Jake wasn't the only one in a bad mood. I had been as well. Still, Hans had come through with understanding and kindness and now I felt we were stronger than ever. He'd given me space when I asked for it, but kept in contact, never letting a day go by without telling me he was thinking of me.

I'd also had a gallery showing at his friend's gallery that was wildly successful. I'd been in talks with Glenn as well, but nothing was set in stone yet. It turned out that Nelson had been full of shit. That wasn't really a surprise. Glenn had been interested in my work for years, but Nelson had told him that I was the one who didn't want to get into gallery work.

That had been one of the reasons for my bad mood— dealing with my feelings about Nelson. I ended up seeing my own therapist over it. I was working through all the issues I had with my relationship with Nelson, as well as learning how to have a healthy and successful relationship with Hans.

Selina's trial had started a week earlier, and Jake and I were both due to testify, seeing as she was pleading not guilty by virtue of temporary insanity. The idea of that made me see red. She wasn't temporarily insane. She was a psychopath. I wanted her to spend the rest of her life in a high security prison that she couldn't ever escape from again.

Hans, Jake, and I were on our way to the courthouse. Jake didn't come with us every day, but he was going on the stand first. He'd met with the prosecutor a few times to learn how things worked in the courtroom, and he seemed to understand what he'd be asked. I was nervous for him. I didn't want Selina's lawyer taking advantage of him and manipulating him. The prosecutor, Ms. Greene, assured me that she would shut that down quickly if it happened.

The three of us sat directly behind the prosecutor and listened to the cops give evidence of what they found at the scene when they arrived.

Then Jake was called. I rubbed his back as he stood up.

"You can do this, kiddo," I whispered.

An hour later, after telling everything he'd seen and heard, he was dismissed from the witness stand. He'd been brave and held it together throughout the experience and did exactly what Ms. Greene suggested when Selina's lawyer tried to ask him awful questions meant to hurt him. He'd kept his mouth shut and let her do her job by calling objection. The judge agreed every time.

"You did awesome," I murmured, giving him a smile.

We had to come back several more times before it was my turn to get up on the stand, and I didn't think I did as well as Jake, but Ms. Greene did her best to help me out as much as possible. Still, I had to answer embarrassing questions about my relationship with Nelson. I was glad Jake wasn't there to hear it. Having Selina's lawyer accuse me of only being his guardian so I could get my hands on his money was the final straw and I nearly lost it.

"I have practically raised Jake since he was four. I didn't care about Nelson's money when he was alive, and I don't care about it now that he's dead. The money is Jake's. It's been put into a trust for him, and he gets an allowance," I said vehemently.

Her lawyer did more to try and insinuate that I was only ever after the money, but Ms. Greene and the judge shut down that line of attack and I was grateful to them. I went on to talk about what Selina and Danny had done to me the night of the attack, as well as the previous attacks from Danny, since Selina was being charged with accessory to those as well.

"Thank you, Ms. Michaelson. You're dismissed," Ms. Greene said a little while later.

I returned to my seat next to Hans and turned into him, hugging him. Being up there on that stand was brutal and I never wanted to experience anything like it again.

Over the next several court dates, Selina took the stand. Despite the fact she was trying to plead temporary insanity, it all came out. She just couldn't contain herself or keep herself from angrily sharing everything.

She explained how fucked-up her childhood was, the abuse from her father, how she and Amanda killed him to get away from him. She then spoke of her hatred for Amanda after she wouldn't help her kill her husband and that she'd had to rely on her lover, Danny.

Yes, Selina admitted that she was in a sexual relationship with her cousin Danny and had been since they were kids. I wanted to vomit over it. She had been horribly abused and I wondered if it was that abuse that turned her into the monster she was, or if the monster had always lurked there beneath her skin. Either way, I still wanted her put away for life.

She declared that she was only taking what she deserved and that she hadn't meant to kill Danny; she'd been trying to kill me.

Soon after that bit of testimony, Ms. Greene put me back on the stand to rebut what she'd said. I told the court about my conversation with Danny and again about how they'd fought about her end game. I told them that Selina had pulled a second gun and shot him point-blank on purpose.

There was no way she could have been aiming at me when she'd done it. Ms. Greene even showed a diagram of where I was standing and where Selina and Danny were when they'd been fighting.

Once again, I was dismissed from the stand and returned to my seat.

The jury didn't have to deliberate for long. Selina was guilty as hell, and they knew it. Still, I was nervous to hear their verdict and we all stood as they and then the judge reappeared in the courtroom.

"Madam Foreperson, has the jury reached a verdict?"

"It has, Your Honor." She handed a piece of paper to the bailiff, who carried it over to the judge.

The judge read over the paper and then set it down. "Ms. Andrews, please stand."

Selina and her lawyer stood, but Selina looked defiant as she stood there, her arms crossed with a petulant mewl to her lips.

"Madam Foreperson, for the three charges of first degree murder, how did you find?" the judge asked.

"On all the charges of first degree murder, we the jury find the defendant guilty."

The court went on to find Selina guilty of three counts of first-degree murder, two counts of attempted murder, fraud, identity theft, and conspiracy to commit murder. They also added charges for escaping prison as well.

"Sentencing is set for next week," the judge said, then added, "Ms. Andrews will be remanded to the local prison until that time." He banged his gavel and dismissed us all.

I was a nervous wreck for the next week, thinking Selina would find some way to get out and come kill us. Of course, that didn't happen, but it didn't keep the nightmares of it occurring from messing with me every night up until the sentencing.

I sent Jake to school that morning. He had wanted to go to the courthouse and hear what the judge decided, but I felt it was more important for him to be in class. I told him I would text him the minute we found out.

Hans and I sat down in the courtroom and waited for the judge. Selina was back, looking disgusting in her orange prison jumpsuit and straggly hair. She hadn't bothered with the nice attire this time. I wondered if she'd given up.

She turned and stared at me as if she'd known I was looking at her. Her evil gaze narrowed on me, and she said, "I will kill you."

I shivered and Hans pulled me closer.

A bailiff moved closer to her, standing right at her side, and he jerked her to her feet when the judge walked in. I noticed then that her wrists and ankles were shackled. She wasn't going anywhere. She wouldn't be able to get to me.

I sighed as I rose along with everyone else.

"Ms. Andrews, throughout this trial you've shown no remorse, and from what I understand you are still making threats. With all of the current charges, as well as the previous charges, this court is sentencing you to life in a maximum security prison without parole. Do you have anything to say?"

After her lawyer leaned in and said something to her, Selina shook her head.

"You may take her way," the judge directed the bailiff. He went on to thank and dismiss the jury and then it was over.

The bailiff gripped her arm and started to pull her away from the defense table. "Get your fucking hands off me! This is assault! Rape!" Selina screamed. "I'll sue! I will sue all of you! This is a travesty of justice! I want a retrial! It's not fucking fair! I deserve to have Amanda's money! That bitch didn't deserve to be happy! It should have been mine!" Her words echoed in the courthouse hallways as she was dragged away.

I realized that after today, I would never have to see or hear of Selina ever again. I finally felt like a weight was lifted from me. I hadn't realized how much stress I'd been feeling until this moment.

Hans wrapped an arm around my waist. "Ready to go?"

I leaned into him, happy to have him by my side. "Definitely. Lunch?"

"Absolutely."

Smiling, we headed out of the courthouse, finally free to live without the threat of Selina hovering over us. Reporters shouted questions to us, but we both ignored them as we hurried down the steps to our waiting car.

I pulled my phone out and sent Jake a text.

> You don't have to worry anymore. She got life without parole in a maximum security prison. She won't be bothering us ever again.

Yes! Ice cream party?

I laughed.

> Absolutely, kiddo! See you after school.

EPILOGUE

Six months later

"It's official."

I stood in the kitchen, the phone in my hand, my jaw on the floor. "Really? You're not joking?"

"I would never joke about something as important as this, Carly. Jake is officially yours. The adoption papers have gone through. Jake is now Jake Carter Michaelson."

My hand went to my heart, and I sobbed happy tears. "Thank you, Mr. Durham, thank you so much."

"You'll have to come into town and sign the papers, but as far as the court is concerned you are now his adoptive parent."

I couldn't believe it. There had been a while where the family court had searched high and low for a relative, but other than Selina, there was no one. Then they'd wavered over the fact that I was a single woman, but Mr. Durham had argued that I'd been in Jake's life for nearly seven years and that I was the only adult he trusted. They'd even gotten testimony from Jake's therapist and from Jake himself that he wanted to live with me. Wanted me to be his new mom.

"This is amazing news. Thank you, and I'll be there tomorrow after I drop off Jake at school."

"We'll see you then."

I hung up and turned to Hans. "He's mine. Jake's mine." I grinned as he picked me up and swung me around.

"We should celebrate. How about we invite Blaine and Dave to my place for dinner?"

We tended to spend most days at my place rather than his because Jake was comfortable here, but he wasn't opposed to going to Hans' apartment. "All right. That sounds nice."

"I'll order in. You see if they can come." He leaned in and kissed my cheek. "I've got a couple of errands to run. I'll see you tonight?"

I nodded. "We'll be there at six."

"Perfect." He pulled me into his arms and kissed me before leaving.

I grabbed my phone and texted Blaine.

> Dinner at Hans' place tonight. Six p.m.
> Don't be late.

Blaine wrote back immediately.

> What's the occasion?

> Jake's adoption went through!

Woo hoo! I'm an uncle! Tell the kid we'll be there.

I grinned. I still had work to do. I was meeting Glenn to go through more of Nelson's studio. I grabbed my keys and headed out to my new car, courtesy of Jake. He'd told Mr. Durham what happened to my car, who insisted that I buy a new one. So I clicked the button on my brand new Mercedes SUV and got in. It was luxurious and had all the bells and whistles.

"Glenn?" I called as I entered the studio.

"Back here," he answered.

I headed for the storage closet in the back. "What are you doing in there?"

"Did you know there are more paintings back here?" He came out carrying a stack of framed canvases.

"Nope. Nelson didn't like me being in his space. He said my vibes didn't mesh with his." I rolled my eyes.

Glenn chuckled. "Help me look through these. I'm setting up a gallery showing so we can sell the rest. At least the ones worthy of being sold. Does Jake want to keep any of them? I should have asked." He suddenly looked concerned.

"I don't know. Let's look and see what they are; maybe there is one he'd like."

We went through them and found an abstract that was simply gorgeous. Nelson really had been a very talented artist. And Glenn was right, Jake deserved to have something his father had painted.

"This one," I said, looking at the abstract. It had swirls of blue, violet, pink, and pale green. It was calming and soothing. Something Nelson rarely was. Probably why it was in the storage closet. I snickered. "I bet he hated this one."

Glenn studied it. "You're probably right. He always trended toward brighter, more exciting colors and images. Maybe this was an experiment?"

"Maybe, but I actually love it. I think Jake will too. We'll keep this one."

"Great. These others will all go to the gallery. Speaking of... when are you going to agree to let me represent you?"

I smiled. "I'm considering it."

"Carly, please?" he begged.

It was funny to me that he was begging when I'd actually already decided that I wanted him to be my agent. I was just teasing him, and I nearly burst out in laughter. "What kind of shows have you lined up for me?" I knew that he'd been busting his ass trying to line things up for me, but he hadn't shared yet what those places were.

"Pending your approval, of course, I've got shows lined up at Maxim, Gill and Fortney, another at Pelham's, and a fourth at Vaux."

"All right, Glenn, you can be my agent." I glanced over at him and grinned.

"Yes!" He grabbed me in a big bear hug. "Let's do this!"

I laughed as I helped him pack up the last of Nelson's paintings. It was kind of sad seeing the space so empty.

"You should use this space for your own studio."

I considered it, but in a way, Nelson was right. This wasn't my place. I didn't feel any harmony with the room. "Nah. I might need a bigger studio, but this isn't the space for me. I'll find something."

"If you're sure. Putting it up for sale seems such a waste."

"It's fine. I want to stay in Brooklyn. That's where Jake is, and I want to be close by."

Glenn nodded. "I get that."

We finished up and I turned out the lights with a final goodbye to Nelson. I put the painting for Jake in my trunk and headed home.

Jake arrived not too long after and then we got ready to head over to Hans' place. I hadn't told him yet about the news. I was waiting to surprise him. He did, however, love the painting and we hung it on his bedroom wall before leaving.

I unlocked the door to Hans' place, and was astonished when we were greeted with a round of "Surprise!"

"What is all this?" I questioned, seeing some of our friends from the bar, as well as my brother and Dave, Mr. Durham, Melanie, as well as Viv and Glenn. "Glenn? You didn't say you were going to be here tonight."

He grinned.

Hans moved toward us and lifted Jake in his arms, then reached for me and hugged us both. "This is a celebration of the best sort. I thought everyone should be here for it."

He was the most wonderful man I'd ever met. I hoped he'd always be in our lives.

"What are we celebrating?" Jake asked, looking around.

I grinned. "Your new name."

Jake frowned. "Huh?"

"The court approved your adoption, Jake. You're now officially Jake Carter Michaelson."

He gasped and threw his arms around me. "Can I call you Mom?"

I laughed. "Absolutely, kiddo." My heart was full of love for both him and Hans, but also for all the people here with us.

Blaine and I had grown closer since the night I was

nearly murdered. He and Dave had even bonded with Jake more, and Jake had taken to calling them Uncle Blaine and Uncle Dave. It warmed my heart at how Jake had basically bounced back from all the trauma in his life. He still had nightmares occasionally, usually about his dad's murder and Danny nearly running him down, but they were getting better.

Hans found us after dinner and said, "I have something to show you and Jake. Can you come with me for a few minutes?"

"You want us to leave the party?" I looked at him curiously.

"Just for a few minutes. Blaine knows where we're going. He'll hold the fort."

"I will. Go, Carly. You too, Jake. You're going to love it."

Now I was really curious, so I agreed.

Hans led us out of his apartment to the elevator. He pushed a button and the elevator rose three levels and then the door opened. He took my hand and pulled me down the hall to a door and then unlocked it.

"Why are you showing me this empty apartment?" I asked, looking around. The space was huge. Like his apartment, there were floor-to-ceiling windows along one wall. It had an open floor plan for the living area, dining room and kitchen.

Jake headed down a hallway. "Wow, these rooms are big," he called, his voice echoing down the hall.

"Hans?"

"I thought, maybe, if you're ready... we could buy this place?"

So many emotions flooded through me. Joy and happiness were the strongest. "You want to move in together?" I asked softly.

"There's a huge bathtub with jets," Jake shouted.

I laughed at his exuberance. I turned to look down the hallway as Jake came toward me, but when I turned back, Hans was on one knee, a ring box in his hand.

I gasped. "Hans?"

"Carly, I've fallen in love with you, and I really don't want to spend another minute without you and Jake in my life. Please, will you marry me?"

"I—" My hand went to my mouth to cover my half-sob. I wasn't unhappy, just overwhelmed.

"Carly! I mean, Mom. Say yes!" Jake demanded.

Tears slid down my cheeks as I looked from him to Hans. "Yes."

Hans stood and gathered me in his arms, kissing me. Then Jake's arms wrapped around the both of us in a tight hug. Hans pulled back, grinning, a moment later. "I love you, Carly. You too, Jake. So much." He picked Jake up and Jake hugged him.

"Now we have to do it all again." Jake sighed.

I frowned. "Jake, what do you mean?"

He looked between us. "Well, I just became Jake Carter Michaelson, and if you marry Hans, you'll be Carly Wohlers. I want to have his last name too then."

I started laughing.

"I have no problem with that. I'd love to be your adoptive dad, Jake. I couldn't ask for a better son." Hans hugged Jake tightly.

"I think we had better get married first before we go filing that paperwork." I grinned.

"Promise it will be soon?" Jake asked.

"We'll see. I don't even have the ring on my finger yet," I answered, flashing my teasing gaze at Hans.

"Oh." He set Jake down and opened the box to reveal a princess cut diamond surrounded with tiny emeralds. He pulled it from the box and slid it on my ring finger. "Perfect."

Another tear slipped down my cheek. "Yes, it is."

"So, what do you think of this place?" Hans asked. "There is even a room you can use for a studio." He took my hand and led me down the hall.

He was right, there was a gorgeous space that would work well for a studio, with a bank of floor-to-ceiling windows along two walls. "This is amazing."

"It was an office for the previous tenant."

"What do you think, Jake? Would you want to live here?"

Jake considered it, tilting his head to one side as he looked around. "I think it will work. There's more than enough bedrooms. You could even give me a little brother or sister and there'd still be room."

"Jake," I started laughing, "we just got engaged, kiddo. Not sure I'm ready for a baby yet."

"Yet?" Hans eyebrow quirked up as he grinned.

"Hush, you." I blushed.

Jake grinned too. "I know, but I would like a brother or sister. And this place would be great."

I smiled as I looked between them. "I think you've got your answer."

"I'll tell the estate manager we'll take it." Hans wrapped his arm around me and kissed my temple.

The three of us headed down to share our news with everyone else and I couldn't help but be grateful for how my life was turning out. I'd found the love of my life and gotten my wish to be Jake's mom. I was sad that Nelson and

Amanda had to die for that to happen, but I swore that I would raise Jake to be the best man he could be to make them proud.

My heart was full, and I couldn't ask for more in that moment. Life was a gift, and I was going to make the most of it.

THANK YOU FOR READING

Did you enjoy reading *Not My Mother*? Please consider leaving a review on Amazon. Your review will help other readers to discover the novel.

ABOUT THE AUTHOR

Theo Baxter has followed in the footsteps of his brother, best-selling suspense author Cole Baxter. He enjoys the twists and turns that readers encounter in his stories.

ALSO BY THEO BAXTER

Psychological Thrillers

The Widow's Secret

The Stepfather

Vanished

It's Your Turn Now

The Scorned Wife

Not My Mother

The Lake House

The Detective Marcy Kendrick Thriller Series

Skin Deep - Book #1

Blood Line - Book #2

Dark Duty - Book #3

Printed in Great Britain
by Amazon

42060964R00169